# TOUCHES
# of TIME

## LoRee
## Peery

This is a work of fiction. Names, characters, places, and incidents either are the product of the author's imagination or are used fictitiously, and any resemblance to actual persons living or dead, is entirely coincidental.

**Touches of Time**

**COPYRIGHT 2016 by LoRee Peery**

Contact Information: www.loreepeery.com

All scripture quotations, unless otherwise indicated, are taken from the Holy Bible, New International Version(R), NIV(R), Copyright 1973, 1978, 1984, 2011 by Biblica, Inc.™ Used by permission of Zondervan. All rights reserved worldwide. www.zondervan.com

Cover Art by Delia Latham, Heaven's Touch Designs

Grace & Victory Press
ISBN-13: 978-0692647875 (Custom)
ISBN-10: 0692647872

**Published in the United States of America**

## What others have to say about *Touches of Time*

LoRee Peery always writes with tremendous heart. I knew this from previous forays into her works. Still, I was impressed by the sheer depth of angst written into the pages and between the lines of *Touches of Time*. The book was inspired by the sorrow and frustration experienced by her own family following the as-yet-unsolved murder of the author's father. The storyline—and the manner in which it is shared—allows the reader to experience those emotions and, to some degree, feel the mind-shattering, heartbreaking, soul-chilling effects of loss with neither the chance to say good-bye nor the satisfaction of seeing the guilty brought to justice. The quiet romance between the heroine and her detective hero provide the perfect touch of relief from the constant shuffle through journals and news accounts and memories. *Touches of Time* is the self-proclaimed "book of (the author's) heart." The truth of that claim is evident in the writing and the powerful emotions written into its pages. —Delia Latham, Inspirational Romance Author

A cold case, a search for God, and a new life soon to be born. From an old journal to tracking down leads, *Touches of Time* follows the journey of a 35-year-old unsolved case. As time is running out, Ford and Sarah must figure out who killed her grandfather. You won't be able to put this one down.
—Sally Shupe, Reviewer and Aspiring Author

My heart went out to Sarah. Her fiancé died. Her mother died. Now she's pregnant and alone, sorting through records of her grandfather's unsolved murder, trying to find the killer before her baby comes. What answers will the cold case investigator have for her? Author LoRee Peery accurately captures the jumble of emotions of grieving, pregnancy, and falling in love in *Touches of Time*. —Catherine Richmond, Christian Author

*Touches of Time* turned out to be a page-turner! One in which I could not turn the pages fast enough. Mystery, suspense, intrigue, and love, a passionate story that will keep you turning the pages and fill your heart with such deep emotion for this family and the closure they need to go on. LoRee Peery has ever so eloquently written a story that is very near to her heart with courage, faith, and unconditional love from our Father.
—Sharon Dean, Avid Christian Romance Reader

*Touches of Time* is more than a murder mystery with a twist. It's an emotional ride with a happy ending. —Frenchy Dennis, Writer

This is another gripping read from LoRee Peery. It pulls you in from the start and won't let you go. I both laughed and cried while reading *Touches of Time*. Unputdownable is a word quite often bandied about these days, but this book really does that. The fact it is based partly on the author's own experience, makes it an even more powerful and cathartic read. If you only read one book this year, make sure it's this one.
—Clare Revell, Christian Romance Author

*Touches of Time* is a gripping story that pulled me in like a magnet, engaged my emotions and driving desire to find out the ending. The suspense builds increasingly as the pages go by. I didn't want to put it down, with so many impending events. The story was woven together well, and encouraged my spirit. I am so glad I read it. LoRee Peery puts her heart in her books. It's easy to find that heart while reading. —Barbara A. Kennedy, author of *My Cowboy Knight, My Boaz*

LoRee Peery's *Touches of Time* strums the heartstrings, and its beautiful melody lingers long after the final page has been turned. —Mary Manners, Award-Winning Romance Author

Two cold cases, a grieving single mother-to-be, and the cold case investigator who could tie them together. *Touches of Time* by LoRee Peery is a story of mystery, love, and faith. An engaging plot and well-developed characters bring the reader to a satisfying and heartwarming conclusion.
—Cheryl C. Malandrinos, The Book Connection

*Touches of Time* by LoRee Peery is based on the true-life unsolved homicide of the author's father, a fact that offers a gut punch to her Nebraska-set story. One expects church suppers and cornfields, not murder and a drug culture gone wild. This is definitely a book for those who love Christian fiction. Ms. Peery offers an appropriate scripture verse in her chapters, but also seamlessly ties fitting verses into conversations and introspection.
—Tanya Hanson, Award-Winning Romance Author

# *Other Titles by LoRee Peery*

**The Frivolities Series**
Moselle's Insurance
Rainn on My Parade
Sage and Sweetgrass
Found in the Woods

**Dollar Download**
Lezlie's Lifeline

**Christmas Extravaganza**
A Blessed Blue Christmas
Christmas Rescue Route

**Stand-Alone Novels**
Creighton's Hideaway
Paisley's Pattern
Where Hearts Meet

## Acknowledgements

I especially thank my husband Bill for his patience and understanding over the years. Writers can be hard to live with. My head is often in the lives of fictitious people and I know I have a glazed look on occasion when I need to switch to life "right now."

Several friends have read this story in varied versions, and helped with the final product. Thank you ALL for your input and your varied talents, not to mention your patience as I've worked through this trial. Frenchy, Stephanie, Yvonne, Melissa, Andria, Montanna, Jamie, Emily, Jessica, Julie, Mary, Barb, Delia, Pam, Rachel. If I missed anyone, I profoundly apologize.

With every ounce of my being, I thank my heavenly Father above for choosing me to be one of His children. I could not have handled this writing project, or the aftereffects of murder, on my own strength.

Dedication

*To my brothers and sister in memory of our parents. Also, to the generations before and after us.*

*I'd like to think we are all overcomers, though in imperfect ways, and wish above all else that we corporately experience our Lord's peace in those times He chooses not to give us answers.*

# One

The walk to the park took more effort than ever.

Sarah left the trail for her favored picnic table, fanning and flapping her shirt away from her body to dispel the heat. She sank onto the bench with a sigh.

Her mother's last days, followed by what she called her celebration of life, had kept Sarah too busy for strolling outside her apartment complex. She'd missed summer, teeming with new growth. Did nature grieve?

She closed her eyes to clear the fog, and sought warmth from the sun.

A thud on the table snapped open Sarah's eyes. She covered her rounded stomach with one hand and batted away an intrusive soccer ball with the other.

"Sorry about that." A buff guy with a killer grin toed the ball from midair, and then dribbled it away, running backwards.

Their gazes remained locked until one of his buddies called, "Hey, Melcher, the game's this way."

*I need to close my gaping mouth and quit gawking. If I had a man like that around, I'd be inclined to rejoin the living.*

Since he caught her eye, did that mean she rode the swell of coming out of her funk?

Events marched on whether she took an active role or not. Her brow tightened. She must be waking up to notice the hunky guy, sweat and all. He had to belong to some lucky woman.

His renewed attention drew her back to his wet black hair and brilliant blue eyes, increasing her pulse rate. Her breath hitched as though he sent invisible vibes through the summer air.

Forget taking another look. He had a life. She had a life. Sarah inhaled as deeply as she could and forced herself to break connection with his magnetic pull. Sliding across the table bench, she turned her back and wished for her waistline to return. She sauntered the way she'd come, grinned and grunted at the idea of taking the path closer to term. The mental picture of her waddling would be worth the trouble, since she'd soon have a baby to love and nurture. The prospect lightened her heart.

*Love and nurture.* Mom's words. Family had mattered so much to Mom.

Sarah sniffed. Time to somehow scrounge up the energy to check on the status of a job assignment she'd put on hold.

Digging into Mom's writings had crowded in on Sarah's call to return to work. Would Mom's words bring back the flood of tears, or give her comfort?

"I need to snap out of it. Baby and I will soon be a whole new family unit."

*Somehow, I'll tackle that promise I made you, Mom.*

*£*

Ford dribbled the soccer ball in circles. He could have taken a kick in the head the way a mere glimpse of a distressed soul sparked electricity. He ran sideways with the ball between his feet, wanting nothing more than to kick that thing out of the park and run after her.

He wanted to call out to the lovely lady whom he still trailed with his gaze.

He wanted to rest beside her for the duration of the day, peer into the allure of her golden-brown eyes and get to know the reasons behind her aura.

He wanted to search out the sense of familiarity, the air of mystery that shot awareness to his nerve endings.

The beauty eventually rounded a curve where bushes hid her from sight.

Why was he drawn to her? What had caused her to be so lost in thought? One glimpse of her eyes, and he'd detected deep sadness, unguarded susceptibility, yet strength. At the same time, she nudged him to adventure.

Did he know the woman from somewhere? She carried a hint of lingering intrigue.

He shook off the knockout's woeful expression to get his head back in the soccer challenge.

Chan stole the ball with his sturdy shoulders and skilled feet. He shouted over his goal in the imaginary net. "Snooze, you lose, Melcher."

Ford grunted at the jolt. He ran to kick aside a hand-off pass.

"That's what I get for daydreaming about a mysterious lady."

Her face tickled by wisps of hair the color of her pretty amber eyes had reminded him of someone. The time enhanced picture of a young girl in a file on his desk. A girl who disappeared from Hardin years earlier, the subject of the latest Nebraska cold case he'd immersed himself in.

£

In her apartment, Sarah tried to shake the handsome athletic guy's image.

Her stomach gave an excited turn. Then her abdomen rolled as the baby somersaulted. A gulp of cucumber water refreshed her.

Sarah took the crushed ice to her studio where she plunked into her desk chair. She booted up her computer and stared at the screen, lost in absent thought. Two e-mail messages replied to, she ignored anything that required taxing her mind, and logged onto her social networking sites. Energy gave way to sudden fatigue.

"Oh, my little one, I hope and pray you will never have to experience such a double loss in mere months. Except for you, I'd feel lonely." She closed her eyes and tried to picture the life nestled beneath her ribs. "If you can sense my sorrow right now, I'm sorry."

Sarah rubbed her belly. "Speaking of waiting, it's hard at times. I promise to tell you about your dad. And I promise you'll always have me."

*Promise me.*

How long would she hear Mom's voice in her head?

Or live with the guilt of finally saying yes when Travis offered marriage? Who would have thought he'd get himself killed? Sarah lost her life-long friend as well as the father of her baby.

Mom claimed God planned each and every child and had assured Sarah, "The Lord will work out the details. You'll learn to love Travis as your husband."

Children were supposed to have two parents.

Sarah's brother had always liked Travis, called him a friend the way she had. And her sister was thankful Sarah would soon have the baby to fill a void.

Her mother cried with her when Travis died. No one cried with her now over the loss of her mother.

Grief lived. Grief hurt. Grief remained an unseen presence.

In order to go on, Sarah pushed the loss of Travis behind. Her true feelings for him may as well have been written on the wind.

"Stop feeling sorry for yourself," she muttered. The command thundered through her head.

Facts were facts. The baby would enter the world without a daddy, and without grandparents. She and her baby would survive.

*Come to Me, and I will give you peace.*

Where had that come from? She swiveled her chair. Could Mom speak to her? Or did the voice belong to God?

Mom never stopped praying and claimed to know she was headed for heaven.

But how could Sarah know the reality of heaven? She'd never explored getting close to the God Mom knew as Lord. Maybe someday.

Her mind remained too distracted. Her heart too full of hurt to accomplish any kind of design work on this given day. She scrubbed at familiar drying tears and pushed forward to follow her belly out of the chair, grabbing the glass of lukewarm water.

She bypassed the mound of Mom's memories on the table and opened the mail.

Sarah fanned new sympathy cards, mostly from her mother's friends, and added them to the stack. She opened the top envelope and pulled out the card: *You are invited to be our guest at a pot faith (we don't believe in luck) dinner. Please join us for a friendly evening of fun and fellowship.* The stamped return address read Plains Bible Fellowship, Grief Support Group.

Her mother knew grief. Thirty-five years earlier, she'd received the traumatic news her father was murdered. Sarah set aside the invitation and immersed herself in her mother's world.

£

Murder on a Country Road by Lena Stanley Bishop…

*Scenes from* In Cold Blood *wove through my restless dreams. Did the jangle of the phone belong to my dream world, or was it real?*

*My husband Leighton and I had stayed up late to watch that jarring television movie based on a true crime in Kansas. I'd gone to bed with a stomach more sour than usual, due to scenes of cold-blooded murder.*

*Off and on throughout the night, my broken sleep felt as heavy as my bloated belly. All I've wanted since I hit thirty-eight weeks is to have our second child. Everything I do takes more effort and energy.*

*Leighton's half-awake greeting turned jovial. "How's my favorite brother-in-law?"*

*I groaned at his early morning breeziness, so like the tone he used when he spoke to the baby in my stomach. I tried to roll to my other side.*

*Leighton stayed me with a hand on my hip. "Don't get up, I'll talk to him."*

*Our mattress rolled and resettled as Leighton rose to take the call on the phone in the kitchen.*

*I scooted to his side of the bed, too fatigued to say hello to my brother, though I hadn't heard Connor's voice in months. At the clicking sound of Leighton picking up the kitchen extension, I replaced the phone in its cradle.*

*Then I dozed off to his indistinct conversation. Soon, silence helped me drift back to sleep, without questioning why I'd heard the kitchen door open and close.*

*Fifteen minutes later, according to the alarm clock, Leighton quietly shut the back door. He came into our room and touched my shoulder. I clumsily tried to raise my swollen body from the bed. My left leg tangled in the orange chenille spread. I fought the sheet and cover, then gave up.*

*Leighton rubbed my calf through the light blankets. "You believe in God, don't you?"*

*What a weird thing for him to say. Groggy, I wondered why he'd left the house for that contemplation. But I managed to nod. "Where'd you go?"*

*"I went next door and rang Connor back so I wouldn't disturb you." He swallowed. "Honey, Connor called with bad news."*

"*Sorry I'm so sleepy this morning,*" I said. "*Does he want me to call him back? How is he?*"

"*Not good. There's no easy way to say this.*" He swiped his eye. "*I'm so sorry, he called to say your dad is dead.*"

*Not sure I'd heard right, I became fully awake.*

*Leighton brushed my bangs to the side, smoothing the wrinkles in my forehead. His shoulders slumped.* "*Your father is dead.*"

"*Wh-a-at?*" *It couldn't be.* "*How?*"

*Dearest Leighton choked on his words.* "*He…he was found in a ditch.*"

*With those words, the real nightmare began. Shock rocked through me. I went with the first thing that popped into my mind.* "*Heart attack?*"

*Nothing made sense. I interrupted my own thoughts before he could answer.* "*Car accident?*"

*Leighton shook his head.*

"*A stroke?*"

*Another negative response.*

"*Somebody hit him over the head.*" *He cleared his throat. With tears in his eyes, he finished,* "*Dad was murdered.*"

*How does anyone grasp such a thing? I fought the blankets again. Leighton helped unwrap them from around my legs.* "*I don't…what do you mean?*" *I searched Leighton's eyes.*

"*He was hit in the head and killed.*"

# Two

Sarah rose from the couch. She needed a break from her mother's descriptive account of an event that hadn't mattered to Sarah until now. She walked to the window, shut the curtain, and returned to pick up where she'd left off.

"Mom, forgive me. It may take some time, but I'll read what you entrusted me with."

*The phone rang throughout that Saturday. Leighton made plans with Uncle Willis Stanley to arrive tomorrow and give me a ride. I managed to eat cereal for dinner and pack for the four-hour trip to Canton. Shocked and numb, I went about doing laundry, arranged for pet care, and waited for my OB-GYN to call me back.*

*My mind never stopped circling. I often ventured a guess as to how Mom spent the hours before Dad's body was found. Had she wondered where he was? Why he hadn't come home? Who'd held her when she heard the news?*

*"Oh, Mom, I'll be there soon," I said to the dishes in the sink.*

*What was she doing as I busied myself in my Lincoln home? Did she pace the living room, or take something to knock her out so she was oblivious, asleep in her room?*

*Way more questions than answers. I prayed I'd be exhausted and able to sleep later that night, relieved the doctor finally called. Since I was so close to term, he advised me to lie in the backseat for the long drive. Sitting so long could wrap the umbilical cord around the baby's neck.*

*It's Sunday already. It took forever to fall asleep. While other families prepared for Sunday church, I woke up alone. How had Leighton slept on Mom's couch?*

*Uncle Willis has always been one of my favorite uncles. He speaks little. Family lore claims he read and started school at age four. He also read every book in the Canton Library before he was out of junior high. I've seen him work the crossword in the daily newspaper in mere minutes.*

*I finally opened the door to him. His welcoming hug made up for the wait. I'll never tell him I wanted to leave the day before.*

*"I take it you talked to your doctor?"*

*"Finally. About nine-thirty last night. He called me and advised me to ride in the back, lying instead of sitting. He also asked if I wanted a tranquilizer."*

*"No way," we said at the same time.*

*It felt good to share a chuckle.*

*We immediately sobered.*

*He patted me on the shoulder. "We can laugh. We have to keep living, Lena."*

*We headed northwest through farmland alive with signs of impending harvest. From the backseat of the antique DeSoto, I tried not to gag from the smell of sweaty bachelor and stale cigarettes. I tried to get comfortable on my side, wished I had a pillow for between my knees. After a short while, I concluded I was as comfortable as I could get.*

*It was hard to imagine what transpired late the previous Friday night and into Saturday morning. No doubt Uncle Willis wondered as well, because silence surrounded my racing thoughts.*

*Time slowed and the quiet embraced me.*

*The idea of someone killing Dad was incomprehensible. Too much to understand. People killed each other in big cities. Other people. Strangers. Had Dad hurt someone enough to warrant getting hit in the head? Was it an accident or deliberate? A drunken fight? Maybe Dad was caught with another woman. Based on rumors I'd heard all my life about his womanizing, a father or husband may very well have lost his senses in a jealous rage.*

*Without intent to kill, I'd like to think.*

*Murder might have been the goal. Could it have been a professional hit? Drugs were big business in the country. Had Dad overheard something in the tavern and been shut up?*

*Tears trickled into my ears, one or the other, or both, as I rolled my head from side to side. Movement couldn't shake away the horror.*

*I resettled my baby weight in an attempt to get comfortable in the back of that car. I rested my tailbone against the tall bench seat, knees bent with my purse now between, and my hands cradling the mound of my precious baby.*

*A thump-thump of baby's fist or foot moved my belly and raised my hand. I smiled through my tears. The world continues on, even when life is snuffed out. Dad would never know this babe, whom I had convinced myself was a boy. Dad and grandson would never check fence together, count livestock, or ride the tractor. They'd never fish for rainbow trout in icy winding creeks.*

*Tears flowed. My nose plugged up and ran in turn. How could this be real? Homicide in my family?*

*I went back in memory to the Easter Sunday visit of a few months earlier. Dad's voice over the phone that spring morning sounded in the forefront of my thoughts. "You doin' anything special today? I thought we'd run down and see you, and then stop in at your sister's."*

*He sounded sober. I smiled as I remembered his teasing tone.*

*When he sought Joyce and me for our last visit, had he sensed he was going to die?*

*He and Mom arrived, and I vividly recall stepping out on the back stoop into bright yellow sunshine. I gave Dad a long hug.*

*"I had to see for myself if you're as big as you claimed to be in your letters." He patted my tummy.*

*I lifted my shirt and showed him the unbuttoned waistband.*

*"You've got a little pregnant bump, all right." He flashed his one-sided grin, and his deep hazel eyes sparkled. "Your mom did the same when her pants wouldn't close. Just wait, you'll be showing to the world soon."*

*Dad would never tease any of us again. He'd never hold my baby.*

*Yesterday, Mason called. He told me that on Friday, Dad bought cattle for Connor, and told Mason he didn't need to drive Dad anywhere again.*

*Did that statement mean he was getting his driver's license reinstated?*

*Before they left that weekend, Dad confessed he didn't know what to do about Mom drinking so much. Dad liked his beer, and he was putting her down for overindulging?*

*My heart broke for her when we talked yesterday, the way she'd sobbed on the phone. She said she should have taken Dad home after they left Rusty's Place. He wanted out at the stop light. A witness last saw Dad walking away from the VFW club. Did anyone else see Daddy early yesterday morning between one and three a.m.?*

*Lying in the back of that old car, my rounded middle felt every bounce and ridge in the highway. My troubled mind attempted to picture Daddy's body lying face down in a ditch outside Canton, near the driveway of Mom and Dad's home.*

Sarah's hand trembled as she set the pages underneath the rest of Mom's story. In honor of her mother's memory, she'd accept the church invitation. After all, she might meet someone to point her in the direction the rest of her life should take.

# Three

Later that week, Sarah arrived at the grief group dinner.

She'd been caught in a weak moment, to have said yes to the telephone follow-up regarding the church invitation.

"What can I bring?" she'd ventured.

"You're considered a guest, just bring yourself."

Mom would have encouraged her to attend, so Sarah now stood on a stranger's sidewalk.

A tanned teenaged girl with braces met her in the driveway. "Go around to the side gate. Everyone's out back."

"Thanks. Do you know how soon we're eating? My dish needs refrigeration." Though she'd been informed it unnecessary to bring anything, she didn't feel right about not contributing.

"No problem. There's a fridge in the outdoor kitchen." The girl bounced back to the sidewalk and said hello to another arrival.

It seemed forever ago that Sarah had been so carefree or energetic. She drew a quick breath and walked through the open side gate.

Milling people chattered on the enclosed patio, spilling onto the yard beyond. Some faces looked vaguely familiar, no doubt from her mom's celebration of life service.

"Hi, so glad you could come." A brunette with an asymmetrical haircut welcomed Sarah. "Mmm. Caprese is a treat. I'll see that your plate is kept chilled. Our resident grill master has yet to give the signal to serve."

Sarah handed over the platter of basil, seasoned tomato slices, and mozzarella. "Thank you for hosting and having me here."

The kind woman shot her a beaming smile, spoke her name that Sarah didn't catch, and yelled. "Hey, everyone, this is Sarah Bishop, Lena's daughter. Help me make her feel at home."

From behind Sarah's shoulder, the hostess said, "Sorry about the deluge of names. I never thought of nametags."

The next few moments passed in a blur of greetings. The only way she'd meet these people again was if she'd attend Plains Bible Fellowship, or visit the bereavement group. Funny. No one acted all mournful at this gathering, especially the hostess.

Sarah aimed for an empty picnic table not far from the grill. The table would soon be in the evening shade.

She caught sight of the dude manning the grill. Toned and fit. He wore a black T-shirt that accented his muscles, and beige cargo shorts above tanned, sinewy calves. Judging by his concentration as he unstacked burgers with precision and placed them in neat rows on the grill rack, he took care with what he did.

The sight of his face made her suck in air so fast she almost choked. The heart stopping soccer player from the park. He swiped his brow and closed the lid. A new kind of nervousness hit her stomach. How could she keep her mind on any of the others at this backyard gathering?

*Get real, Sarah. Forget these crazy hormones and put your focus back on making the best of your time here.*

Their gazes clicked.

Recognition slid into his expression. He shot her that engaging grin and waved her over. His rapt interest hit her like an invisible soccer ball.

She didn't have far to travel, just around a circle of patio chairs and the length of a picnic table.

His friendly regard remained on her face. "Hi there. We meet again. Sorry about kicking that wild ball. Do we know the same people?"

"A member of the church grief group contacted me. Guess that's why I'm here. My mom recently passed. Plus my brother strongly suggested I come. Then he said the hostess is married to an old classmate of his and suggested I check out this grief group in a setting other than a meeting at the church."

"Your mother passed away."

"Lena Bishop. I'm Sarah." Her shirt clung too close for her to feel at ease. She would have been more comfortable indoors, though she loved summer in Nebraska. Was this guy causing her contradictory thoughts? "What brings you here, besides having to man the grill?"

"Others could do it just as well. My name's Ford Melcher, by the way, and I spend time with those in the grief support group. It helps to know others care and understand what one goes through."

"You've lost someone, or are you a counselor?"

Meat juices hissed from the open grill and perfumed the air. He swung his focus to the fragrant burgers. His gaze flicked back to Sarah as he snagged a squirt bottle. "I need to mind my job. Let's talk later. Save me a place in line. We can eat together."

By the time he shut the lid, two guys took seats next to him. They commented on his skills, or lack thereof. He responded with a good-natured grin and waved at Sarah.

He was slow to lower his arm, which gave her a flash of the way Ford had run backwards at the park, while keeping eye contact. Their glances met again now. She grinned, and meandered to the modern outdoor-living area.

Time passed while she helped set the table with chilled salads, veggies, and fruits. She waited to step into line until Ford set the heaping platters of burgers and hot dogs on the buffet table.

Those platters were the signal for a short, but upbeat prayer.

Sarah bowed her head. Instead of closing her eyes, she stared at Ford's white feet balanced atop red, white, and blue flip-flops. Just above the anklebone, the color of his legs was bronze. She raised her head at the "Amen."

Noise ensued all around.

Ford moved with efficiency and precision, as he swiped a plate off the pile and handed it to her. Conversation eddied around them, but they were encased in a bubble.

He leaned close. "You asked if I'm a counselor. No, just a friend. I make myself available to come alongside and listen. On the job, I deal with people whose grief has spanned years."

She frowned, unclear what he meant.

"That didn't come out right, judging by the face you made. I'm a cold case investigator with the State Patrol. I like to think I deal with facts and files rather than emotions, but some hurts never go away entirely."

He understood somewhat then, accustomed to people who dealt with feelings of loss, old or fresh.

*Promise me.*

Bells dinged through Sarah's mind. Would Ford be familiar with Grandpa's case? "We should talk about your job some time."

"I'm sure we will. Who's your mom again?"

"Lee…" She cleared her throat. "Lena Bishop. Mom recently died from cancer. I was her constant companion until the end." What did he mean by grief spanning many years? This joy-stealing loss would last a long time?

"You have my condolences. You can be proud of your mother. Most of us who knew her, respected her. I had classes with her a time or two at Plains Bible." He flashed a grin that put warmth inside her chest. "But I don't remember ever seeing you there. Which worship service do you attend?"

She swiveled, prepared to say she didn't go to church.

Standing too close, he moved and rammed his plate against her belly. "Oh, I'm so sorry. Did I hurt you?"

She bit her cheek to keep from laughing. "It's a plastic plate. My front precedes me these days."

He excused his reach and grabbed a napkin from behind him. "I still should have been more careful. Here, there's some of my salad dressing on your, um, front."

"So there is. It's my shelf now and I hit it with stuff on occasion myself." She swiped at the smear.

"Let's talk while we eat, I didn't plan to meet anyone in particular tonight and I don't see a person off by themselves, so let's load up our plates. I'm hungry."

Sarah quivered inside, tried to keep up with the whirlwind of feminine response he created. Heat followed cold through her veins. Life did go on, ready or not. Was she ready to spend time with another man?

$$\mathcal{L}$$

Seated at the picnic table, Ford granted Sarah his full attention. *This gal pulls at my insides. But she's pregnant! Why now, Lord?*

He'd spoken to those they'd passed by. Most of the experienced mercy counselors of the group knew a one-on-one pairing was critical during the early stages of grief. It didn't bother him that he and Sarah sat apart from the others. He intended to make her feel as if they were the only ones who attended this backyard barbeque. "These gatherings can be awkward the first time or two. I hope you don't mind the way I've monopolized you. I want you to feel at ease."

She rolled her eyes and patted her stomach. "Uncomfortable goes along with this stage of my life. Sitting on a picnic bench is familiar."

"Aw. The park." He hadn't seen her rise from the table the first time he'd seen her, but took note of her narrow hips as she left on the path. She carried her pregnancy well.

He blinked a fast shot at her left ring finger. Unadorned. Where was the baby's father?

"Yes. I'm fine. The women seem nice. Vaguely familiar. I may ponder later what I was doing here at a grief support group. A church one, no less. I have my moments of crying jags, but I think I'm doing fine on my own."

Ford chomped a chip. "This is a terrific bunch of people. God puts us in the world together. Fellowship keeps us from feeling alone."

"Mom believed that. Toward the end of her life she spent a lot of time sharing Bible verses with me, and I met some women she knew from church."

"It's good she had you to spend time with. What else did you and your mom talk about?"

"The emotions she went through over the years because she never knew who was responsible for ending her father's life. He was murdered and the case is unsolved." Sarah cleared her throat.

Her words stunned Ford.

Sarah took a drink, met his gaze over her glass. "Now that Mom's gone, I guess I'm the patrol's family contact for Granddad's case, since neither of my uncles lives in Lincoln."

"I'd like to hear about it. I'm desk deep in another case, but here's my card. You can give me a call later this week. Once I'm familiar with the details, I'll try to answer any questions you have."

They sat for a time in affable silence, smiled at one another during the moments laughter rose around them. His heaped plate dwindled down the hatch much faster than her sensible servings. It took concerted effort to focus on her face and not her obvious pregnancy. Sarah drew more than his casual interest. He wanted to know her story.

"Sorry again for bumping your front with my plate. At the picnic table in the park, I didn't notice that you were expecting. I must have been dazzled by your gorgeous face."

She sputtered.

"Oops. This is not my usual professional self. Forgive me." He wasn't a nervous teenager, blurting out whatever caught his attention. Usually. He guzzled his tea, and then played with the condensation on the plastic tablecloth.

Sarah ran a cucumber slice through dressing and plopped it in her mouth. "I've eaten more cukes this summer than I have in my whole life."

"Cravings." He waited for her to swallow. "I apologize if this is too personal, Sarah, but what does your baby's father think of you coming here alone? How would he react if he walked up to us?"

"That's not going to happen, him walking up. He died a few months ago in an accident."

Ford wanted to kick himself. He wasn't in top form with this woman. "Again, I feel for your double loss. I hope you give these fine people a chance, take the time to meet them. Most have lost someone."

"I'm taking life a day at a time. I can only dream of having as much strength as Mom showed, right up to the end."

"We just met, but I'd venture to guess you have equal strength, considering your mom's death on top of losing a man dear to your heart."

She gave him another frank look in the eye. "He was hit while jogging across the road."

"Tough." He attempted to remain casual. "Does the baby's father have a name, or does it hurt to talk about him?"

She leaned back, rolled her shoulders, and sat taller. "Travis and I spent many hours in the park over the years, at that picnic table where your soccer ball bounced. We called it our spot when we were teens, and discussed everything from homework to hot dates. Then after college, I moved to within walking distance. We still met at the same picnic table. He'd sit on the tabletop instead of the plank bench, where he'd rest his feet. He drank his caffeine-laced sodas while I indulged in the iced caramel-laced espresso topped with whipped cream he often brought for me." Sarah gazed off in the distance, lost in thought. Then she giggled.

"What's tickling you?"

"On one of our last stops, it struck me that my belly would hit the table a few months later and I'd have to sit backwards. Look here, I still fit on the bench of a picnic table."

"That's a good thing." His sister made remarks like that, but she'd been carrying twins. He caught a smear of mustard on his finger and scrubbed it with a napkin. "Travis, you said?"

"Yes. Travis Clifton."

"The graphic novelist?" He studied her face, those eyes. *So attractive. So sad.* "I've read his book, if it's the same guy."

"No doubt."

"Very good, if you're into that genre. I heard about his accident. What a waste of artistic talent."

She finished her water and let the last ice cubes slip back into the cup. "I'm convinced he would have been a good father. We'd already discussed baby furniture, including a changing table, and where it would fit in my apartment. Neither of us even knew what to call that vital piece of furniture before I got pregnant. Never got around to shopping for one. I need to get busy. It's past time to check my work deadlines and jot in my calendar time to shop for those big baby items."

"What do you do for work?"

"I'm a graphic artist. I work out of my apartment studio." She met his gaze again and her cheeks turned a pretty pink. "My goodness, I can't believe I've told you so much about my fiancé, let alone my personal life. You must be good at getting information out of people."

"Observation becomes second nature. Your water is gone. Shall we clear our plates and get more drinks and check out dessert?"

"The only dessert I can think of at the moment is one of those lovely coffee drinks, blended and icy enough to freeze my brain cells." She heaved an exaggerated sigh. "But caffeine isn't good for the baby. I'll have to settle for water."

It hit him with all the force of a major break in a cold case. Sarah was the model for the heroine in Travis Clifton's graphic novel. No wonder she seemed familiar.

# Four

Sarah could have been posed like one of her stock art models, sitting so fixed and still at her table. Except for her fingers. Shame washed through her as she twirled the business card over and over. *Ford Melcher, Investigator, Nebraska State Patrol.* She should have sympathized more when Mom talked about the old murder. Why hadn't she paid closer attention to spoken details regarding Mom's attempts at moving along the investigation? Her grandfather's unsolved homicide had worked on her mother off and on over the years. Mom was gone now.

Time to move on. Sarah needed to occupy her mind for the sake of her baby. Read everything her mother left. Pick up the search for answers. "No more melancholia, woman. Do this for Mom."

A dry lump in her throat tried to choke her as much as the guilt that assailed her.

Murder had been too big for Sarah to grasp as a young girl. But now on the brink of giving birth, she found herself compelled to learn the details surrounding Grandpa Stanley's death.

Had Mom ever been scared in her pursuit?

Sarah grasped her cell phone, heaved a fortifying breath, and tapped the numbers with a firm touch. A surprising calm washed over her. Had she given him enough time to check on the case?

"Lieutenant Ford Melcher."

Her heart picked up its beat. "Hello. This is Sarah Bishop. We talked at the grief support barbeque."

"Of course, how are you, Sarah? Hope all that good food and fellowship settled well with you."

"The food was terrific and the company great. Thanks for asking."

"How can I help you?"

"Remember I mentioned my grandfather, an unsolved homicide victim, I didn't give you his name."

"It's all right. I followed up using your mom's name and it led me to Dieter Stanley." His voice exuded warmth.

Proactive. She liked that.

"I've become familiar with the basic circumstances of your grandfather's case." His voice invited her to confide, his sincerity hitting her on some gut level of intuition. He sounded friendly, yet professional at the same time.

"It happened some time ago. My mother's family never gave up hope of resolution."

"I wish I could give you something to go on now, but as I said earlier, I'm deeply involved with another case. Interestingly, it happened in the same part of the state. I'll need a little more time to really get into the details of your grandfather's death."

Keyboard taps and a mouse click sounded through the phone.

"Could I have your contact information then, please?"

She gave him the info he requested, including her date of birth.

He asked nothing more, so she braved a question. "Has there been any recent activity, like from the crime-ads? Or has any new evidence come to light?"

"Not that I'm aware of, but remember, I need a closer look. In cold cases, we'll consider information as long as it comes in. Going back to your question, I saw no indication anyone responded to the latest published notice."

"Oh. I hoped for some hint, anything new to make the case active again."

"A homicide case is never closed until it's solved."

"I do realize that. Thank you again for taking my call."

"I'll check into this for you as soon as I can."

"I'm reading through Mom's records and diaries now. Would they be helpful to you?"

Sarah heard more keyboard noise. She didn't know what else to say.

He spoke instead. "I'll be away from the office for a while. Maybe something will pop up in your mom's stuff, or spark a new lead. I'll give you a call once my case doesn't demand so much time here in the office."

"I've some of my work to do as well. Good luck with whatever you're involved with. Thank you so much."

"Of course. And again, I really am sorry about your losses. A call to someone in the grief support group may be helpful."

Could a heart splinter? Wouldn't she just reawaken her sorrow if she talked nonstop about losing Mom and Travis? She ended the call, and wished for nothing more than to wrap her arms around Mom.

Several times already, Sarah had intended to call, only to stop and remember. *Mom's gone now. I can't just pull up her listing from my phone.*

Sarah never knew her grandparents. She'd listened to stories, seen pictures over the years, and tried to imagine Grandma attempting to hide from the awful incident. Did Sarah's aunt and uncles have nightmares? Probably so. The subject of murder without answers had come up at family gatherings. Mom and her siblings lost their father at such young ages. The family had discussed their unanswered questions, how the murder still plagued them at times. How had they continued to live with the unknown?

That fateful blow of long ago changed the lives of a lot of people.

"I'll get to know you, Grandpa, through Mom's words. And maybe, just maybe, with Ford's help, we'll discover who killed you."

*The unsolved homicide of Dieter Stanley* trickled icy fingers over Sarah's senses.

£

Sarah spent two weeks reading her mother's material, her mind still unsettled, she'd have to read it again. She entered Ford Melcher's office with one of Mom's journal entries on her mind. Her mother had described walking into the FBI's office in downtown Lincoln. By her description, Sarah believed her mom must have had a panic attack.

Jittery nerves hummed in Sarah's stomach, caused more by the man she was about to face than the account of her mother's past experience. She hoped to suppress them so the baby didn't sense her agitation. She had nothing to fear.

Ford concentrated on an open file on his desk, giving it the same undivided attention he'd given a gas grill loaded with burgers. He wore a button-down salmon tinged dress shirt, sleeves rolled up to expose tanned muscular forearms. "Come in. Be with you in a moment."

The friendly expression and genuine smile of the man who greeted her could be beaming from the proverbial boy next door. Or the park around the corner, as on their first encounter. He rounded his desk and extended his hand in one athletic swoop. The warmth of his palm seared her clammy fingers. *Dratted nerves.* "Pleasure to see you again. Have you been well, you and the baby?"

"We're doing well, thanks for asking." She sank to the offered chair, grateful for the support against her back. She lifted her eyes to meet Ford's piercing gaze. Up fluttered the nerves.

His heart-stopping features would make women of any age give him information he sought. He must be a gentle terror when it came to interviewing women. Ford's sincere azure eyes calmed her, erased all her nervousness regarding the reason for her visit. His short summer cut had grown out enough to make his coffee-colored hair appear on the untidy side. His gaze swept her abdomen.

Had she grown since the barbeque? *Oh, to have a picnic table to hide behind.*

The zing of attraction screamed for attention. Such a skittery feminine reaction hadn't surfaced since her very first crush. *Pull yourself together. You're pregnant. You're here for your family.* She swallowed. Nothing in her mouth but dryness.

How long could they sit with their gazes on one another? He gave her a slight nod.

"Thank you for seeing me. I'm wading through Mom's records concerning my grandfather's case, and trying to make sense of it all. There are so many names I finally had to create a list. As I said on the phone, I'd like to see if anything can be done to resolve such an old dilemma."

He relaxed his shoulders, gave a slight headshake. "Lists and notes are a good way to puzzle things out. I'm sure part of your process as a graphic artist is doing the same. You're closer to the subject than I am to my cases."

She set her purse on the floor. "What I do for a living can't be as complicated as solving old cases that cross your desk."

"Regarding your grandfather's demise, I've picked up on bits and pieces, but no one thing has jumped out for me to start assembling this puzzle." Ford settled a pair of thick-framed, black-rimmed glasses on his nose. It took a few facial motions and head movements for him to get things adjusted.

To keep from staring, she surveyed the space surrounding him. A photograph of two children perched on the mezzanine, a girl and boy about four, with a golden retriever. Everyone had a personal story, but she saw no picture of a woman, and no ring circled his finger.

"Scanning through these notes," Ford began, "it seems nine months ago was the last time a published notice appeared in Swanson and neighboring counties."

"Did anything come of it?" He shook his head, her anticipation deflated. "Is there any hope for a break in the case, so it'll be solved?"

"We always hope, and search for that one missing clue that breaks things open. For the record, this case was active not that long ago. We had an undercover officer in the area. No rumors or mention of your grandfather were ever discussed." Self-confidence spread across his features, along with a smile she took as personal.

Her tummy flip-flopped in reaction, as though the baby had jumped at her response. "You sound like my mother." She couldn't help but answer his smile with one of her own. "I won't give up then. Are you the one to reach if I run across any details of interest, or is someone else in charge of Grandpa's file, since you're working another case?"

"Please call me. I've meticulously gone over the available details we have. But little points to the initial investigation, other than a note that says a large number of people were given polygraphs."

"Is it normal for that many people to do lie detector tests?"

"We have to follow up on every possibility. We look at and rule out family first, of course, which can make them feel suspect. Murder is often personal. Most victims are killed by those they trust, or at least viewed as posing no threat."

"In other words, family, friends, even a child or a spouse."

"That's an ugly statistic, but yes. As for the polygraphs, each person who supposedly saw or could have been with your grandfather that night was questioned."

"Is there anything at all to bring this case to light?"

"After so much time, it comes down to a matter of proof."

"As in DNA?"

"DNA can still show up, but it's often contaminated after so many years. A reliable first-person account would do it. We've learned to consider that one person's memory may be a contradiction, or even disbelief, of another's." He consulted the file. "There's reference to an unreliable witness, but only the perpetrator knows the details."

"What makes a witness unreliable?"

"Different factors come into play. The rush of adrenaline can shut down brain cells. A witness to a crime or victim of trauma goes into survival mode. Memory can be faulty because of individual perception, more so with the passage of time." He met her gaze with a furrowed brow.

Why the frown?

"To elaborate on your question, investigators work toward a personal, reliable confession to any killing. If there's some kind of back-up proof? That's what we dream of. It's rare those dreams come true."

He rattled off all that information as though he were training others. "Do you know about the playing cards in prisons and jails?

They aren't being distributed to the general public, though the images can be viewed on the Patrol's website."

"What are they?" Sarah grew unsettled again over continued eye contact.

His compelling presence made it hard to look away. "The Patrol received funding to place cold-case homicide playing cards for inmate access. They feature pictures and profiles of unsolved victims and stats. Other states have found their use effective. Your grandfather's information is on one of the cards."

"That's good to know. What are the chances a prisoner will come forward as a result of the cards?"

"I'm not a man who follows conjecture. Many playing cards have been a waste of time and money. Yet in other states some cases have been solved." He sat back in his chair, removed his glasses, and pointed them at her mid-section. "Is it wise to put yourself through this now? In your condition, I mean?"

Her heart melted another notch over his protective nature. She raised her shoulders, and rubbed the mound away from where the baby kicked against a rib. "I'm healthy, and so is my baby. Since I started digging and learned what supposedly happened to Grandpa, this crime won't let me go. I need answers for this to be over and done with. My mom never rested easy about my grandfather's murder, if rest is even possible following such a life-altering event."

Sarah had made her mother a promise. She refrained from voicing the true-to-life image of Grandpa bleeding out in the gravel and browning grass at the side of the road. Mom had carried that image in her mind more than half her life.

"You're the only one who knows if this is the right time for you to get involved."

"I've seen a lot, what with how graphic forensic programs are on the television any given night. Head injuries bleed. Little is left to the imagination. Blood, bruises. Splinters of exposed bone. Are investigators actively searching for Grandpa's killer?"

Ford didn't respond.

"Has anyone done a reenactment?"

"Is it relevant?" His response sounded like a line from a script. He'd gone all professional over her probing.

"Too bad I'm growing as big as a horse. I could move to Canton and go undercover as a tavern worker, pay attention to local gossip."

The tough cop emerged. All friendliness disappeared from Ford's face, his features turned hard and formidable. He leaned forward, yet appeared taller. The narrow gaze and concrete expression, complete with an indented vertical line between his brows, matched the seriousness of his tone. "I would not advise that, Ms. Bishop."

Instead of discouraging her with his input, she preferred to think that Ford spoke from a cautionary perspective.

"You mentioned documents your mother kept."

"Correct. Mom saved news articles, photos, and letters. She poured out her feelings in journals. I'm reluctant to part with them but you are welcome to read through them. I think a chunk of my grief process is going through all the information." She stopped to gain control of the chokehold closing off her throat.

He waited her out.

"I don't know what you're working on, but I think I was around twelve when Mom told me about the disappearance of a girl my age from Hardin. That case somehow affected my mother. Authorities considered it a supposed kidnapping. I found a letter in Mom's things from a stranger who wrote he thought the cases may be tied, that girl's and my Grandpa's. The whole thing haunted Mom because of the girl's resemblance to me, and it took place in a neighboring county not far from where Grandpa lived. As far as I know, the case was never solved."

"I may need to look at your mother's documents."

"As soon as you're free to come, I'd like you to see everything. You have my address now."

Would it seem strange having a man other than Travis sitting at her kitchen table?

# Five

At the mention of the probable kidnapping of the young girl, and Sarah's mother's interest, Ford's nape hairs had stood straight up. If he grew antennae they would've elongated like Pinocchio's nose. He'd followed hunches on the job. Instinct came into play on those occasions when facts appeared coincidental. The timing and the proximity fit. The names of thugs crossing county lines, tied up in various criminal activities. There might be something connecting his current case of Neely Stallcup's disappearance with the murder of Sarah's grandfather.

Dare he hope he'd find something for the case he was embroiled in, such as Lena Bishop's mention of the names Easter and Kruz?

Sarah waited at the top of the stairs as he climbed the steps to her apartment door. He focused on her face. She had more color in her cheeks and her eyes were bright, less weary. Pretty. *Stop that. She's pregnant.* He entered her apartment and scanned the open room. Orderly, tan and light brown accented by blues and greens. A pitcher and bowl sat on the coffee table, peacock feathers swaying out the top. "Nice."

"Thanks. I've always enjoyed blues and greens. I rearranged Mom's pretties when I was little. I'd visit my aunt's or a friend's home, and move around their knick-knacks." She fell silent.

The door clicked shut. He regarded her with intensity, seeking a reason for the effect she had on him. How long should he fight the impulse to draw her close, offer protection? He found no answer in her eyes. But the strong pull told him he needed to pray for control.

"What does your wife think of you visiting a single woman in her apartment?"

"Excuse me?" He frowned, puzzled. "I don't have a wife."

"There's a picture of kids in your office."

"Oh." He relaxed his brow.

She shot him a winsome crinkle that did crazy things to his system.

"My niece and nephew. Tyler and Tanya."

He plucked a copy of Travis's graphic novel off the raised counter dividing the room, and traced the author's name on the cover. "Did Travis have a habit of taking that west route on the Pacific Trail?"

"Yes, outside the city limits. A car hit him three months before my mother died."

"I take that path myself, and switch off running the Pacific Trail south and west of town. Did you put the memorial cross and flowers there in the ditch?"

"Mom and I did."

"I got the impression Lena had a strong faith. I imagine she gave you rock-solid support, and helped you get through what happened with your Travis."

He waited for her to fill in the blanks.

She didn't. "Come in and sit at the table. Coffee or something cold?"

"Thanks. Coffee if you have it."

The mess on her table belied the order in the living area. It looked as though she'd done a lot of digging.

He turned his attention on her as she frittered around the small kitchen nook, and talked in spurts. "After Travis, Mom supported me as much as I did her the last few months of her illness. She never reprimanded me for getting pregnant without being married. She couldn't understand how we let it happen, but was excited about becoming a grandmother."

He pulled out her chair and she sat with a thud, no doubt due to extra weight she wasn't used to carrying.

"We wondered if we had ruined our friendship by getting intimate, until Travis and I talked it out." She waved her hands and shook her head. "Oops. Way too much info."

It touched him that she was comfortable enough to speak her innermost thoughts to him.

"Imagine that was awkward."

She kept her eyes lowered. "We did love each other. He agreed to be a daddy, and he proposed, shortly before he died."

"You have my condolences. Again, you didn't have to go into all that."

"I figured with your inquisitive mind, I'd get it over with so you wouldn't wonder. I don't want you to be distracted from all of my mom's records here."

"Appreciate it. So what do you have for me?"

"This stuff fills a couple storage crates, consisting of diaries or journals, whatever you want to call them. There are copies of correspondence and news clippings. I remember Mom writing all through my life. The whole family called her the historian, the way she kept scrapbooks and photo albums and memorabilia. So, yes, if you count all those, she saved boxes and more boxes. Family mattered to Mom. Sorry, I'm a little nervous. I think I have things in chronological order. I read again this morning what she said about getting the call, so you can keep those pages to yourself. Next is her trip to Canton and her description of the memorial service."

He accepted the typed pages she handed him, stalled by a glimpse at an open journal. "I like knowing your mother was a Christian, and that she used Bible verses in her writings."

Sarah ignored the Bible comment. "Please pick up at the top of this page, it's still during Mom's ride to Canton."

He read, turned the pages over as he went, until he reached the page she'd indicated. "Do you want me to read aloud?"

She nodded.

"It can't be easy for anyone to write about murder on a county road, especially a victim's family member." Ford unfolded his glasses and adjusted them on his nose. "Your mother's perspective may give me a new slant on what happened."

She drew in a ragged breath, reminding him of a child who had been crying hard.

He closed his eyes for a moment. *Lord, give me the stamina to deal with this grieving beauty. Help me set my job ahead of the way she pulls at my heart.*

Then he began.

"*How bloodied and battered was Dad's body? How about his eyes—open in fear or surprise, or closed? Had he had the chance to defend himself? Had he known his assailant and trust showed in his eyes?*

"*I shook off the image, drawing back to the last time I saw him at my backdoor, and the picture I preferred to keep.*

"*Uncle Willis' voice made me jump. 'Did you know the milk truck driver was the same one who picked up milk for the Canton Creamery when you lived on the farm?'*

"'*I remember Mr. Chapman. He'd joke and tease until I blushed.' I smiled at the memory. 'How do you know that?'*

"'*Connor told me.' Uncle Willis returned to his private thoughts.*

"*The ride seemed to take forever, but Uncle Willis and I finally arrived at my parents' home west of Canton, where I'd never lived. Guess it's just Mom and Mason's home now.*

"*I moved as fast as I could into the house to see Mom. I found her lying in her darkened room amidst rumpled bed clothes. Her hair was flat on one side and knotted in the back. Her face was red and swollen, her speech incoherent. Zoned out on what? I hoped it was only a tranq of some kind and not vodka.*

"*She murmured and talked as though continuing our phone call from yesterday. 'I couldn't sleep all night. He didn't come home. When I looked out the kitchen window and saw the stopped cars in the road, I knew. I knew.'*

"*I could hardly breathe, I cried so hard.*

"*Mom started to speak, then choked on words that seemed stuck in her throat.*

"*We clung to one another.*

"*Her eyes told me she was in lala land, out of it and no doubt unaware of activity in the rest of the house. I smelled her hangover, though vodka isn't supposed to smell.*

"*I'd attempt to escape reality, too, if I were walking in her shoes. And not pregnant. My soul dripped sorrow as I witnessed Mom, the beautiful Pearl Stanley, at this wretched time of her life. I tried to make her as comfortable as possible before I left her room.*

"*Then I did what came naturally. I took over, and kept myself busy with all the household duties. Interesting how I slipped right back into the mode as the oldest child, doing what needed to be done. I felt I had to be the doer. The one who took action, the one who tried to be strong for my brothers and for my sister.*

"*It felt so wonderful to have Leighton hold me. Through those remaining hours of Sunday, I walked as though in a fog. He was my strength, my rock, and my family looked up to him as a leader.*

"*All the while I cleaned and tidied up and answered the phone and accepted condolences and dishes of food at the door. Law enforcement was absent. I prayed that meant they were on the hunt for Dad's killer.*

"*All through Monday we tried to comfort one another, Joyce, Connor, Mason, and I. Each of us remains independent to a fault, no doubt due to the building alcoholism in the family. We held in more sorrow than we dared reveal to each other.*

"*The men kept coming and going. Leighton, my brothers, and their friends.*

"*The women came in a parade of twos and threes. I greeted them at my mother's door, then moved my pregnant body back a step or two. Compassionate smiles and condolences ushered in their offerings of casseroles, sandwiches, desserts, and cans of coffee. Most of them were strangers to me, but friends to the family.*

"*Mom stayed in her room.*

"*Connor went to pick up Uncle Walter, who flew to Omaha from San Francisco. He'll get to the bottom of this. He's a cop.*

"*I'll carry a wonderful picture to bed tonight. First, Leighton assured me that Leah is playing with neighbor kids and doing okay.*

"*He pulled me in close. 'You'll never believe what happened last night. I pulled off the highway onto the blacktop to get here, and a vision simmered up the road ahead. Don't know what else to call it. Within the beam of headlights, and about twenty feet tall, I saw my dad and yours. They stood with their arms around one another's shoulders. They were laughing and having a grand time.'*

"*I smiled and cried at once.*

"*I lost yesterday. Now it's Wednesday. I want to go back to bed and escape wherever Mom does so as not to feel the pain.*

"*Dad's body arrived at Oakwood Funeral Home. The autopsy was done in Lincoln. Family was allowed to view the body. Don't ask me why, I chose to see Daddy twice.*

"*Leighton didn't want to take me into town the second time. He must have known I'd come close to collapse.*

"*The body looked like my father, lying there in the silky coffin, yet it didn't. The makeup failed. I saw underlying bruises across the right temple and behind the ear through his thinning hair. His beloved mouth held the familiar slant of his crooked smile. Did my eyes need to see the bruises for my mind to accept the reality?*

*"What noise I made, I can't name. It sounded more animal than human.*

*"I believe my body went into some kind of auto pilot. At the house I swallowed tasteless food, responded when spoken to. Or I didn't say anything. While awake, I walked through the kitchen and living area where Dad had been only days before. Was I dreaming, and he'd come through the door again? The echo of his voice followed me through the rooms I'd never lived in.*

*"My life will never be the same.*

*"My family will never be the same.*

*"Disaster. Disbelief. Shock.*

*"It's true. Someone unknown crushed in my dad's skull. And took him away from those who love him. The funeral is tomorrow. I need to seek rest for the sake of my baby.*

*"I need to pull myself together. It just seems as though life has stopped."*

At Sarah's gasp, Ford paused and looked up from the paper. "Sure you're ready for me to continue?"

Sarah needed to pull herself together. She'd seen her Mom do that very thing through her last days. She'd start to sag, then close her eyes. Did Ford also pray? He liked Bible verses.

*I want to believe in what the Bible says, the way Mom believed.*

Mom was gone now, and Sarah had a promise to keep. She squirmed. Arms on the table, then hands on her stomach, returned to scrunch close to the table. *Enough wallowing.* She bolstered her shoulders against the chair back.

Ford showered her with concern.

"Ready as I'll ever be." Sarah set her shoulders, slanted him a look. "I'm compelled to be strong, no matter what. It may hurt at times to hear Mom's words, but they comfort as well. Could you go on with the funeral?"

"You can't help but wish for your mom to be with you, rather than the words she left behind."

"Just do it." Sarah's jumbled insides zeroed in on the rich timbre of Ford's voice, which pulled her into the scene her mother related.

*"Thursday, the day of Daddy's funeral. Flashes over the past hours let me know I'd been in the Congregational Church, yet I remember no face from inside the jam-packed church. I can visualize my body convulsed with inward wailing, silently screaming for normalcy. Dad loved the hymn, 'How Great Thou Art.' But I couldn't sing.*

*"People were everywhere. Farmers poured in from their harvest preparations. The church overflowed to the choir loft and into the basement. Mason's whole sophomore class attended, even though school wasn't in session yet. As for the rest, were they curiosity seekers, or did they really care about my family? Murder had shocked the whole village.*

*"Had the killer attended the service?*

*"One face stands out. While I sat in the limo waiting for the ride to the cemetery, my ex-husband and I had an eye-connect.*

*"My soul will always remember the strength Leighton gave. He was my lifeline. Throughout the day, he remained by my side. I leaned on him for support while we walked down the aisle of the church, picking our steps across the wet grass at the cemetery, and then downstairs for the food.*

*"I forced myself to take bites of a sandwich for the baby, not for me, back in the church basement. Why didn't I ask Leighton to take me to the house? Grief talking. The whole town would have added that disrespect on my part to the homicide gossip. I felt their gazes. I didn't care what they thought.*

*"I have no other memory of the memorial service.*

*"My heart remembers concern from relatives for my advanced stage of pregnancy.*

*"Rain greeted us at the gravesite. Leighton helped me to a metal folding chair under an awning in the front row by the casket, then he stood behind with a hand on my shoulder. Mom quietly sobbed beside me. Connor stood behind Mom, with Joyce and her husband Vern on my other side.*

*"I flinched at the shots of the twenty-one gun salute. The recited words from the Bible comforted me. As with the church service, I draw a blank as to what scripture was read by the pastor."*

Ford paused for a drink. "It was a military service then?"

"Yes. Grandpa was a Korean War vet."

"Aw. That explains the VFW reference." He picked up where he left off reading.

*"A blue break in the clouds punctuated the possibility of hope. A glimpse of sunshine broke through and momentarily penetrated my numbness.*

*"Later, out the window from the backseat of the limo as we left the cemetery, I couldn't believe my eyes. A rainbow was perfectly arced over Daddy's grave. Tears washed my cheeks at the sight of God's symbol of love and mercy. What an unbelievable sign of comfort. I felt as though He assured me of His presence. The rainbow is a physical sign that God keeps His promises. Somehow, I also took it to mean that He has my life in His hand.*

"*Hours have passed. I'm numb, and still wearing the purple maternity dress I sewed from fabric Aunt Verlene gave me as a wedding shower gift. Back home in Lincoln, I'll put the dress in the trash.*"

"Stop. Please." Sarah's body tightened as taut as her belly during Braxton Hicks contractions. She couldn't tell if Ford's reading made the story easier or harder. Mom's emotional turmoil spilled into Sarah as she tried to absorb the story.

# *Six*

The poignant account of her grandfather's murder blurred Sarah's vision, but she blinked away the tears. Her soul filled with Mom's frustration, her anger, her sorrow. "What Mom endured has flowed from her into my heart and taken root. At times, I feel as though I'm going through it alongside her. Hearing this account makes me remember getting the call about Travis."

"I'm so sorry. I wondered how much you could handle." Ford removed his glasses and rubbed his eyes.

Her heart plunked and her throat filled. Focus fixed on Ford, she drew on the strength he offered simply by being with her. "I don't know why some things come to mind when they do, but I remember Mom's emotions. Actually, my first memory is wrapped up with feelings. I recall sitting in the backseat of the car while my sister, Leah, rode in the front and talked to Mom. Mom said something like, 'I'm sorry I still get sad over his death. You know how my Dad was killed. We'll have answers when God says so.'"

Sarah paused. Ford reached out as though he wanted to touch her, but withdrew his hand and nodded encouragement.

Composure retained, she went on. "I clammed up, so devastated I didn't say a word the rest of the day. But I'll never forget how glad I felt to see Daddy come through the door that night. I went running into his arms and yelled, 'I thought you were dead!'"

"How awful for you." Ford paper-clipped the pages and set them down. His hand nested over Sarah's. "In other words, you heard your mother refer to her father being killed, and you thought she meant your dad."

She flipped her hand over. Who could feel lonely soaking in his offer of solace? "I plan to talk to my little one about his or her daddy. I'll use Trav's name, especially if I'm fortunate enough to have a new live daddy for him or her."

Sarah kept her eyes on their clasped hands so he wouldn't read anything into her comment. She braced herself, sat taller. "It won't be easy. In weak moments, I've wondered what it would be like to go to sleep. Let all that time pass and wake up later to bring my baby into the world. Have you ever thought what an escape that would be, to sleep in a place where heartache didn't exist? For me, it'd be followed by waking up to the exhilaration of new life."

Ford opened his mouth, but she went on without giving him time to say anything. "I promised Mom I'd pick up the pieces where she left off, and try to find answers to what really happened to my grandfather."

"A promise like that gets under your skin and turns to an obligation. We'll go through whatever information you want, but it's not your job to solve his case."

Guilt smacked without warning. "I listened to Mom and her siblings over the years. I never tried to empathize. Before reading about the details of Grandpa's murder, the unsolved homicide didn't sink in. But it's remained a blight that affects the whole family. Thanks to Mom's account, I now understand what drove her adult life. How could she have gone through such heartache? How did she survive?"

Ford ran a comforting finger over the inside of her wrist. "I believe God gave the gift of strength to your mom. She loved her Lord. She somehow had the gumption, while enduring cancer pain, to relive an event that impacted numerous lives. You'll get through as well."

"One thing's for sure. I'll tell the people in my life how important they are, and how much I love them." She downed cucumber water to chase away a sob. The constant ache of loss throbbed with no foreseeable cure.

Ford's presence took the edge off, dulled the sharpness, enabling her to endure. He reached for her other hand, warded off the chill of her fingers from contact with the glass.

"She was pregnant with your brother at the time of your grandfather's death?"

"Yes, my brother Jeremiah. He lives in Aurora, Colorado. Leah and her girls are in Valdosta, Georgia. Mom and Leah's dad were married a short time, separated shortly after Leah's birth. She's nine years older than me."

"You've got to feel especially close to Lena at this time of your life, considering your pregnancy." Ford drew Sarah to her feet.

"And speaking of time, I think I'll call it a night. Thanks for sharing your mother's writing with me, Sarah."

"She'd want that."

"Let me know when you're ready to continue." He released her hands as though it was the last thing he wanted to do. "You'll be all right?"

"I dig deep and get through it most of the time. Thanks again, for everything. I'll see you out."

"No need, unless you have to latch the door. Thanks for including me, for allowing me to get into your mother's thoughts with you. But if we come across anything significant, I'll need to take it in as evidence. You'll get it back."

She couldn't help herself. As soon as Ford left, Sarah returned to the spread of her mother's life on the table. She unfolded a sheet of paper from inside the cover of the first journal.

*Mid-August.*

*It's the middle of the night so I don't know what date to enter. I've lost count of the days since we've been back in Lincoln. I don't even know what day it is (guess I wrote that). School starts shortly. I float through the days as though in a numbed dream. Somehow, I get the meals on the table and tuck Leah in at night. Leighton often heads back to work in the evenings, trying to get ahead so he can help when the baby comes.*

*I try to talk to Mom every day, but she's self-medicating with vodka. Mason said she often babbles and he doesn't know how to take care of her. I think Connor is going to move back in to help.*

*How does one know what to do? How to act? Physical needs stop their signals to my conscious mind. Instead, the spirit of survival kicks in.*

*My baby has slowed his kicking. My back hurts. I feel so heavy. I'll soon have a baby to bring into the world. And I'll be busy taking care of my increased family.*

*Leighton and I have agreed it seems as though Dad was telling us good-bye that sunny April day we last saw him. We shared statements Dad made, and the way he acted. Could he have guessed his days were numbered? Maybe premonitions do exist.*

*One thing for sure, I need to live in the present. I plan to embrace the love of my expanding family. We are as prepared as we can be for this newborn's entrance into the world. We'll all be involved in caring for him. Or her.*

*I also need to be available if Mom needs me. I feel like I'm revealing my naked heart and at the same time burying my emotions. There's one thing I need to get down before it's another vague memory.*

*Sometimes it's hard to determine what's real and what's imaginary. I still don't' know if this was a dream, or a vision like the one Leighton saw of our fathers, but something nudged me awake during the night. It looked as though a yellow night light glowed from our bathroom. There was no electrical light.*

*Dad stood smiling, framed in the doorway, backlit in gold. He said, "It'll be all right, Lena."*

*And then he faded away.*

*What exactly is a vision? A trick of the mind, or a spiritual sign? Other worldly, for sure. Anyone in either realm knows the spirit world involves either God or the devil.*

*This vision had to have come from heaven. There can't be happiness in the other place.*

Sarah's vision blurred, the words swam from eye strain and tears. So many tears. Grief hurt physically, beat her down, as she ached for Mom. But she'd settle for her sister's voice in her ear rather than her own thoughts.

Sarah picked up her phone and selected Leah's number. "Hey. Do you know the time Mom began writing about her life?"

"Hey back, Sis. Let me see. It was around the time of Jer's birth, soon after Grandpa was killed. She claimed her life changed forever with Uncle Connor's call. What are you doing? Reading the journals instead of getting ready for the baby?"

"Guilty. Reading them brings her close," Sarah whispered. "I believe she lived as happily as she could. She somehow made the most of the hand she was dealt. I'm trying to…do the same."

"I know how you feel, no way to ask her things about the kids…your baby, all that stuff." Leah's voice wobbled. "We're left with reading her journals and by extension, finding out about the family's 'tragic event.'"

"At least you knew Grandpa Stanley." Sarah's voice grew stronger.

"And it's sad you and Jer didn't get that opportunity. I stayed with Grandma and Grandpa and have a few pictures. His death had such far-reaching effects…it's like that door never closed, as if something has been left undone all these years." Leah's voice softened. "But life continues on."

"Will missing a loved one always hurt?"

"I'm sure it fades, but can hit strong at times…" Leah's voice trailed off. Then she sighed. "You've had a double whammy. As shocking as Trav's accident was, at least you know what happened to him. And Mom, too. But Mom never had that blessing with Grandpa."

"It's crazy, isn't it? The way I was oblivious to the injustice of it all. Mom lived her adult life haunted by unanswered questions. She was so brave. How would we have dealt with the unsolved homicide of our father?"

"Mom kept busy raising a family. Thank God, I have my girls. Sarah, soon you'll have your baby to keep your mind on happier things."

"Sweet baby can't come soon enough. I keep thinking how hard it must have been for Mom to overcome the ugly facts of life so young."

"She kept on keeping on."

Sarah attempted to imagine the shock. The unreality. The hunt for evil intent. "Yet she never understood. Now I don't get it. Why didn't they ever make headway, at least find one person of interest? Something's wrong for it to have gone on so long."

"I'm guessing the answer is meant to stay with God. Maybe it's not His plan for us to make sense of Grandpa's death. Like Mom always said, the Lord is in control."

"I wish I could believe that, Leah. For some reason, I'm driven to seek an answer to Mom's tangled turmoil. I feel her words spill off the page and into my soul."

"You're using her colorful wording. Maybe you should be a writer." Her sister interrupted with an audible sigh. "Be careful of your emotions, Sarah, they can upset the baby."

"I try. Could be Mom's words have soaked into me somehow. I've peeked into most of what she left, there's this guilty sense of snooping, but I wanted a sense of order." Sarah cleared her throat and blinked away the tears. "I promised Mom I'd do whatever I could. I understand her anger, her sorrow. Even her thwarted efforts. Listen, I'm really tired all of a sudden. Thanks for listening."

"Call me any time." Worry tinted Leah's voice. "But don't let those documents get under your skin and make you sick. I feel for you, that obligation to keep such a promise may turn into a burden. Love you."

"Love you too. Give the girls a hug for me." Sarah set down her phone and resumed reading.

Grandpa had been likable, talented, and a hard worker with an enjoyable sense of humor. Then his health went, and he medicated his pain with booze.

After a time, Sarah left the kitchen and wandered into her studio. Trilling her fingers over the swiveling chair back, she stared at the blank computer monitor, uninterested in any looming deadline. She couldn't put off work much longer, but for the present, graphic design was beyond her brain.

Through the window, the clear blue sky called for serenity. Treetops swayed above the creek that flowed behind the apartment complex, the creek that led to the park where she'd first seen Ford.

He sought answers every day. How many cases did he solve by unearthing hidden clues?

# Seven

Ford took the stairs three at a time. He'd be a fortunate man, coming home to Sarah every night.

"My turn to read," she greeted him. "While I pour our drinks, you can read that unfolded sheet of paper."

He finished, tucked the paper inside the journal, and handed it to Sarah.

She began as she slid onto the chair. "*It's been twelve and a half years since my father was murdered.*

"*I regret I didn't keep a journal while the kids were young, but life was so busy.*

"*Now, I'm wondering, and seeking answers again as to what happened to my father.*

"*Where have the years gone? I know my time has been spent in raising my children, my three precious children, while continuing on life's journey. For several months I've been missing home. Dad's been gone over twelve years, and Mom eight years now. I'm thinking how wrong it is that someone is walking around free when he should be serving time behind bars.*

"I've considered how Mom got through the first months after Dad was killed. I know how she tried to cope. She hit the bottle harder than ever, and the alcohol finally took her.

"Connor, Mason, and Leah haven't talked about how we really dealt with our loss. They no doubt kept on keeping-on, as I have.

"I'm doing what I'm compelled to do now—combing through the pieces in order to find peace.

"My soul will not come to order until I try to sort through what happened to Dad. I think of my life as before the phone call in 1980, and after the call. That one event changed or impacted generations of the Stanley family. Conversations often start or end with the statement of time referring to Dad's murder as the demarcation.

"How much more do any of us know after so many years? The emotions, the speculation, the possibilities, and the questions have roamed through my thoughts time and time again.

"The incident came seventeen days before giving birth to Jeremiah. I can no longer ignore the lack of action on the lawmakers' parts, or answers. He and Sarah are no longer small children. As preteens, they aren't as dependent on me.

"Is there any way to discover whether our lives can be fixed? The circumstances around Dad's death gnaw at my guts. That unknown killer has clouded our lives for too long. Who was responsible for swinging the fatal blow? I want to search for who did it. Too bad I don't live closer to Swanson County, where I could easily jump in my car and return before the kids get home from school, after I did some digging.

"It's like churning up debris from a mud puddle, releasing the sediment to swirl around before it settles back down again. It doesn't go away. The swishing *mixture of events rests on the bottom of my heart and in the back of my mind. The murky details turn my life muddy when they float to the surface.*

*"It's a new year, the thirteenth anniversary coming this summer. We have no answers. It's a cold case. There is no statute of limitations when it comes to homicide, though. I'm contemplative after spending time with the family over the holidays. Now, at the beginning of a new year, I need to get my feelings out to them on paper."*

Sarah set down the journal and leaned back, shoulder blades against the chair. She put pressure on the mound of her baby within her belly.

Ford swallowed. Suze allowed him to experience his niece and nephew's movements himself. "My sis used to do that. Babies act like they're playing soccer in there at times."

She made a *squee hee, hee* sound behind her teeth. "In the early days, when I first started to show, I could cover my baby with one hand. Now a basketball goes before me. I think of Mom ready to deliver, and then getting the news someone killed her father."

He sighed inwardly, thankful to know she belonged in the moment, aware of him and her surroundings. He took a drink of tea and the ice clinked against his front teeth.

"Sometimes I wonder if this baby nestled inside senses my sadness."

"You'll pull through this, Sarah. You're as strong as your mother."

The Bishop women, Mom and daughter, had an undefined element melding them close. He sensed it entailed more than being pregnant at the time of loss. He worked his tongue from cheek to cheek. The action proved unable to help him wrap his head around parallel lives a generation apart.

At the moment, he wanted to know more about the daughter than the family history.

"Mom talked about her new life in heaven a lot. I had time to prepare for her death. There's a huge contrast when it comes to someone slowly dying and sudden death due to an accident like with Travis, or my grandfather's murder."

"Don't discount the added physicality of being pregnant at the time of your fiancé's death."

"As far as Trav's accident, that's not the same as murder. I asked to meet the van driver who ran into Travis. The woman wasn't at fault. She'd been headed east and blinded by the rising sun. Travis either didn't see her or thought she saw him. He coded on the way to the hospital and was pronounced dead upon arrival." She sat up straight and scrubbed the hair back from her face. "Let me splash some cold water, take a bathroom break, and we can get back to this."

Moments later, Sarah returned and handed the funeral account to Ford.

He took a turn reading where Sarah left off. The sorrowful words of one imaginative grieving daughter, while he listened to the sniffles of another dedicated daughter dealing with loss.

*"Where were Mason and Connor when Dad was killed? What did they think, feel?*

*"My anger has erupted a couple times over the past years. That's how long it's taken to totally face God's answer as a probable no.*

"*Am I ready to accept that?*

"*I'm not angry at God. I've never asked Him why. It's the mockery of the sheriff's investigation at the onset that gets me going. My anger may not be right.*

"*Humans need to face the past. Before letting go, I believe a person has to come to terms with what happened earlier in life, right up to the present time. It hurts way too much when I let the grief and unfairness bother me. I wonder sometimes if I'm grieving now instead of years ago.*

"*All that considered, I refuse to live with a bitter heart.*

"*I admit I've been angry at my mother for suppressing the whole incident and refusing to talk about it. One time she said, "Oh, Lena, there's so much you don't know."*

"*Did she ever say what she knew? No.*

"*What the heck did she mean? She offered no explanation when I pressed. Was there something going on that endangered their lives? It hurts to realize she knew something that she never talked to me about.*

"*Could it be my father had an affair that went violently wrong?*

"*Mom had to have held some secret close. Maybe that's why she turned to the bottle as a means of escape. She couldn't live with what she knew.*

"*I realized at some point I couldn't have helped Mom. She succumbed to a dark place under the cover of prescription drugs and alcohol. Even after she knew her liver was diseased, she chose to continue drinking. I haven't been angry with her for many years, but I have been sad.*

"*Forgiveness heals.*

"*Ever present is my Lord. He showed Himself at Dad's funeral, but I had yet to turn my life over to Him. What a difference a relationship with Him made when I faced Mom's death four years later.*

*"I'm getting sidetracked. Writing this all out is a terrific avenue for unloading. I have the compulsion to follow my quest, try hard to fill in the missing blanks with more details concerning my questions about what happened to Dad."*

Ford stopped, and glanced across the table. Without thinking, he reached over and wiped away Sarah's tears.

She cried harder.

He scooted his chair away from the table and offered her a tissue box from the edge of the counter. He couldn't resist resting a hand on her shoulder, and stifled the urge to gather her in his arms.

"Thanks, Ford." She pulled in a sob, which reminded him of his niece Tanya after she skinned her knee.

"Being pregnant I can identify with Mom's emotional and physical state. It makes all the difference in the world to have you next to me. I don't have to face this alone. Okay, deep breath." She inhaled and they exchanged a smile.

"Do you need to take a break?" He noted the time. "We can come back to it later. Or, do you want to eat something?"

"Please stay. I have plenty to eat, whenever you get hungry. I need to get through this."

"If you're sure. Mind if I help myself to another drink?"

"Please, make yourself at home. Grab some water or tea from the fridge."

"Cucumber slices and seeds floating around in water? I don't think so." He refilled his glass and closed his eyes.

*Lord, You've brought Sarah into my life for a reason. I'm praying You are guiding this hunch that her mother's documents will help my current case.*

*Provided it's Your will, reveal to me anything that may help resolve her grandfather's murder too.*

Never in Ford's life had he wanted to solve a case so badly. For the memory of Lena Bishop, and now for her daughter's peace of mind, before Sarah's baby entered the world.

"I found this note in Mom's Bible. 'Happiness is in the here and now, God will replenish my joy.' That's a lofty assumption."

He resumed his seat and circled his glass between two fingers. Feeling like a witness to a heart that was, quite simply, breaking. Pain stabbed his own chest. "We all need Jesus, Sarah. He heals the brokenhearted. You can find Him in your mother's Bible."

She didn't look at him. Had she heard him?

The Lord reached hearts. Sarah Bishop had touched Ford soul deep and turned his involvement in the current case personal.

His instinct screamed she could no doubt use a hug, but he held himself back. Such an act would be a breach in his profession. She pulled at him as no woman ever had. Her loneliness and pregnant state called for him to protect her.

"I'm here to help you, but I don't want to intrude on your personal space." He scrubbed a hand through his hair. "This is rather personal, but you've opened up to me. I wanted to protect Suze, my sister, during her pregnancy. She resented my interference and said I couldn't control her life. I did the best I could, but felt responsible as her big brother, while my brother-in-law Marty was deployed."

Sarah rose from her chair as though she found it easier to stand, flapping the paper with her fingers. "As far back as I can remember,

Mom said God is in control. And she believed it. I just don't understand how she could be so sure, especially after reading all of this about Grandpa."

"I know she believed it. I also believe He's in control." Ford had to touch her, let her know she wasn't alone. He clasped her wrist and urged her to sit. He tucked her damp hair behind her ear, lightly brushed the back of his fingers over her wet and swollen cheek. "My sister Suze somewhat acclimated me to the world of pregnancy. I say you need a rest. I would think mourning your mom takes enough energy. According to my sister, babies kick at all hours of the night and can prevent adequate sleep."

*Lord, watch over Sarah. Show me what You want for me to do in her life.*

He nudged her hand, encouraging her to edge closer.

Beauty and inner strength shone through her drowning eyes. She lowered her gaze.

"Please, try to rest now." Still holding onto her, Ford stood and escorted her to her bedroom. "How about I buy you dinner after a bit?"

"No, thanks. I'm not up to going out."

"Okay, then. You have pasta in a cupboard? I could cook something."

"That sounds nice. I give you free rein in my kitchenette."

"Fine. While things are cooking I'll sift through some more of your mom's documents."

She grew quiet behind the door he'd left ajar.

He sat again, bypassed a three-ring binder of miscellaneous keepsakes related to the event, and picked up the journal recorded twelve years after the crime. *I need to find a missing piece waiting for me to go "Aha!" More than anything, I'm curious to see if Lena noted the names I'm seeking.*

# Eight

Sarah pulled back her tufted emerald duvet and then sank into the welcoming cushion of her mattress. She dozed off to the comfort of Ford's hum, a hymn her mother sang.

She woke with a start to the sound of Ford clanging pans and running water, which took away the sting of her mother saying in a dream, "*Someone really did crush my dad's skull, and took him away from those who love him.*"

The journals invaded Sarah's slumber. Many times over the years, whenever Mom and Sarah saw a rainbow together, Mom shared about Grandpa's rainbow, the one that appeared on the day of his funeral. Reading the words in Mom's handwriting made them come alive, almost tactile.

A rainbow was supposed to be a real picture of a promise from God. Mom had also believed God collected tears in a bottle.

Sarah had enough of her flowing tears.

Dare she follow Ford's and Mom's examples and allow Jesus to be in control of this whole trip into the past?

The rainbow story related to what Mom wrote about Grandpa's service. The funeral brought her sister to mind. Sarah rose, visited the bathroom, and opened the door further to wave at Ford. She placed the call. "Everything still good in Georgia?"

"Hi, Sarah. You just called. You doing all right, still going through Mom's stuff? I remember how huge I felt at your stage of the pregnancy game. Good thing it's summer. Since you live alone you don't have anyone to tie your tennies." They shared a sisterly laugh.

"Wearing sandals, thanks. I'm fine." *Because you're right, I've met someone.*

"Oh, how I remember that business of not seeing my feet." The humor left Leah's voice. "What's up?"

"Yeah, I wish you were here to help. Anyway, I'm still reading, just finished the funeral."

"Did Mom expound on why she didn't allow me to go?" Lingering pain coated Leah's tone.

"I'd like to take away the hurt that still affects you. Mom once told me she'd made a mistake in not letting you view Grandpa's body or attend the memorial service. She felt bad when she understood how you felt. Mom probably had her hands full trying to keep herself together, and didn't want to disappoint or fall short in taking care of you."

"We talked about it and she told me the same thing. But I needed to be with Mom. You get that, right? I do understand it eased her mind to know I was safe so she could deal. All is forgiven, Sarah. I still have a gap of longing, but then I try to picture Grandpa in heaven. She did what she had to do. We don't know what we'd have done in such a situation."

73

Sarah waited through the pause.

"As a parent you can only do the best at any given time. We all look back and wish we could have had more insight, or dealt differently. Anyway, do you have any clearer idea as to what happened to Grandpa?"

"I've only skimmed the other documents. Speculation worms all through the info Mom kept. We have to remember, or at least hope, the investigators have combed through all this as well. And speaking of investigators, I've met the cold case guy with the State Patrol. He's been great."

"Something afoot here? I can tell by the tone of voice you find him attractive. Is he married?"

"Not married. And yes, he is a hunk. Back to serious business. I wonder if Grandpa could have been the man who knew too much, based on the drug theme. Maybe in the tavern he overheard names or a drug exchange and it was a pro hit."

"I remember my dad mentioning a deputy sheriff being in the mix. Or it could have been an accident as well. Who knows what happened besides God?" Leah's open SUV door dinged, so it came as no surprise to hear her say, "Gotta go, Sarah. Love you."

She'd had such high hopes for some kind of breakthrough from Leah's memory.

$$\mathcal{L}$$

Sarah took her place at the table, smoothed her fingers over Mom's words, attempting to refocus on the entries. She read a notation on an open journal. *Secrets inside secrets, like nesting dolls. What secrets accompanied my father to his grave? Did Mom know more than she ever told us kids?*

Ford closed the journal and made room for their plates by stacking one pile of journals on top of another.

"May I say grace?" Ford stilled Sarah's wrist. "Like a watch in the night, You guard over us, Lord. Thank You. And thank You for bringing Sarah into my life as a new friend."

She put three penne pasta noodles that she'd speared before he touched her, in her mouth.

His words didn't reach her heart any deeper than Mom's prayers had.

Sarah returned to the journal and read while she ate, immersed in the gritty resurgence of her mother's questions. The last paragraph came out in a croaked whisper as tears ran down her face. *"It's a cycle of life. Someone dies and another is born."*

Ford handed her a tissue. She'd rather take hold of his hand, the way she craved his touch at the moment.

"I know it's a cliché, and I don't mean it to sound that way, but time truly does heal. Your mom left this earth with a peaceful heart and she is physically free of pain in heaven now."

"I'm glad you believe that, Ford. But my heart hurts. I miss her so." Should she follow instinct and double over with the gut-wrenching blow of loss? At times, grief stole life-giving oxygen.

"It's hard to come to grips with my grandmother not warming up to my brother. Could she have believed Jeremiah replaced my grandfather here on earth? Maybe that was a twist, considering the family lived with this tragedy without receiving justice."

"I understand wanting justice. To know what happened becomes a need." Ford lifted his glass and gulped. "The unknown affects body, mind, and soul. Grief can suck out life if you let it."

*If you let it. Maybe letting go was the key.* How does a person do that?

Various clippings were tucked inside the filled pages of a three-ring binder Sarah opened. She swallowed a bite she'd held in her mouth too long, continued to turn pages while Ford looked on. A glance at the bold, red-framed wall clock told her twenty minutes had passed in silence.

The headlines were noisy, blinking through her brain, eerier than a neon sign in the fog. Once past the opening sentence, the names meant nothing. The words inquest and autopsy stopped her. At least she hadn't had to go through anything like that with Travis or Mom. Sarah speared a chunk of tomato covered in the meat sauce, and mindlessly played with it.

*Dieter Stanley, fifty, of rural Canton, was found dead at 8 a.m., Saturday, August 5 in a ditch one fourth mile west of Canton.*

Once past the opening sentence, Sarah's mind zeroed in on the highlights.

*...time of death between one and four a.m. Saturday...survivors Pearl Wingate Stanley, and sons Connor and Mason Stanley, daughters Lena Stanley Bishop and Joyce Stanley Halverson...brothers Willis and Walter...*

Further details turned her stomach. She set down her fork. "I miss her so, Ford." She gazed down the hall and studied the photograph of Mom on the wall above the computer desk. "I cannot imagine living with an unresolved murder hanging over a person's head. She lived with an empty hole in her heart, all those years."

Sarah refused to let the ugly facts of the past choke her, but she'd had enough for the day.

Ford broke into her thoughts. "It's a nice evening out there. Why don't you finish your tea on the balcony, and I'll clean up."

"You are spoiling me, Ford. You're the kindest man I've ever had in my kitchen." She reached out and tapped the shirt pocket covering his heart. "Better watch out, I could get mighty used to this."

"You deserve some pampering, after all that's happened over the past months." He opened the freezer and plunked a couple more ice cubes in her glass. "Now, scoot."

Sarah eased past without entering the studio, and opened the slider. Ford called it a balcony, even though two people could barely stand next to the matching chairs and tiny table.

*He's right about the weather.* The flawless blue sky matched the clarity of Ford's eyes.

*I created them both.*

Ignoring the Voice, she scanned the parking lot three stories below. A mother helped a little girl out of her car seat. The girl looked up and waved. Sarah's eyes filled. Her mother would never see her first grandchild.

Ford swished the door open, releasing a rush of cool air, and stood behind her. His body heat shimmered through her as though he touched her.

"If your baby is a girl, she'll be every bit as pretty as that tot down there." The calm assurance of his voice so close to her ear made her shiver.

Sarah's eyes drifted closed. Dare she acknowledge the thrill? His nearness touched an empty place deep in her very soul. Were her senses on hyper alert due to grief and hormones?

"You've had quite a day. You may not think you need to rest easy, but tomorrow is a new start. I'll let myself out and talk to you later."

The area was too small for her to turn and see his face without her belly pushing him back against the slider. How could she meet his eyes anyway? Awareness kicked her heart into high gear, coursing through her veins like a movie drama's musical score. She settled for a quiet response. "Thank you, Ford. For everything. You've gone way beyond the call of duty."

"Here's a flash, Sarah." He stopped, and waited until their gazes connected. "I don't consider *you* my duty." His eyes held tenderness as well as firmness. "I'm here because I have guys in the field. I also have a gut feeling your mother's materials hold a link to that case."

*Settle down, heart of mine.* Why did such a man appear in her life now? Cold air kissed her legs through the open door.

"See you soon."

"Wait, Ford. Mom organized a chronological order of events, and what she did when, in that three-ring binder. The summary helped me gain perspective. It may help you as well. Maybe you'll see a name that means some connection."

"I'll look, thanks."

Her mind finally went blank as she remained on the balcony. Once she'd relaxed, she went inside, and caught a whiff of his lingering scent. She closed her eyes for focus and inhaled, but the fragrance remained unidentifiable, a masculine reminder of Ford's presence. Her apartment seemed emptier and larger without him. She latched the slider and turned toward her studio.

She ran an eye over computer, printer, and the design layout work for her current project, all spread in readiness. The piles of reference material, ideas, books, and magazines needed to be sorted. Who procrastinated more than creative people?

Trav would have doodled to get going.

She'd struggled over not being in love with him. She rebelled at first because she thought life with Travis Clifton would have been like marrying her brother. By some factor beyond her, he'd remained her best friend in memory. Since his death, she'd tried to put their one-time status as lovers, as well as his fiancé status to please her mother, out of her mind. The baby wouldn't allow that to happen. She carried Travis with her.

Settled in her desk chair, she pulled up the project file, and was soon sucked in, all her attention riveted. The mouse moved as an extension of her fingers with photographs and Internet searches for other book trailers. She circled, pointed, right and left clicked the mouse, selected, sized, juxtaposed photos and captions. Without the Internet, she wouldn't have a job. Sarah read and reread impenetrable words, creating captions.

The phone rang. She jumped. She didn't answer for a beat, took time to save her file before rising.

Ford.

"How did you know I needed a break?"

"Does that mean you're working hard?" His chuckle gave her comfort.

Were they so in tune already?

"Not really. I've actually been designing. It pays the bills, you know. I love the process of getting all excited while putting together a new project. It's easy for me to lose track of time, even reality. I still plan to go through more of Mom's journaling before I call it a night." *Even if it unsettles me.*

"Don't forget to get adequate rest, Sarah, for the baby's sake."

"I get the impression you know a lot about babies and expecting moms."

He laughed outright. "You could say I've had experience. With the twins in the picture you asked about. I didn't just watch over Suze while Marty was gone, I went through delivery with her because he was serving in Iraq when they were born."

She yawned.

"That's it, time for you to get some sleep. Doing anything in the morning? I can come by about ten, and then we could go out for a Runza at lunch time."

That woke her up. "Never."

"Oh, sorry, someone else is coming by?"

She couldn't help but make a face. "No, silly. I meant go to Runza. Those things smell wonderful, but I don't eat cabbage and beef rolled inside a bun. Onions either, at the moment."

"Some Lincolnite you are. We'll talk about it tomorrow. Valentino's, then."

"Mmm, thoughts of quadruple cheese pizza will keep me awake. The sauce upset my stomach the first couple months. Not now. I'll crave that Lincoln tradition until I bite into a slice."

"Sweet pizza dreams, then. See you tomorrow."

Would some small detail leap off the page and give them a clue to pursue together? Instead of crossing the apartment to her room, Sarah went to the table where her mom's notes waited. At some stage, she'd highlighted phrases from an article in the state's largest paper, date unrecorded, but details had yet to sink in. Sarah regrouped and deduced the report took place shortly after her grandfather's death.

She caught a hint of Jeremiah's features in the deep-set eyes of the grainy photograph of Grandpa. She breezed through the article and took away her own points:

*Foul play is suspected...death of a rural Canton man....Dieter Stanley...found face down in a ditch a quarter mile west...spot half way between his home and town...Max Chapman, a milk truck driver from Oakwood, discovered the body at the beginning of his route. He went back to Canton Creamery in town, where he notified the Swanson County Sheriff...caused from a blow to the head by a blunt instrument...Stanley was found lying face down with several bruises to the head...time of death was early morning Saturday following time spent at Rusty's Place and the VFW Club...Sheriff reported having several possible leads...Stanley often walked to his rural Canton home because he did not have a driver's license...witnesses in Canton said they had seen him earlier in the evening at the tavern...he's reported to have played poker later at the VFW…autopsy indicated cerebral hemorrhaging as the cause of death…investigation continues by Swanson County Sheriff's Department and Nebraska State Patrol Criminal Investigators.*

How had Mom dealt with the newspaper accounts? Every few years, someone did a feature on unsolved crimes and her grandfather's murder showed up in the articles. These first articles mentioned the sheriff, but didn't go into his perspective or any details the police might have released about the case.

Did her mother ever become used to it, or had pain stabbed her afresh at every reminder?

Were the law enforcement officers still alive? Had Ford talked to any of them? It sure would be something to know the sheriff's reaction, his initial thoughts from that day. Perhaps he knew something that never made it to the articles.

The possibility she or Ford might be able to trace an important angle filled her with hope.

# Nine

Late the next afternoon, Sarah hurried to release the door for Ford.

His trimmed, but tousled dark hair stood spiked above his open expression. The load on her shoulders lightened so much she wished for him to open his arms and give her a hug.

Make that a kiss. She missed the easy way of touching she'd had with Travis, missed masculine arms around her. She shook it off, determined to concentrate on the reason Ford came to visit. "Thanks for calling me earlier. I put what I've read in a separate pile for you. Can you really take so much time off your work?"

"That's why I wasn't here first thing this morning. I had to be at the office." He slanted a smile her direction and brushed against her shoulder. He reached behind her chair and set the tantalizing pizza box on the counter. "I'm never really off work. I've also sent out another investigator, so we're good for now."

"That relieves my guilt some."

He helped himself to a drink from the tap. "You're still determined to do this now? Rather gruesome words to ingest, wouldn't you agree?"

"The facts do sound gruesome. And cold. But for some reason, it's fascinating as well. I feel like Mom is still here when I hold her words in my hand and hear what she's written. The news accounts are like reading about a stranger. I count on getting to know Grandpa through my mother's perspective."

She'd been in her mother's world most of the day. *"Grief is at the forefront of my days. I'll soon have a baby to bring into the world…we've heard nothing from Uncle Walter about the investigation.*

Sarah sensed Ford's compassion as he pivoted, touched her arm. "Let's eat while it's hot."

"Mom wrote with such detachment at times. I guess it was her way of coping, as though she were an observer, rather than spilling her guts and revealing how she felt emotionally. She opened up toward the end of her life, but in a subdued, verbal way, rather than expressed with passionate energy. I wonder if I would detach that same way, under similar circumstances."

"You know, I'm happy to say I'm not under any circumstances. Ever since a strong Christian speaker asked those in the audience, 'What on earth are you doing under them anyway?' I quit using that expression. Life will always hand us trouble. Attitude has a lot to do with how we deal. Paul the Apostle tells us we can rise above any situation."

"You sound like my mother." With a sigh, Sarah sank onto a chair.

Ford placed strong fingers around her wrist and bowed his head.

She wanted to experience the joy he talked about, and the thankfulness.

He prayed the way he talked to a friend. "Lord, please give Sarah and her baby health and strength."

His sweet consideration melted her emotions into a glob. He met her open gaze. "So, how much do you think your baby weighs?"

"Right now? Probably about four pounds." She chewed the crust before biting into blistering cheese. "This pizza hits the spot. You'd make someone a good wife."

"Not funny. Does it bother you to talk about Travis? He had talent. I believe I figured out why you look familiar. Were you his model for the heroine of his graphic novel?"

"I can talk about Trav. Remember how you made the connection that he was the author of the graphic book?"

Ford nodded.

"Well, I got really sick of that graphic book. He asked me for help all through the process." She wouldn't admit her embarrassment over being the model for Trav's heroine.

"Okay." Ford held up a slice of pizza, tilted his chin, and lapped the string of mozzarella. "Tell me about your design work then."

She talked while he gave her his undivided attention until one pizza slice remained. "What you can pull out of me is uncanny. Sorry I got so carried away. I must be gearing up for a few hours of creative work."

A peek at the clock told her she'd yakked for thirty minutes. She stood and handed him a paper-clipped group of Mom's papers. "Any chance you can read that bunch of Mom's stuff while I clear the table? Let me know what jumps out at you in the three-ring binder." She tried not to clatter dishes as she went from table to counter to fridge. She filled the dishwasher to run later, and took her seat at the table.

"Your mom gave a personal perspective in what we first read. These news articles reveal details made public."

He held a clipping titled *Services held Thursday.*

"Mom and I planned her celebration of life while she still lived. I'm so glad we live in these days. Just the word celebration gives mourners a greater sense of hope. Funeral sounds too depressing."

"Can't argue with that. Some small town congregations still use dark organ dirges at services. It puts me on edge rather than makes me feel better."

"Leah was upset that she didn't get to tell Grandpa Stanley good-bye. She had wanted to be with Mom and Dad when they were at my grandma's house."

Ford raised his head, causing his eyelids to disappear beneath his brow. The youthful expression touched her soft side. "Where did they take her?"

"With relatives, she said. A great-grandmother and aunt on the Wingate side, who died before I came into the family. Remember, my sister and I have different fathers."

Ford nodded and gave her a one-arm hug across the shoulders. "We can do this another time, unless you need me to read this now."

"I do. I'm deep into the story. And you know what to look for that might be a lead." She sat taller, sighed, and talked around an ice cube. "More and more I realize how strong this kind of drama must make a family. At the same time, it tears some members apart. I would think being together brings back painful memories. Plus, I'm getting to know Mom on another level, her role as daughter. My throat is dry from reading aloud, though." Sarah got up and went to the fridge for drinks. He scooted so close the hairs on his arms tickled her skin, raising goose bumps. She breathed in his spicy scent as she set down the glass.

"Shall we read to ourselves?"

They read the news clipping and Mom's few notations, so in sync they turned the pages at exactly the same time, knowing when the other had finished reading. She paid no attention to those who provided music, or the pallbearers. She figured they were either deceased or in assisted living by now.

Ford muttered, then peered above the rim of his glasses. "Sorry, talking out loud. I do that sometimes. You come from a big family. Hard to keep track of them all."

They took turns reading the list of survivors out loud.

"A big family I know few of. Mom had cousins she only met once or twice. And check this out. One great-uncle was a big detective in San Francisco at the time of the murder. Mom said he stayed in Nebraska for about ten days after the service. She expected results, so naturally she felt disappointed through the years because her uncle ignored her letters and phone calls. She never had satisfactory answers to what she asked of him."

"Do you think your uncle figured out what happened?"

"That's part of the mystery. He retired early and they lost contact. I've never met him or heard his voice on the phone."

"Could be it ate him up, the idea he couldn't solve his own brother's murder. It would get to me." Ford wiped condensed moisture where his glass sat. "Once a cop, always a cop. And his brother's case remains unsolved."

"I never thought of that. No wonder you're involved with solving old mysteries."

Ford raised his brows and drilled her with an intent look. She cleared her throat and lowered her eyes to continue reading a more recent entry. "After she was diagnosed, Mom referenced the first chapter of Ephesians, verses three through seven. I'll read what she wrote:

*"I'm humbled and thankful anew that God chose me for Himself. I would have been a nut case, no doubt thrown away my life by letting this unsolved case get to me. But You, Oh, Lord, redeemed me with Your blood, and carried me through everything I faced in life. I'm eager to spend eternity with You. And my prayer will always be that my children and grandchildren join me in heaven one day."*

Heavy silence took on a life of its own.

"She did have a strong faith," Ford agreed. "I'd hope the same thing for any of my children."

Ford tucked Sarah's hair behind her ear. He searched her face with that soul deep, penetrating gaze again. "What about you, Sarah? What do you believe?"

"I went through a ton of teen angst at the big church we attended. I thought the kids were stuck-up and hypocritical. I never felt like I fit in during any of the activities. With my shyness, I turned a deaf ear to any teaching."

"I can't imagine you shy, struggling with such inner feelings."

"You don't want to know. Thankfully, I moved beyond. None of that fazes me now. Could you please read this out loud?" She handed him the journal.

*"It's closing in on thirteen years. I have no idea why I'm bothered by unanswered questions at this time, but I have to do something. I've had headaches. I'm fighting depression, and not sleeping much.*

*"I wrote a letter to Connor, Mason, and Joyce wishing them a Happy New Year, and said it was wonderful spending Christmas Day with them.*

*"Then I spoke from my heart and wrote that one of my goals for each of us was to have peace about what happened to Dad. For our individual maturation, each of us needs to come to terms with the murder, since it's still an unsettled issue for all of us.*

*"I told them I'm planning a trip to the State Patrol office to ask a few questions. I also hope for a response to one of my editorial letters to the Gaylord and Hardin papers.*

*"NOW WOULDN'T THAT BE A MIRACLE?*

*"I believe judgment is ultimately the Lord's so we all have to deal with the necessary forgiveness. We were created as emotional beings. It's all right to admit hate, guilt, and anger. I don't like the depression that settles over my heart when I have so much to be thankful for.*

*"Next, I asked them to respond to three questions. Where were they the Friday night in August when Dad was killed? How were each of them told about the homicide? And, what happened when the officers talked to them. (I can't imagine how hard that was.)*

*"I told them about that awful movie Leighton and I watched, how the scenes got mixed up in my head, and made me sick to my stomach.*

89

*"The crime has been weighing on my mind. I so hope they respond. I don't want them to think I'm nosy or prying into their business. I want it to help us all."*

Ford stopped reading and handed her a tissue. "I think it's time to call it a night. You've got to be tired."

"Just read the rest of the page, please, where she wrote Mid-February."

*"Things are happening. A reporter from Hardin News and Dispatch called me.*

*"When I received Mason's response to my letter, I cried and cried reading about his last day with Dad. Mason's statements tore at my heart. Now I believe Dad told Joyce and me good-bye that Easter Sunday.*

*"And I wonder anew, had Dad planned on meeting someone that night? How much longer will we wonder?"*

Ford closed the journal and stood to open his arms.

It came natural for Sarah to lean into his hug. His belt buckle pushed against her tummy. She wanted to bottle this feeling of security, preserve the moment, yearning to keep his arms around her for a long time.

But after what seemed like mere seconds, he patted her shoulder and left. The click of the door, his tread on the stairs, and then quiet.

"All my years with your daddy, he never churned my insides the way Ford does." She rubbed the spot on her tummy where she'd had contact with Ford. "I'll always consider Travis a friend and remember the way he stood by me while your grandma went through cancer. But it's time to move beyond the past. First, I have to face what your grandma dealt with." She shook her head and laughed at herself. Soon she'd be talking to her sweet baby for real, rather than talking to an empty room. Was it much too early to think Ford might fill the void of companionship Travis left?

She had yet to pick up the mail. She traipsed the short walk down the stairs, supporting her baby weight as she concentrated on each step.

Back inside, she opened a sympathy card from one of Mom's friends in her Bible study, who recommended the grief support group at Plains Bible Fellowship. Sarah burst into tears. "Oh, Mom, I miss you so. I wish you had found answers."

During one conversation about prayer and believing in Jesus, Sarah recalled what she'd told her mother. "It isn't that I don't believe in God. He's just never been personal to me the way He is to you."

If she could believe at that moment, she'd ask for divine help to find the answers Mom sought.

*That's why you have Ford now. You have only to ask for Me.*

Sarah ignored the temptation to allow more tears to flow.

She passed a roving glance around her apartment, and wondered about her Grandma, left alone after Grandpa's death. She was alone now too.

Sarah's stomach growled and the mental gymnastics faded away. She rummaged in the fridge for some fruit, and tried to imagine Ford's whereabouts.

The phone rang.

"I'm heading out of the parking lot." Ford's voice assured her she wasn't alone. "Leave the burden of this case with me, Sarah. It's my responsibility. You take care of yourself and your baby."

"I've been a big girl for quite some time. Good night."

And how should she refer to Ford's orders? Caring friend? Or controlling he-man?

# Ten

**F**ord tapped his phone against the steering wheel. He didn't want to sound like a control freak the way Suze accused. But his sister had been only twenty when the twins were born.

He scrubbed his fingers over his scalp. Was he being honest with himself?

Sarah, in the same position of need as his sister had been, caused him to think of both women in like situations. Who else did they have but him?

Since meeting Sarah, he never felt whole unless they were together. Corny as it sounded, she completed him. If only she'd get things straight with the Lord.

His thoughts returned to why he was meeting with Sarah. He checked his rearview, no one behind him, and swiped his cell phone. "Hey, Chan. We've got our guy in the cell block where K.K. is now?"

"Affirmed. If anything comes up, I'll know on Bible study night."

"You call me with the smallest bit that might be important. Any names you catch. Got it? Anything."

£

Sarah forgot searching for a snack and jumped into her mother's next journal entry. She missed reading with Ford and realized she'd absorbed nothing of her mother's words. She drew Uncle Mason's letter from its plastic sleeve, and her mind went back in time.

*Dear Lena,*

*I have a confession to make—this past October I sent a letter along with a photocopy from the Canton News of Dad's death explaining the incident to a TV show. No reply.*

*My approach was a little different than yours—my thinking was give it national exposure, and maybe someone would take enough interest to come forward. How do we know this killer is still in Swanson County? Or Nebraska? Or even the Mid-West? Or the States?*

*The reason I did it was simple . . . my daughter, Torrie. Why should she go through life never having a grandpa and grandma? So many times I sit and stare at her and imagine Dad or Mom holding her, being the proudest grandparents in town. But no, she'll never know them. And maybe the killer has grandchildren . . . is that fair?*

*No, but life is not fair.*

*I learned that at age 16, when Dad was taken from me, from us, from this world. I had spent the whole day working with him, a Saturday . . .*

*He woke me up late, about 9 a.m. (that was late for Dad). We drove his new Ford pickup to Grandpa Wade Stanley's farm to begin work. (Actually, I drove because Dad did not have a license at the time. I didn't mind, hey, a 16-year-old kid driving a brand new pickup?)*

94

*Pulling into the yard of Grandpa Stanley's farm, we had a trucker waiting to unload some cattle Dad had bought for Connor. They were beautiful. I remember Coop Paulson passing by minutes later, then after driving around the section once, he stopped in and expressed his approval of the herd.*

*As the cattle were coming down the chute and getting acquainted with their new environment, I remember Dad saying, as clear as day, "These are the last cattle I'll ever have to buy for Connor."*

*We worked all day, getting the cattle settled in, moving dirt around the watering tank for the hogs. (They enjoyed rooting after the thaw of a long, cold winter.)*

*As I recall, we didn't break for lunch. Dad seemed to be quieter than normal, and was preoccupied with something. I didn't think a lot of it, however.*

*At about 5:30 p.m. we were heading home. Dad told me to drop him off in town. I tried to persuade him to stop at home first, eat some supper, change, and then I could take him in. No go . . .*

*As I parked in the back parking lot to Rusty's Place, Dad looked me straight in the eyes and said, "This is the last time you'll have to drive me anywhere, Mason."*

*He didn't say good-bye. But worse than that, I never got the chance to tell him how much I loved him. All the years at home with my own father, and never once did I tell him that. It hurts. That's why never a day goes by that I don't tell my daughter that very thing. Life on earth is too short to live that way, with such emptiness . . .*

*Anyway, I went home and showered, ate supper, and later went to a drive-in movie with some friends in Gaylord. I got home late, about 1:30 a.m.*

*I was lying in bed, trying to sleep, and got up to get a drink or something. As I went into the bathroom, I saw lights and heard sirens on the road between home and town. I rushed to put my clothes on and dashed downstairs . . .*

*When I reached the bottom of the stairs, Mom's room was empty. I ran into the kitchen, I heard her starting to sob. I noticed a car pulling out of the driveway, and asked who it was. She explained the county sheriff had just told her Dad's body was found in the ditch. He was dead.*

*Dead? What do you mean, dead? How? When? Where? Do you think I thought to ask myself who? No. Why should I?*

*By now, it was getting light outside. Mom kept crying. At some point, Connor came in. he got on the phone to call our sisters and others in the family.*

*That morning, people started coming by with food, expressing their sympathy, saying how sorry they were, etc.*

*Monday, Connor, Mom, and I went to the State Patrol office in Hardin. Every time I drive by it, the memories come flooding back.*

*They gave us all a polygraph test, and even asked "Did you kill your dad?" I couldn't believe it. How stupid!!! Me, kill Dad? Were they crazy? I loved him. I never got a chance to tell him so . . .*

*That was only the beginning of a nightmare that has not yet ended, and may not ever be over.*

*Mom. What about my own mother? The wife of a man for what, 20 or 25 years? Taken from her? Why?*

*Only the Lord knows that answer. Only He knows who it was, and it may stay with Him, if that's what He has chosen to do. But why make Mom suffer for so long? Why make us kids suffer? Why should we have to wake up in the middle of the night to the sounds of Mom crying her heart out, pleading with God to take her from this earth? She was the one who never understood why, and who lived a life of hell on earth for another four years. She is another one who deserves to know who. But maybe the Lord has already told her . . .*

*I accepted this because I have always believed the Lord makes everything happen for a reason on this earth. I think it is inevitable we will one day get justice here on earth.*

*Why, after 12 and a half, almost 13 years, do I decide to write all this down and send it to a network news station?*

*Why, months after I did that, does my wonderful sister send me a letter, interested in finding out the ultimate goal I, too, am seeking?*

*The Lord does work in mysterious ways, and I love this one! My pen hasn't been able to keep up with my thoughts this whole letter, so my apologies for the occasional sloppiness!*

*Love you lots, and call or write when you hear anything, even if it is nothing. Let's make next year's era of depression easier to cope with. And, with the Lord's help, that will be a reality.*

£

Sarah's stomach turned sour reading her uncle's letter. She went to bed hungry and woke up hungry. *Baby must be growing.* She fed them both a healthy omelet and puttered around.

She listened to some bluesy piano while she stretched. The house needed a good dusting. Soon, the music swept her away from the lyrics and settled her with soothing saxophone notes.

Once the kinks were out, she headed down to the trail behind her apartment complex. It took many blank minutes of walking before she became fully aware of her surroundings. Where had her mind been? On nothing, and it felt good.

Down the line, there'd be an end to the numbing fog of grief. She noticed the soft breeze while she greeted others on the path. She tuned in to musical refrains that repeated through her consciousness.

Another glorious summer day, the kind the weatherman placed in his top ten. Sunny, deep blue sky, upper-seventies, with a slight breeze. As usual, her mind clouded over and returned to Mom. Mom's whole life had been colored by losing a parent in a way that was never resolved. Yet she remained joyous with her children and strong in her faith.

*God, You were real to Mom. I thank You for allowing her grace to live in the moment, participate, and have peace as she faced the end of her life on earth.*

Wow. Had she prayed? It wasn't that hard.

Had God heard?

At a forked spot on the path, she turned around instead of going on to the park. The whole world seemed brighter on her way back to the apartment. A yellow swallowtail butterfly tipped its wings as though greeting her, and the chittering of birds sounded in the branches. Baltimore oriole, house wren, goldfinch, and the scree of a hawk in the distance. Sarah identified them all.

"Beep, beep, Ms. Bishop." Buck from the next building slowed his scooter.

"Where are you off to today?"

"The library. Checking out inventions." Buck whizzed by, ever present smirk in place revealed the glint of braces. At twelve, did his mother have to remind him to wear sunscreen?

"I have so much to learn when it comes to parenting." Sarah sniffed, missing her Mom even more. She scanned her surroundings, soaking up life. Nature continued on, living and dying in due time. She reached down and sandwiched her belly, from the bottom where the baby suddenly felt heavy, and over the top, where a foot or elbow poked. Life.

Once inside, she dropped onto her computer chair and did an Internet search on Dieter Stanley. At first, nothing in the Nebraska cold case search showed up, other than a notification article about the playing cards the State Patrol sponsored.

His picture appeared with the click of her mouse.

She shivered, swallowed, and blinked. Nothing new, minimum details listed on the back of the card.

The lack of discovery filled her heart with deeper resolve.

No matter how long it took, she'd set her eyes on every word piled on her kitchen table. And if there was some small thing she could do to force the ball to roll again, she'd do it. For Mom, for the whole family, for herself, and her baby. *But really, for you, Mom.* "I'm turning your quest into mine."

Mom's letter to her siblings yanked on Sarah's heartstrings.

Uncle Mason answered right away. Uncle Connor responded later the same month.

Her uncles' ravaged emotions twisted Sarah's empathy.

Mom finally admitted anger, pouring it out on the page, but not at God.

Sarah cradled her baby and let the crying have its way, angry at her own emotions.

Traveling back in time and experiencing her mother's grief, expounded on through her uncles' letters, hit her hard. Set down in black and white by her elders, the composed details drew a hormonal reaction. The upset, the continual tears after losing Mom and Travis, exacted a toll.

"How long do I have to put up with this?" The ceiling answered with a mocking, silent glare. "I need to pull myself together. The mess of a mommy-to-be out of control can't be healthy for either of us, little baby."

A half snort, half laugh escaped. "Now I'm talking to myself, and sounding like first Travis, then Ford, the way they've told me to carry on."

Ford made it easier to deal with these distasteful details. She chose to tackle the next family letter with Ford by her side, and broke for lunch.

She boiled eggs and then prepared tuna salad. She sliced through a ripe tomato. Thoughts of Ford and his lunch menu intruded. Another sign her soul was on the mend, she found pleasure in the company of a certain handsome Cold Case Investigator. She set the tomato on a sea of greens and stuffed the tuna salad into the tomato petals. Her meal looked almost too pretty to eat.

After savoring her salad, she settled down to work in her studio. The client needed to approve the music she'd selected for his trailer, so Sarah made that call, explained what she wanted him to check after she sent the attachments.

Throughout the afternoon, Uncle Mason's private thoughts to Mom played peekaboo with Sarah's attempts to immerse herself in her own activities. It was like reading an outstanding novel, where the characters popped into her thoughts while she lived in their fictitious world.

*What about your life?*

Sarah set a glass of grape juice on the table. Nope. She'd wait for Ford.

She picked up Mom's journal, carried it to the door to answer Ford's buzz. The sight of his face warmed her to the core.

"Figured you've had your caffeine allotment for the day. I brought you a loaded fruit smoothie."

Her heart skipped a beat and the baby leaped in tandem. Good to know she had approval of the new man in their lives.

Ford set the cups on the table, and went for paper towels from the counter. He folded them and tucked a sheet under each cup.

"You are a thoughtful man. Thanks." She focused on the drink. Yep. Sarah could get very used to having this guy around.

"Ready to move forward?"

"I keep going back and forth between journal entries and letters. This journal includes references to the sheriff's investigation, and Mom's frustrations over not getting her questions answered. You might find a clue, or name, or possibility to follow."

"Appreciate it. You want me to start with that?"

"I'm getting ahead. Check out Uncle Mason's letter first, for yourself, then please read Uncle Connor's while I listen."

He lowered his eyes and recited Mom's Bible verse copied in the open journal. "'*So do not be afraid of them. There is nothing concealed that will not be disclosed, or hidden that will not be made known. —Matthew 10:26.'* That's a terrific verse to consider when I'm working cases."

Sarah closed her eyes and concentrated on relaxing her muscles. After a few moments, Ford cleared his throat and she jumped.

# *Eleven*

Sarah reached for her go-cup and sipped on the frozen fruit. Hands free, she set her shoulders back and down. "I'm ready for you to read Connor's letter."

Ford's smile and soothing voice drew her empathy for another grieving uncle.

"*Lena, I was living in the hotel efficiency in Canton, working full time at the Creamery and helped Dad whenever he needed me, totaling 80-90 hours a week. Dad wanted to get more land and cattle to keep me busy so I could quit the town job and have the means to survive from farming.*

"*We talked about me getting married, settling down, and fixing up Gramps' house to move into. All Dad wanted was for me to farm, have a family, and be happy. He believed Mason would follow my example. We already had a lot of hogs together. Mase also worked with Dad and me, taking care of our livestock. Boy, did we have big plans. We were looking into renting more land for pasture and farming.*

*"I had to work at the Creamery that Friday, so Dad and I agreed he'd go and buy me 50 head of cattle. We talked to the banker, who was ready to back us on anything.*

*"I went to my apartment after working Friday to change clothes from whites to the blues with brown spots. I was to meet Dad at the farm to do chores and look at the cattle. Those he picked out were beautiful and probably the best buy of the day. Tears flowed from my eyes just like they are now. I had to sit down on the tailgate of the pickup.* Dad really does love me, *I thought.* He wants me to follow the Stanley farming tradition. Do what we're born to do.

*"I chored and piddled around, waiting for Dad to show up. Found out later I just missed him, so I went back to my apartment. I had a date and arrived home late.*

*"I was awakened next morning by a banging on my door. The town cop greeted me. 'There's been an accident. They need you for identification.'*

*"He took me west of Canton, almost home. There were several vehicles stopped midway between town and home. The cruiser stopped. A deputy opened the door, pulled me out of the car, and walked me to the edge of the road, not saying a word.*

*"I looked in the ditch, recognized my father's cowboy boots. You remember, you gave them to him when you worked in Hardin. I thought,* someone stole Dad's boots.

*"It hit me, this body was my father!*

*"Then everyone started yelling and asking me questions.*

*"'When did you see him last?'*

*"'Did you kill him?'*

*"'I have to tell my mother,' I said, and started walking.*

"*The deputy grabbed me and put me in the car. We went to my parents' house. Mother was looking out the kitchen window. We walked in.*

"*The deputy blurted out, 'Your husband is dead.'*

"*Mom's legs folded and she collapsed. The deputy sheriff reached for one arm and I put my arm around her.*

"*We hugged and cried. I guess the deputy left.*

"*Eventually, I had to have some air. Left the house. Couldn't stand sight of cars on the road. Went back inside. Mason was there. The three of us hugged and cried.*

"*Then I got on the phone and called all the relatives.*"

Ford reached over and cupped Sarah's hand underneath his.

"Finish." Sarah stood and leaned on the table. "I feel as though I was right there. I've never seen the place."

Ford gave her hand a squeeze and did as she asked. "*I quit the Creamery. I moved back home to take care of my mother and brother. I took over the whole farm.*

"*Something told me Mom wouldn't recover. She really wanted to die so she could be with her husband. I tried helping Mom and taking care of my brother.*

"*I fixed up the house of my gramps and moved in.*

"*Mason stayed with me. I tried giving and doing. I wasn't his father. We were all looking for the right path.*

"*We moved back home for a time.*

"*Mom drank herself to death.*

"*Mason stayed with me, then he went away.*

"*I was all alone and very lonely. I was slowly dying myself. I knew I had to get away. There was no help for me. Not in Canton, Nebraska.*

*"One thing I do believe. Only two people know who killed Dad. God, and the guy who did it."*

Ford fit the letter back where it belonged in the three-ring binder. "I approve of your uncle's wording. Quite a delicate description of manure-splattered jeans."

Sarah snorted through her tears over the reference to denims with brown spots. She and Ford were on the same wavelength, gleaning humor from Connor's dreadful story. "Uncle Connor's outlook brightens my mood to this day. He always makes me feel better after I spend time with him because of his positive attitude and wise counsel."

"Connor's telling of the last day he wanted to spend with his father, but didn't, is no doubt a bittersweet memory. The way he was treated the next morning is an insult against my profession."

"Each of my uncle's letters is hard to take in. I need to walk a bit." With effort, she pushed away from the table to pace around the apartment, and landed in front of her bedroom window.

Ford came up behind her. "I'll do anything I can to help. We'll get a break. I'm sure of it. God will give an answer, one way, or another."

"I don't know about answers from God, but I have a decision to make about the here and now." She swept the room with an outspread arm.

"May I suggest relaxing a bit?"

"Let the pregnant lady vent, please. Travis planned to help with all I have to do to get ready for the baby. We would have been married by now, living in a house. I won't have his income to help. I have yet to figure out where the baby's crib and little dresser should be placed. We'll eventually outgrow the apartment space."

"Whoa. Deal with today. You're not in the hospital having the baby. I can help with furniture and other stuff." He took a step closer, gentled his tone. "I've had experience, remember? I believe God will show you the way. Life doesn't get easier when we believe. But relying on God's provisions eases the pressure. I—"

"Walk with me outside?" Sarah interrupted him.

"Sure. Change of scenery sounds perfect."

Outdoors, she made an effort to be more aware of nature's blessings. "I'm thankful the developers left a creek and existing trees for us apartment dwellers and other neighbors to enjoy. Mom reminded me I should appreciate the cottonwoods, swamp willows, birdsong."

"And the surprise of a cottontail bunny." He pointed, and took her hand.

She smothered a laugh so as not to disturb the scurrying bunny as it hopped away, and kept it in sight until its white cottontail disappeared under a low hanging pine branch.

They followed the trail through the common area behind the blocks of apartment buildings.

"Mom loved to be outside. She'd come over just to walk. She could name birds, flowers, grasses. She used to talk about the pasture on the farm where she grew up near Gaylord. She'd sing praise songs from church and mention verses from scripture."

"I'm sure she's enjoying nature in heaven." Ford gently nudged Sarah's side. "Your mom's pain is all gone. That should give you comfort."

"I have trouble picturing heaven clearly. Does Mom have a job there, or is she simply basking?"

Ford didn't respond at first. He squeezed her hand. "She's basking over the reunion with your father and her parents. The book of Revelation points to us having eternal responsibilities that bring glory to God."

She scanned the horizon. So heaven existed for Ford as it did for Mom. Her attention refocused on where they strolled. She felt more cumbersome than usual, more exerted, on her walks now.

Ford released her hand and wove to the side so a neighbor and her Brittany spaniel had room to pass. Then he moved close again, and they circled to enter the park. They ended up at the picnic table where Ford's soccer ball almost hit her.

"Do you believe it was an accident for us to be here at the same exact time?" His raised arm brushed against her as he waved to the open grass. He cupped her shoulder and trailed his fingers down her arm.

Same wavelength again, but she didn't respond. She lowered her gaze to study the way his strong grip covered her hand. He offered a silent life force via a simple touch. And she loved it.

They sat on the bench leaning against the table edge.

His thumb on the back of her hand gave her tingles. "I think God places us in the paths of those we meet. So I've never thought our first meeting accidental. And to recognize you later at the BBQ, anyone could have knocked me over. Such a surprise to see the gorgeous lady from this picnic table walk through that backyard."

"I'm glad God brought you into my life. I've lost so many people. My whole life lately was wrapped up in Mom toward the end of hers. I'm glad I had her to replace my time spent with Travis."

"You've got friendship and support from me."

Sarah sensed he left something unsaid, and wished eyes could speak. He made her feel all kinds of stuff she didn't want to name. She looked away. "I appreciate your friendship. Guess I'm feeling a little melancholy today. Dad died suddenly when I was in high school. I'm able to see his picture or his name in print, without a single sense of remorse. I miss him, but I feel warm instead of lonely with my memories of him."

She tried to suck in some fresh air, humid rather than refreshing. Baby kicked against her ribcage and she attempted to sit taller, must be awfully tight for baby tucked inside.

"Do you think your baby feels cramped in there?"

"Are you sure you're not a mind reader? I just wondered if it feels tight to the baby."

"You're so much smaller than my sister. Suze's belly stretched bigger than I could fathom before she delivered those twins. I thought they'd burst through her skin. She had blue veins showing everywhere. And her belly button stuck out no matter what she wore."

Sarah burst out laughing. It surprised her and felt good at the same time. "Can't imagine the stretch marks. Poor thing. I know about the belly button. It's embarrassing. She must have been miserable being that huge."

She forced away the smile for a serious expression.

"What's wrong? Does something hurt?"

"I'm fine. I'm glad I have my baby for company. Yet, I sometimes feel hollow inside. Most days I keep too busy to dwell on what could have been. Now with Travis and Mom both gone, I can hardly wait for my baby to fill the huge gaping hole yawning in my heart."

"You just said it. You'll have your baby for company. It's so good to hear you laugh." His eyes softened and the lines around them relaxed. "Hope you don't mind me saying, your sadness and your beauty kept my thoughts captive after I saw you here that first time. You aren't hollow or empty inside. It's natural to miss your loved ones, to feel sad over not having them around any longer. I pray the Lord will fill those empty spaces. He does fill the void, but we need to invite Him in as we wait."

Sarah refused to go there. Ford talked about the Lord the same way Mom had. It hit Sarah with force. She was an orphan.

Thoughts of her mother sent her back to the crime. Who had hit her grandfather so hard it killed him?

She glanced skyward to view as much gray as her mind.

"There's always been speculation about the weapon in question, according to those first newspaper articles." Ford's thoughts proved in sync with hers again. "The article with the picture of your mom and aunt, any chance I could copy that and take it with me? There are a lot of names I'd like to check into."

"Sure. I still don't know how you do this on a daily basis. It's enough to cause depression, which Mom dealt with sometimes when I was a girl."

"It's my job and I have to get back to it. You ready to hit the path again?"

Sarah stretched the kinks from her back. How could she possibly change, or fix, or help, such madness as Mom dealt with? She'd waited more than half her life to know who killed her daddy. Had she waited for nothing?

They retraced their steps, lost in individual thoughts.

Ford waited at her building door while she made a copy upstairs and returned to his side.

"I believe Mom felt the unknown was worse than dying with no answer. Wish I could believe she's really happy in heaven."

"Sarah, you're seeking. I believe you'll be with her again someday. As per the case, let me deal with this, won't you? It's too bad the original investigator has passed away. I'd like to talk to him. I'll call you once I've read and done some follow-up." He squeezed her shoulder with his free hand, and walked away.

Sarah took the stairs at a snail's pace. Since it was still open, she read the journal entry related to the article she copied for Ford. *Wiletta Reynoldson from The Hardin News and Dispatch called. She asked Joyce and me to come into the paper's office when we're in Hardin.*

Mom's note wasn't detailed in her journal, only that they went. *Joyce and I had a nice visit en route to Hardin. Except, I became ill thirty miles out. Nausea. Nerves. Discombobulated.*

*We met with State Patrol Investigator Richard Randall and a sergeant, whose name I never did get straight. We were there for under an hour. They said they'd follow up on a couple leads and keep in touch.*

*Next, Joyce and I were interviewed at the newspaper office. Will the killer get shook up?*

# Twelve

**F**ord opened his men's devotional Bible to read a passage in John's gospel, and prayed. "Dear Father in heaven, You are mighty, You know all. Please guide me as I read this newspaper interview with Sarah's mom. I ask You to give Sarah peace and draw her to your saving grace. She needs You, Lord, like we all do. I ask for protection and blessing on Sarah and her baby. In the name of my dear Savior, Jesus."

He chose a green highlighter and perused the article.

*Seeking Peace after Thirteen Years…probe into father's death is revived …for thirteen years, Lena Bishop has sought answers…revisiting details in regard to her father's murder…Stanley's killer has yet to be found…Mrs. Bishop, of Lincoln, recently sent letters to the editors of area newspapers, with the desire to ignite renewed interest in Stanley's unsolved death…Mrs. Bishop wonders why she never heard of anyone coming forward with reliable information regarding the crime…*

"I also find it strange no one has slipped up and it was reported to the Patrol. As with everything, it's in your hands, Lord." Ford went back to the article.

*...according to the Nebraska State Patrol's spokesperson, an investigator is checking into the Stanley case to decide if further investigation is called for...some alleged robbery may have been a motive following the incident, former sheriff Frank Eldon of Gaylord disagrees.*

*A car possibly struck Stanley as he walked home early that morning. "In the middle of the night when a driver was as intoxicated as Stanley reportedly was."*

*Pathologists agreed at approximately three a.m. severe head injuries caused Stanley to die of cerebral hemorrhaging. One examiner thought it possible a vehicle caused Stanley's fatal head injuries, but a second said no.*

*One theory was that Stanley accepted a ride home by an enemy who struck the fatal blow.*

Ford hoped to find copies of those reports.

*Another theory, according to initial investigators was death may have been inflicted by a blow from a heavy frying pan.*

*...the Swanson County sheriff and his deputies did their best with nothing conclusive as a result. The case was turned over to the Nebraska State Patrol. Eldon confessed his surprise no one had ever slipped up by blabbing when he was drunk.*

*The Patrol conducted polygraph interviews of several people. Numerous leads were checked during the initial investigation, but nothing conclusive was learned...the original investigator retired two years ago and lives in Hardin.*

*Eldon said, "I don't know the events leading up to Stanley's death." He reminded this reporter that homicides are never considered closed until they have been solved. Leads continued to come in some time after Stanley's death, and the State Patrol fully investigated each new piece of information.*

*The sisters from Lincoln, Mrs. Bishop and Joyce Halverson, came to Hardin to visit the State Patrol investigator recently assigned to the case, seeking any updates on what happened to their father. Mrs. Halverson said it was their idea to meet and they were encouraged not to give up...the sisters described their father as a good provider with a great sense of humor, and who was proud of his children...they disclosed he was an alcoholic, whose closest friends were his drinking buddies...he was a disabled Korean vet who was receiving 100 percent disability benefits and supervised the farming his sons helped with.*

*"We can speculate all we want, but we have no concrete idea why someone would want to kill our father, Mrs. Bishop said. "Such a traumatic shock churns up your emotions. No family should ever go through what we have over the years."*

*Mrs. Halverson added, "An event like what happened to Dad hovers over the whole family, and has affected three generations. Whatever the end result may be is immaterial, we only want to have peace."*

Due to the personal connection, Ford's stomach gave a turn. Lena Bishop now experienced the peace Sarah's aunt referred to in the article. A peace that only comes when a heart is at rest in Christ.

It would be a long night. Ford planned to look up every name referred to in the article.

Sarah greeted the next day refreshed and renewed, relieved Ford accompanied her on this journey. No denying it, life seemed brighter today. Two walks the day before and Ford's company had changed her perspective. She'd gone to sleep with a lighter heart.

She turned on Mom's laptop and searched for Uncle Connor's phone number. Instead, she found an e-mail address, and sent a quick message.

*Uncle Connor, I feel like my heart is breaking. I read your letter to Mom about where you were when Grandpa died. I read Uncle Mason's letter as well. Have you given up on finding out who did this cold-blooded act? After I got through a crying jag over losing Mom, and empathy for all you guys, I became angry for our family all over again. Has everyone lost their desire to ever find justice? If so, looks like it's my turn to dig.*

Sarah signed off and was soon engrossed in work. So much global information only a click away helped to make work quick and fun. This particular ad campaign featured horses, Kentucky, a little bluegrass music. Her day improved as she worked away. Eventually, she found herself so focused on craft, she grew woozy from skipping lunch.

The phone rang, the baby kicked.

"Hey kiddo." Uncle Connor's voice lifted her spirits. "Thanks for the message. Your mother kept all that stuff, huh? I haven't thought about those letters in years."

"It's so good to hear your voice. How are car sales?"

"Used vehicles are moving like hot cakes, never seen such prices. I might have to hire you to design some kind of computer ad for my business." His contagious laugh drew a smile from her.

"I'd be glad to. Are you still in contact with anyone investigating Grandpa's case?"

"Not really. Last time I was in that part of Nebraska, I heard only the usual rumors."

"Rumors? What kind?"

"The same gossip that's been around for years. A deputy sheriff didn't like Dad. An old drug dealer who served time and later went clean. Dad, your grandfather, didn't approve of my old buddies hanging around the house. One guy in particular, whose name I don't like to use." He cleared his throat, spoke quieter. "I've tried to bury that time of my life."

"Did Grandpa's dislike ever end up physical?"

"Oh, yeah." He chuckled low. "Dad didn't back down from anyone. He was tough."

"All these details kind of turns my stomach."

"I hear you. It's pretty hard to move forward while looking behind. Do you need anything, with no daddy for your baby?"

Serious or teasing? Sarah hadn't been around her uncle recently enough to make the discernment. "We'll be just fine. Thanks for calling. Do you have Uncle Mason's number in case I need him?"

"I have it. We text more than talk. Want me to send him your e-mail address?"

"That'll work." Sarah hung up.

She turned attention to her baby. "Oh, sweet baby. Someday I hope to tell you that Ford and I together discovered your Great-Grandpa Stanley's killer. Maybe that person will even die behind bars."

She shuffled pages on the table and read the journal entry before her out loud, her voice flowing into the corners of her living space.

"'There is nothing hidden that will not be disclosed,' according to Luke 8:17. I know I've taken that out of context, but I'm thinking about Dad's case*

**117**

*again. Will details ever be exposed? When I'm in heaven? I doubt I'll even care then, in the presence of my Lord. Should I waste my time now if God takes care of this injustice? I've had years to consider circuitous points. I'd like to think the killer has confessed to someone, blabbed in a bar or jail. I once heard murder victims have no secrets. Maybe their families don't either…"*

Sarah tried to release pent-up emotions. Her mother's distress leapt off the page and into her own being, yet she continued to read silently.

*Regarding the newspaper interview for the Hardin paper, should Joyce and I have smiled in the photo? Too late now… After the feature was published, Connor's former landlady called Joyce. The idea of a frying pan strike, indicating Mom hit Dad, is ludicrous! Talked to Connor. He, Vern, and Leighton have misgivings about that angle. Especially Leighton, who said, "I saw the crease across his forehead. No frying pan made that dent."*

*If some crazed murderer comes after us, Joyce and I accept it as something God will allow. It's that protective instinct men have. Connor didn't understand from the relayed message that we wanted him to go to the State Patrol in Hardin with us…*

*Psalm 37:7 says,* "Be still before the Lord and wait patiently for Him." *v 8,* "Do not fret." *v 10,* "A little while, and the wicked will be no more." *What comfort from the rest of the chapter. I know my Lord will protect me and those involved in Dad's death will be dealt with.*

*I have studied and considered all the grief steps. They are shock, denial, fear, anger, bargaining with God—and I realized that I may not have grieved after Dad and Mom died. God blessed me with infants to care for at the time of each parent's death. I know God's justice will prevail.*

Unlike her Mother, Sarah found no comfort or proof of God. Let alone peace.

£

Sarah couldn't get Aunt Joyce off her mind. According to Mom, at the time of Grandpa's death, Joyce and Vern Halverson lived south of Lincoln and had no phone.

Aunt Joyce had gone earlier that Saturday morning to help friends move and hadn't told her husband she was doing something on her own. She was gone for three to four hours. Dad informed Vern while she was gone.

Ford had advised Sarah to go to the source, so she did. She'd never seen the beach resort where Aunt Joyce worked part time.

Her aunt answered. Joyce sounded so much like Mom, Sarah swallowed a sob. "Hi. It's Sarah. I almost forgot the Florida time difference, you're not at work are you?"

"I'm working, but it's quiet at the moment. Good to hear your voice. You growing?"

"You can say that. When I hit the end of my second trimester, I sure popped out."

They shared a laugh.

"How's your life in the sunshine?"

"Beautiful. Blue sky that calls for descriptive adjectives. You can tell I've been writing ad copy. No clouds. Perfect day for picking up seashells along the Gulf. How are you doing, dear niece of mine?"

"No complaints. Work is good. I've been reading Mom's diaries and all about what happened to Grandpa." Sarah waited, curious as to how Aunt Joyce would respond.

"That subject won't get you anywhere but upset."

Sarah didn't give her aunt a chance to say more, but plowed on. "If you don't mind, I have a couple questions for you. Can you remember back, Mom asked you to write about that night before Grandpa died. Why didn't you?"

"It feels like a lifetime ago." She paused. "I called her instead of writing. It was a dark time in my life, not just because of Dad being killed, but I had an abusive husband. It took all my energy to concentrate on survival."

According to Mom, Grandpa and Aunt Joyce's husband were similar in their appearance and behavior. Whatever that meant.

"Did you ever hear anything that I can pass on to the State Patrol investigator I'm in contact with?"

"Why do you want to put yourself through this? Especially being pregnant." Aunt Joyce blew a sigh. "I suppose you won't let it go any more than Lena. One time I heard Uncle Walter mention they, whoever they happened to be, had a particular suspect at some point. Never a specific name that I recall."

"Was the person of interest given a polygraph?"

"Don't you sound all professional? I don't remember because I chose to put all that behind me."

"Do you remember a friend of Uncle Connor's, whom Grandpa had thrown off the property for bringing drugs on the place?"

"Where'd you hear that?"

"Read it in Mom's notes, but she didn't name him. Uncle Connor did. Your home life sounds so different from the way I grew up."

"Lena did a good job by you, kiddo. Your dad too. Small towns sometimes don't have very much to offer. People in Canton were under the influence of a cocktail of drugs at the time. Even Mom took a tranquilizer. Not to mention the popularity of beer, marijuana, prescription pain meds, uppers, whatever. At least, meth didn't get added to the mix then. Who knows what else the people questioned had been taking? My guess is polygraphs were invalid due to those influences."

"What a way to live. Makes me glad I grew up in Lincoln."

"I think Uncle Walter's cop persona once claimed someone in the family withheld information, but had never come forward, or admitted anything conclusive." Aunt Joyce audibly exhaled. "I'm not sure, memory fades over time. We were probably having a beer or two when I visited California, and speaking of which, there were a lot of keg parties going on at the time of the murder, all around Swanson County."

"You said that already. From what I gather, Grandpa was pretty drunk that night too. Yet, I wish I'd known Grandpa." Sarah hesitated. "What kind of enemies did he have?"

"You captured him. He was a drunk." Aunt Joyce huffed, sounded frustrated with me. "We loved him when he was sober. He liked to tease and tell stories and make us laugh. But he was a mean drunk. He wanted to fight anyone who slanted at him cross-eyed, including my husband and your dad."

"That's so hard for me to imagine. Must have been a difficult way to grow up."

"It's over, why bother? I said the same thing to your mom several times. Just let it be."

"No matter what kind of person Grandpa used to be, wouldn't everybody feel better about finding resolution? No one has the right to snuff out another person's life."

Her aunt expelled that weary-of-the-conversation sound again. "That's a loaded question about potential enemies, and full of possibilities. Husbands or fathers of women Dad had put the move on. I can see why any number of guys would have gone after him. Booze loosens tongues. Made him feel important, I guess. Maybe if he heard what he shouldn't have, and spread those secrets—"

"Did you think of him as a bit of a womanizer?"

"That's a side of him I didn't see a lot. Mom and Dad loved each other, though. Sarah, I hate to cut you off, but I need to talk to some people here."

They exchanged an I-love-you.

"Be sure and call when the baby comes." Joyce disconnected.

Sarah continued to probe into her mother's notes. Who knew the beginning and the end?

*I do. It's always been in My hands.*

That Voice again…

# Thirteen

During the ultrasound, Sarah declined the offer to know the gender of her babe. The amplified rhythmic heartbeat brought tears of joy to her eyes and promised to accompany her while running weekly errands.

Back at home, she held the image of her own sweet baby in her mind, and called to share the progress report with Ford.

"I can't wait to see the picture. Do you feel like getting out of the apartment again? As in, would you like to bring the pictures and meet me for dinner?"

"That sounds wonderful." A date?

"Wish I could talk now, but duty calls. I'll text you." And Ford was gone.

She pondered her Mom's response over the initial disclosure of her pregnancy. No censure, only love and acceptance. Mom never quit praying for all of the family members.

Sarah turned back to old clippings. The quotes from her mother and aunt in the interview nearly did Sarah in. She couldn't help herself, so she continued with journal entries.

*As a result of the newspaper interview, Alexander Gipson called from a pay phone and will call again at 8:00. He spouted tons of garbage that could legitimately be true, but sounds like he reads available information and has an imagination. It scared me, though, the magnitude of what he covered in thirty-five minutes. He claims there's a leak in the Patrol, and he doesn't want me to call Uncle Walter.*

*Gipson asked Leighton and me, and Joyce and Vern, to come to Clayton on the weekend to listen to a tape that lists names, dates, and incriminating evidence. He sounds like a kook. I called Uncle Walter anyway.*

*Leighton's convinced I've put the family in jeopardy. Connor's mad. I trust in the Lord's protection. Someone may be a little nervous, but not apt to come after us. I know nothing that could connect any of us to what happened to Dad.*

*I received a heartfelt letter from a stranger. His name is Christoph Troy, a mortician who helped embalm Dad's body. He was serving his internship in Lincoln and helped with the preparation and embalming. He said he's thought of our family many times, the unknowns, the wondering, the whys. He wrote, "I believe your persistence will one day pay off. Your research of rumors and fact will answer your questions."*

*I also got a letter from Alexander Gipson. He listed "No Telephone" along with his PO Box for Clayton, Nebraska. He included other information based on research regarding dope in Swanson County, as well as mass kidnappings. What in the world does any of that have to do with my dad?*

*Later, Gipson called (from that same pay phone, I imagine). I told him we weren't going to Clayton and that I'd give him Uncle Walter's business phone.*

*He said, "That's who I want to get to anyway, Walter Stanley. I've got an extra one of these tapes, I'll just send it to him."*

*What tape? How did he get a taped recording that concerned my dad?*

*Then Gipson rattled on about a known family in the county that sends cocaine profit to a terrorist group in Germany. He also said that two people knew who killed Dad. The man will probably talk, but the woman (a woman was involved?) is scared to death.*

*Now what if it's Uncle Walter Gipson really wants and he's going to send a bomb instead of a tape??? I suppose I'd better call my uncle tomorrow, for his okay to give out his phone number. But if the State Patrol more or less says Gipson's okay, did I really mess up by mentioning my uncle?*

Sarah looked for names relating to her grandfather. She found Gipson's name in a March entry.

*Received a detailed letter from Gipson that included a lot of names. I have reservations about repeating them here…he claims the reason he never sent a copy of the tape to me (that he sent Uncle Walter), was out of deference to Leighton's fears.*

*I quote, "Your uncle has problems, all right! My sources tell me he was told 'shut up or die.' Just after I sent him the tape, I received a death threat from an individual second from the top in that mess. I have the capability of intercepting would-be 'hit men' and jailing them for prior crimes. I've done it four times. The people who ordered your father murdered are the ones who sicced all four on me. So, I threatened back and it quit there."*

*He went on to say he doubts the people who murdered Dad will stand trial, but they will be put out of business. According to Gipson, Dad and another man were murdered because they went to Omaha FBI with details about a huge cocaine smuggling operation headquartered in Gaylord; run by community leaders to generate replacement income for ____.*

*Gipson's cronies made things so hot another operation was shut down. No murders, only normal cocaine deaths like the guy who murdered his wife and the kid who killed his weird girlfriend, both in ____. (He left these names blank for my protection.)*

*Dad's and the other man's deaths focused attention on rural dope smuggling, warehousing, and distribution. Gipson said heads would eventually roll in Swanson County for current drug activity, but not for Dad's murder. Then he claimed he couldn't tell me what's already happened. As an aside, he wrote cocaine profits are used in part to finance mass kidnappings.*

*What would kidnapping have to do with drugs and my father?*

*Gipson included a copy of his letter to Uncle Walter. With the warning BE CAREFUL WHO LISTENS TO THIS TAPE!*

*He told Uncle Walter, 'I'm one of those people who walk roughshod over everybody. People either hate my guts or worship the ground I tread. My basic approach is massive research. I should say that I left the FBI with egg on their faces twice.*

*"Lena will get all of this except the key items that would reveal names. I would give them to her, but under no conditions in writing. Nor will I let her have a copy of the tape. Too dangerous for the informant."*

*That letter leaves me with even more questions. I'm so confused…Dad and kidnapping and drugs?*

Sarah needed to stop due to signs of headache. She couldn't meet Ford with an aching head. She also couldn't stop reading, and noted lines from March and April journal entries.

*I called the attorney general's office in Lincoln, which I should have done years ago, and inquired about an autopsy report. I was told it's in Gaylord with the Swanson County Attorney.*

*Mortician Christoph Troy called…following are my notes from our conversation: He thought about my family because Dad resembled his dad. He said there were autopsy pictures that revealed the severity of the temple area (Leighton always said the hit was meant to be fatal).*

*Troy said the guilty often return to the grave…maybe we could publicize the anniversary and the Patrol could place a listening device or camera on the headstone. Just an idea.*

*…I went to the library and got books on forensic science.*

*…Received a letter from an ex who was married to a cousin of Dad's. He wrote, "Your mom sent me a letter after your dad was killed and said she was scared because she knew something."*

*…I read two books on forensics. A takeaway —"When there is little evidence left at the scene, a psychological profile is sought."*

*Little evidence is right. Sheriff Eldon destroyed what evidence there was. The initial investigation was such a farce at the scene (no protection, rain washed away any physical evidence).*

*…I read a book on medical detectives and wrote questions to Uncle Walter.*

*…I read a book about autopsies. Why did I put myself through that kind of stuff? I had a hard time picturing Dad's body on a cold stainless steel table. Then sliced into.*

*…Uncle Walter finally called. He's following up on the tape he received from Gipson and he'll talk to a state patrol investigator Monday. When he knows something, he'll call and keep in touch.*

Eventually overcome with her mom's anguish, Sarah gave in to the tears. Again. Would they ever dry up? She wept huge, convulsive sobs that sloshed against her arms beneath her bent head.

She cried for Travis, and for loving him only as a friend.

She cried for Mom and the ravages of cancer.

She cried for her mother's grief. The harder she attempted to shake it off, the more she wept for the sake of weeping.

At last, she needed to call it a day, but couldn't resist one more peep. She rubbed her eyes, trying to stave off a headache, and skimmed the rest of Mom's notes. Nothing made sense.

She had to set the past aside for now, so left the papers on the table and went to get ready, anticipating an enjoyable dinner with her new friend. The friend who tripped her heart into beating as fast as her baby's. She resolutely moved her thoughts to the future.

"No matter the outcome of what we may discover, little one, I'll be done with this quest before I go into labor. You are now and will forever be the light of my life. I promise."

# *Fourteen*

Sarah spotted Ford's pickup parked near the entrance to the restaurant. She needed a hug after the emotional storm earlier. She felt weak, but no headache.

"Hey, sunshine." He opened his arms as though he'd read her thoughts.

She stepped into his embrace.

Touching Travis had been as habitual as slipping into cozy slippers, nothing but familiarity. She'd missed their connection.

The sensation of being in Ford's arms woke up her femininity. She had the urge to pat her fluttering heart, calm it the way she planned to calm her restless baby.

Ford guided her inside with his hand at the small of her back. They followed the greeter to a booth and ordered drinks.

The server approached before their drinks arrived, and took their orders.

"That was fast," Ford said, holding out his hand, palm up. "Let me see."

Likeminded, Sarah knew what he wanted. She dug into her bag, eager to share what he sought, and handed over the black and white picture.

"What a perfect face. I am almost too awed for words. Only God is capable of creating the miracle of life." A glint of moisture shone in his eyes as he passed back the picture.

"Travis and I never talked about the baby attending church," she blurted. Where in the world had that come from?

"What in the world brought that on?"

She shook her head. "It's uncanny the way you seem to read my mind. I thought the exact same thing. Don't know. Church and Bible study were really important to Mom. She'd be quite disappointed if I don't give my child some kind of Christian upbringing."

"Some would say living in the United States makes us Christians. I know better. Each of us must choose to follow Christ. Good idea. I believe in fellowship on Sundays and through the week."

Did Ford think she was a heathen?

Sarah shut off church concepts and studied other patrons. A child behind her chattered away about penguins at the zoo. A couple seemed to be celebrating. She snapped a mental shot and planned for images in their likeness when she needed to depict a joyful occasion in her work.

Ford said thanks to the waiter for their entrées.

Without thinking, Sarah stretched her arm across the table so their hands touched.

Instead of cupping the top of her wrist, Ford covered her hand and interlaced their fingers, forming a tent. "Lord, I thank You for the food set before us. I thank You that Lena is in Your presence, as well as my parents. I didn't know Sarah's dad, but I'm guessing he's with You also. Please become real to Sarah, Lord. Guide her by the Holy Spirit to realize the truth of Your death on the cross. For us. Amen."

"Amen." For the first time, Sarah took his words to heart. She needed to look into a relationship with God. "Tell me about your family, Ford."

She got lost in the details of his face. His kissable lips, the cleft in his chin, and that killer smile.

He sprinkled salt and squiggled a potato fry. "My parents spent as much time at church as they did at home. They went on a missionary journey when I was in college, and were killed by terrorists."

That woke her up. "How awful. Where?"

"In the Mideast somewhere undisclosed. They went to minister to the missionaries there, to offer encouragement."

"I don't know what to say. I'm sorry seems so bland."

"You don't have to say a thing. I've lived with it close to half my life. I grieved, dealt with some guilt, grew closer to the Lord."

She studied his face, and concluded he preferred asking the questions. She'd ask anyway. "I get that. But why should you feel guilty?"

"Because when I first heard about their trip, I wanted to go along. The elders thought since the missionaries were a couple, another couple should reach out, representing our church body here in Lincoln."

"So we're both orphans."

"I wonder how a woman in her thirties with a babe in the belly can even be considered an orphan."

Mom had expressed the same thought. And now, Ford.

Were they meant to be kindred spirits?

"God tells us in His Word that He is the Father to the fatherless. Sure, I miss my parents. But the Lord has filled the void. Our heavenly Father adopted us." Ford searched her eyes, soul deep.

As he reached out to her, seemingly from his innermost being, Sarah perceived sadness, tenderness, gentleness, and even unspoken wishes in his eyes.

Many of Mom's words were centered in the Bible. Those phrases that gave her comfort, were they for real? She didn't understand how God could be the answer to her life's problems. Did turning a heart over to Jesus Christ change things? It sounded way too simple. Sarah turned back to her plate.

"You look tired." Ford gulped the rest of his soda.

"Probably eye strain from hours at the computer, and Mom's material. I had a full day."

Ford ran his fingers over the back of her hand.

A thrilling shiver wound through her. It'd be too easy to get used to his touch.

"Adequate sleep is important. I'm sure your body lets you know when you need rest. You're building up for a big physical feat, you know. As far as your mom's stuff, let me help."

"I appreciate that more than you know. I have a feeling we'll get to the bottom of it this time. Mom's handwriting links me to her. I don't regret the promise I made, so I'm compelled to go after justice. I'll tell her, I always refer to the baby as a she, that her mama and grandma did all they could."

"Well, I'm concerned about your health, so please don't overdo. Agreed?" He dug into his huge burger, chewed, and swallowed. "Tell me how you and Travis got together. Didn't he teach, as well as write and draw?"

"Yes, at community college. Travis and I became friends in high school. Then at university, we took many of the same classes. It felt as though he'd been part of my life forever. Just before he was killed, the students were working on their portfolio development."

Ford held out his free hand and she gave him hers.

"I miss that part of design, drawing the sketches. Using the computer isn't a tactile experience. There's a creative touch element to pencil and pad that has more visceral satisfaction than fingers on a keyboard or mouse." She heaved a sigh.

A toddler too booths away stepped into the walkway. Sarah made a silly face at him. He hid his rosy little face in his dad's arm. Sarah winked. He dipped his chin against his dad's side. His thick, straight black hair brushed against his father's leg each time the boy moved his head. Who wouldn't fall in love with such deep brown eyes? The static standing his hair on end drew a motherly response from deep inside. He laughed again. That engaging smile over tiny teeth made her wonder what her baby would look like at that age.

"Finished?" Ford drew her attention off the child.

Sarah nodded, her thoughts elsewhere. Finished with her meal, she chased away the idea of being finished with Ford.

Ford wanted to say she could lean on him forever. He didn't want their dinner date to end. Dare he hope to keep in contact once she discovered he withheld the name of a probable suspect? He had yet to see it in Lena Bishop's words.

"I haven't reached an entry yet concerning your dad's actions after your parents took the call about the murder."

She undid her ponytail, massaged her scalp. "Mom wrote that Dad said her pregnancy took priority. It's a relief to know Mom had Dad's support afterwards."

"I'm guessing your dad must have been a godly, caring person, a perfect mate for your Mom."

"Yes. Leah often said she couldn't imagine her dad with our Mom." Sarah crumpled her napkin. "My dad died without an inkling he had heart disease."

"It's too bad I can't talk to him. I'd like to know his impressions of the crime." Ford hoped to learn more of him from Lena's pen. "Anything else your mom recalled from your dad's perspective?"

"You think he could have shed some light on what you're searching for?"

"I've had the impression your grandfather knew his assailant, someone who took him completely by surprise. I wonder if your dad had the same thought."

"Mom wrote that Dad, my uncles, and several others stood abreast and walked the field from the ditch to the north and east, toward town, looking for the weapon."

"I'd sure like to see the original file on the case." He made a mental note to follow-up with the first investigator when the cold case division opened up. The man was now retired. It was a long shot he had notes from the original investigation.

"They had to get back to Lincoln shortly after the funeral for Dad to resume work, to pick up their normal life."

"Life does have a way of carrying on."

Sarah rubbed her arms, as if chilled by the topic of their conversation.

"One thing," Ford paused to sign for the check. "If you see names your mom mentioned more than a couple times, would you flag them for me?" He stood and held out his hand, waiting to assist her from the booth.

She accepted his aid while shouldering her purse. "Thanks. Ugh. Bathroom break."

"Meet you at the door."

Outside, Ford guided her through the parking lot to her car.

"I know you miss your folks like I do mine, but the upside of believing in Christ means we'll all be reunited in heaven."

"Couldn't we go one time together without talking about that?" Even as she said it, Sarah felt a twinge of guilt. Hadn't she decided earlier to check into being one of God's own?

"I will always talk about Jesus, talk to Him, unless I'm dealing specifically with a case where talk of the Lord would be out of place."

"Maybe you can help me take believing more serious."

Ford released her hand to open the door and handed her the seat belt, grazing her belly button. Then he leaned in and planted a kiss on her cheek. He patted her arm, wishing he had the right to pat her baby bump.

He left before giving her a chance to react to the kiss, and grinned all the way to his SUV. It would be so gratifying to be a father.

# Fifteen

The tingles of Ford's parting caress lingered until Sarah kicked off her sandals inside her front door. Neither had said good-bye. Their first date. She turned to lock the door, more than ready to rest her weary body in the comfort of her apartment.

As soon as she turned, her gaze zeroed in on the kitchen table. The load of loss landed hard yet again. She and Leah had cleared everything out of Mom's home as soon as they knew she wouldn't go home again.

How would Sarah cope once she and Ford solved the mystery? Would she toss the tangible documents concerning her grandfather, and rely on her memories?

Instead of the rest Ford suggested, Sarah grew anxious to return to the past. The kitchen chair felt good on her back. She placed a small stepstool under the table to take off the load. She pressured herself to drive on with that promise to Mom before the baby began life outside the womb.

She picked up an article with the title, *"Empty No More,"* by Lena Stanley Bishop. Mom noted, "Testimony, published in a magazine gone out of print."

The article began, *"You believe in God, don't you?"* ...the question Dad asked Mom years ago.

And ended with a heart stabbing: *Think about that. God promises to never leave me. I'm never alone. My father's homicide remains one of Nebraska's unsolved mysteries. But every time I see a rainbow, I'm reminded of God's promise. He has never betrayed His covenant with Noah, and He'll never break His vow to remain with me. After all, His later covenant was sealed by the blood of His Son Jesus.*

A sense of something hard to define swept over Sarah. Emotion and tension lifted. Somehow, an unexplained calm rained through her like the refreshing sprinkles of a spring shower. God promised never to send a worldwide flood again.

Mom had put Bible verses on note cards around the house, on the refrigerator, in greeting cards, stuck in mirror frames.

Fragments of what Sarah had read and what Mom said over the course of her last months added to the mix in Sarah's mind.

One of the verses said peace transcended understanding.

Sarah cuddled a handmade notebook and settled on the sofa.

Mom scrawled that she'd made the book at a tall-grass prairie event for writers. Sarah traced Mom's handwritten words. *Every person was created with an eternal soul. I pray, Lord, You have chosen each of my children and grandchildren to spend eternity with You.*

Leah and Jeremiah shared Mom's confidence of ending up in heaven. How did they have that assurance?

Sarah had read parts of the Bible, but it never seemed real. The old words flowed through her, without taking root. "I'll do it for you, sweet baby. Our next venture will be seeking answers from

God's Word. But first, I'll continue seeking that puzzle piece everyone else has missed."

As comfortable as possible, on her side with a pillow between her knees, Sarah circled her hand over her swollen belly. The mound had expanded to give her a larger shelf beneath her breasts. She continued to read, but pictures of Ford's face interfered.

The way he looked at her and seemed to read her mind. The hint of his smile that could erase immediate stress. She'd read her mother's struggles, and wished she knew how to pray that Ford would help her find answers.

To top it all off, the kiss. She licked her lips, and fell asleep imagining his taste.

In the wee hours of the morning, the baby woke Sarah from a dark dream, rolling and pinching a nerve in her leg. She rose to her feet, her leg so numb she fell back against the arm of the couch until the prickles abated.

Seated at the table over coffee with cream and sugar so it wouldn't upset her stomach, she smoothed a crumpled page of Mom's notebook.

Had God somehow spoken to Mom when she copied Jeremiah 1:5? *"Before I formed you in the womb I knew you, before you were born I set you apart."*

"God really plans the life path a person walks? This verse claims He formed us, He knows us. Everyone dear to me has life only because God the Creator and Father ordained it?" Saying it aloud made it more real.

For the first time in her life, she saw the true answer to life, clearly laid out in black and white. Yet at the same time, every color in the room around her appeared brilliant, as if an unreal patina polished her surroundings. The framed edges on each object sharpened in definition and clarity.

How strange for the words before her to pertain to Sarah, written straight to her heart, as though God assured her He knew *her* intimately. He also knew the child nestled beneath her ribs. He planned for the baby she carried to come into the world at a particular time on a given day. He set in motion all the generations of her family, according to His Word.

The knowledge filled her to overflowing, until a sob turned into a laugh. Cleansing washed through her as though her feet, her very security as she perceived it, flew out from underneath her. God was meant to be her foundation.

"I'm a sinner in need of a Savior. Jesus, I've found clarity of mind, and of spirit. Thank You for giving my mother life. Thanks to her legacy of believing in God's Word, I perceive what a transformed life is all about. I believe. For the first time, I really do believe that You are what's been missing from my life. Forgive me, Lord, for my unbelief and all my sin. From now on until the end of time, I give my life to You."

Wow. What a breakthrough.

*I have to tell Ford. I belong to the family of God now.*

She leaned back in the chair, filled with more joy than at any time in her life.

Ford. Little more than a stranger, yet the first person to come to mind to share such thrilling news with. Ford, a man brought into her life because of an event that happened before she was born, seemed more a part of her than Travis ever had. She regarded Ford as intimately closer than Travis. Who would have come up with such a concept?

The author of timed events regarding people and events, God clearly orchestrated with His mighty hand. Today, that discernment came as a thunderbolt out of the blue. God hadn't been in her conscious thoughts, even yesterday.

New life began today. New life in Jesus.

"Oh, baby, we are in for an adventure."

One of Mom's sayings echoed through her mind. "Today is the day of salvation."

She'd find it, if that phrase came from Mom's Bible, the Book with paper thin, fragile pages worn from use.

At the right time, she'd tell Ford.

For now, Sarah rejoiced. God held the rest of her life in His hands.

£

Sarah's eyes traveled the journal entries and noted what her mom did at what time.

*May...I wrote and submitted "Unanswered..." for Nebraska Writing and Storytelling Festival Book...and wrote more about the event during a live workshop.*

*August...I Wrote "The Hidden will be Revealed."*

*September…Trip to Gaylord for appointment with Robert Smith, County Attorney. A waste of both our times. He said the autopsy report is with the State Patrol and he could answer none of my questions.*

*He asked, "What exactly is your part in all this?"*

*I said, "I've had Dad on my mind more this year than the previous ten years combined, and want to have answers so I can put it all behind me."*

*October…*Connor and I stopped at the patrol office in Hardin, but Investigator Richard Randall wasn't in. I left a message regarding Gipson. Randall didn't answer.

*November…still no answers.*

*Sometimes I get so angry I could scream at the injustice of it all. The initial investigation—if you can call it that—was a farce.*

*It haunts me when I remember hearing there were more suspects in this homicide than either of the investigators had ever seen. Does that really mean Dad was hated so much?*

*Someone, somewhere, has kept silent all these years. I know somebody knows the killer. Someone who is too frightened to come forward. I get scared, too, when I think of the implications that this was more than an "in the heat of the moment" manslaughter.*

*I also get angry at the unfairness of my children growing up without a grandfather. Many times I've imagined Jeremiah and Dad fishing next to a small pond. I can even hear the red-winged blackbird as it perches on a cattail stem.*

*Dad would have been so proud of Sarah, the first blonde in the family.*

*I'm glad Leah has memories of him. She was blessed with so many grandparents.*

*Why has Dad's death been bothering me so much? Some years that weekend in August came and went and I didn't give it a thought. For six months now, I think of Dad almost every day.*

*Too many unanswered questions. I'm so frustrated! I have to be submissive to the authority of the State Patrol. I can't but think something could be delved into. Maybe it's simply not priority because it's such an old case. Yet, wouldn't someone seek the notoriety of solving this crime?*

*Lord, give me the peace whether it's solved or not . . .*

*December. . .I wrote to Uncle Walter one last time. I read the list of all my earlier efforts to find out answers to my questions concerning Dad. One of those was "Uncle Walter is working and promises to call back." He never did. I wonder again about that tape. . . I've suspected all along he knew what happened to Dad.*

*Am I looking for something that doesn't exist? I've always believed knowing the truth in any situation is easier to live with than haunting, unanswered questions.*

*I told U Walter my opinion of small-town law officials. I said I'd gone to see the Swanson County Attorney in Gaylord because I'd been told that office could help me. Ha.*

*Don't even know if I journaled that I left three messages for Richard Randall at the Hardin State Patrol office, and finally gave up. He never returned my calls. Maybe it's crazy, but I want answers so I can put it all to rest. Out of courtesy, I thanked my uncle.*

*I won't bother him again.*

*In my Christmas letter, I told my siblings, "I've decided to put all this stuff regarding Dad aside because Leah is getting married following college graduation next summer."*

Sarah couldn't blame her mother for needing to set the search aside. Children put a mother's personal life on hold, no matter if they were about to be born or ready to graduate from college.

She prayed Ford never reached the point of filing away cold cases forever.

# Sixteen

*You turned my wailing into dancing...clothed me with joy, that my heart may sing to you and not be silent. O Lord my God, I will give you thanks forever.*
—Psalm 30:11-12

Sarah rejoiced in the day, a new day to begin with reading the Bible, the same as Mom did. The world around her looked the same, only brighter, noisier. She was different. She decided to hand over all of her mom's stuff to Ford.

As she stepped outside for a walk, she replayed the previous night, galvanized at the mental picture of Ford's face. More than good looks and a brilliant mind, he comforted those in the grief support group at his church. He'd given her hope to solve the case.

With that thought, Sarah realized hope was also a prayer away. Hope in Jesus.

The Holy Spirit drew Sarah to identify with Mom's hope.

Ford shared the same hope.

She searched for words to express her new outlook on life. Her gaze wandered ahead to the park. And there he stood, casually leaning against a tree trunk. How in the world had Ford known she'd be walking to the park at this very time? She approached, their gazes locked.

As she neared, she caught a whiff of the blended icy caramel latte he swung her direction. He held out his other hand to ease her down to the bench, then straddled the seat where she'd sat the first time she laid eyes on him.

"If I didn't know better, I'd think you were stalking me." *That wasn't a very nice start.*

He frowned and reached for his cup. "Stalking is nothing to joke about. Is this business of the case getting to you?"

Sarah drew up a knee and slanted her body in order to face him in comfort. "I feel like I'm just scratching the surface. The phrase 'what a tangled web we weave' keeps traipsing through my head."

"Please watch out for little one here. You can't worry over this old stuff. That's my job."

The baby jabbed Sarah in the rib and she winced. "It's not old stuff to me. I find the idea of what you do fascinating, in a puzzling sort of way. And I'm more determined than ever to see if I can do any little thing to spark solving this thing."

Still frowning, so formidable, he studied her face.

She took a slow enjoyable sip. The icy flavors went straight to her sinuses. "Just what I needed. Now, thanks for the coffee break, but did you really get one for me, or were you planning to drink two?"

"A gentleman never tells." His eyes sparked and he slanted a flirty grin.

She dipped her chin and made a funny face, looking askance above her sunglasses.

"I confess. I saw you head down the path as I pulled into the complex parking lot. So I figured I'd meet you here."

Baby punched as though Sarah's protective womb had turned into an exercise bag.

"May I?" Ford reached out, not quite touching her stomach. His face held such tenderness, it didn't matter that they hadn't known one another long.

She nodded, and drew on the straw. His touch made her gasp. She blamed her reaction on the drink. "That's icy cold."

In contrast to the coffee, his hand was warm, comforting, and familiar.

A touch she could get mighty used to.

The baby rolled and stilled in response.

*Sweet little bit must like having Ford around as much as I do.* She, or he, should know Ford's voice by now. Sarah fought the impulse to cry.

Awe spread across Ford's features and his grin spread. "I admire you, Sarah. Carrying a baby is a mystery to me. I couldn't help but notice the way your shirt just moved. Some babies come early, and with the stress, well, you might be pushing this impending event. Whenever you're ready for our new little someone here, I'd consider it an honor to help set up the furniture."

Had he really said *our* new little someone?

"It's on my list. Soon. Time for me to head back, it's heating up out here. I'll walk you to your car."

An idea sprung when they drew next to a ratty old pickup with a metal bumper. "Ford, indulge me, please."

He shot her an eyebrow lift.

"Remember one possibility of what caused Grandpa's injuries? The car bumper concept always seemed in left field to me. Would you mind getting on your hands and knees?"

"Just don't hop on for a piggy-back ride."

She swatted his shoulder in a playful manner. He shrugged, shook his head indulgently, and handed her his coffee. He glanced at his feet then leaned over to brush loose gravel and a couple twigs aside before squatting onto his knees. This time he raised both eyebrows and showed his eyes above his sunglasses, the way a puppy looks up from below its brow bones.

Her serious thoughts switched to laughter. "I hope my child will so quickly do what I ask."

He wiggled his rear as though he sported a tail, and gingerly placed his head close to the curve of the bumper. Ford sobered, no doubt over a clear conclusion. Odds were against Grandpa being knocked down in such a scenario.

She waved Ford over to the corner of the bumper, and did her own duck squat in order to have a better angle. "A car bumper makes no sense. Grandpa's injuries were front and back, correct?"

Ford squiggled around some more, all the while shaking his head. "I agree. No way."

Their gazes slammed and she knew they shared a like thought. *So how had it happened?*

"Hard on the bod." Ford stood and brushed off his knees. "Do you want a ride back?"

"I'll walk. I have to be in shape for labor, you know. Thanks anyway. There's a lot more for you to go through, or take, next time you come by. Mom received letters from strangers following the newspaper interview."

"Now you've got me curious, Sarah. I'll check out those letters soon." He took his coffee, then turned to wave as he opened his door.

She watched him merge into street traffic, and considered herself fortunate to know the man. An image flashed of the note from the church grief group. Not lucky, more like blessed.

On the return walk she pushed thoughts of the case away and concentrated on work.

A calf cramp dropped her on the threshold. She clung to the door handle, told herself to ease through the pain. Maybe she should have accepted that ride. She figured it as good a time as any to try prayer. *Lord, help me, please, this hurts. I need to get upstairs.*

Some instinct or inner voice told her to lean into the pain and flex her toes. Sure enough, the stretched-out seconds passed and she was soon able to climb the stairs without a twinge. She pondered on what it would be like to carry the baby in a car carrier, a diaper bag, tote a purse, and grocery bags up twenty-two steps. "Hmm. I really do need to pay attention to our very near future, little one."

As soon as she entered the apartment, Mom's scattered documents screamed for attention. Sarah downed a tall glass of water, and picked up a journal.

*Leah's married and living in the South.*

*It's been two years since I shook things up with my letter to family and the newspaper editorials/article. And fourteen and a half years since Dad was killed.*

*I'm taking a novel writing course and plan to write about a daughter's visit back to the small town where her father was murdered. Cult activity has been in the media. I found Peggy Knipplemeier's name for the second time while doing some research at Love Library on UNL campus. Her name is associated with the investigation of cattle mutilations.*

*Today, I wrote to her. She lives near Hardin and may have seen reports about Dad, and our subsequent interview. Since Andrew Gipson contacted me following The Hardin News and Dispatch interview, I'm curious to know if she knows about him. He claimed in one letter he's working on a special task force of the Justice Department.*

*I told her Gipson contacted Uncle Walter, since he's a retired police detective, and all has been silent since their connection.*

*It's a small world in Swanson and Oakwood Counties, I asked if she'd run across anything tied to Dad. I'm aware of most speculations about his death. The frying pan reference in the article still unsettles me.*

*I mentioned I feel Dad's death was drug-related, the way I got nowhere with the investigators, and even a second trip to Hardin. Leighton and I agreed that somebody in high places knows what happened. If there was drug information involved, maybe some cartel was, too, so I needed to lay off to protect my family.*

Sarah leaned back in her chair, shaking her head. "Wow, Mom. Drug cartel, cattle mutilations, cult activity. Your Nebraska had its issues the same as each generation."

A bathroom break, a glass of water, and Sarah resumed reading.

*Peggy answered within a week after I wrote to her...what an encouragement. I wish I could meet her, and copied bits from her letter. She wrote, "...Like you, I wouldn't be able to let this lie. I would have to keep looking for any lead, no matter how small or insignificant it seemed. I would not give up without digging into everything I could possibly find."*

*Then she asked if anyone had told me I could obtain information through the Freedom of Information Act by contacting the regional FBI office and asking for a form...ask them to disclose any information they may have concerning Dad and his death. She says I can request the State Patrol file the same way.*

*She asked if Dad had said, in answer to other people's speculations, anything he may have suspected or overheard. According to Peggy, his being an alcoholic doesn't mean he wasn't upset by the influx of drugs into the area, or other things "wrong" with the world. She believes people who drink are more affected by their inability, or what they feel is their inability to do anything about such things...Having been around when such discussions occurred, politics on a local level are often unfair. People like Dad know far more than most non-drinkers about who, when, where, why, and how things happen locally. Dad may have expressed his feelings to the wrong person. Someone may have overheard, and decided he had to be silenced.*

*Peggy expressed her opinion based on the article copy I sent her. She made me cry when she said she felt she would have liked him. She agrees it isn't right that his death is not solved. She'll be watching for anything that even remotely sounds like a clue.*

*I had to wipe my face and go back to her letter. Peggy said her heart goes out to the family and me. Losing a loved one is never easy. Losing them to a senseless, useless death such as murder, is even more difficult to bear.*

*Amen.*

*She's also not satisfied with the pathologist's answers on the head injuries, and asked if I had a detailed report. (Yeah, right.) One pathologist said he felt the injuries could not have been caused by a vehicle, which she strongly doubts. And asked if the injuries would have meant he was on his hands and knees on the road, facing an oncoming vehicle.*

*Peggy asked if I sat down with the original State Patrol Investigator named in the news feature, or visited with any of his drinking friends. (Not when I had two little ones.)*

*She encouraged me not to be disheartened if I don't find answers to my questions or let it rule my life, but to keep my ears and eyes open. She advised me to remain patient. "God in His infinite wisdom may be guiding you to things not imagined."*

*Peggy added a full page expressing her respect for Alexander Gipson and his qualifications. She finished with, "He has a true hate for any kind of child abuse from physical to mental, and pornography to kidnapping. If suspected, he'll move heaven and earth to get to the bottom of a problem."*

Sarah took a bathroom break and walked around the apartment for a few minutes, not ready to be finished with the entries regarding Grandpa.

*Peggy encouraged me. I had to write a letter to Alexander Gipson...I told him I recently reread the miscellaneous information I have on the death of my father. I reminded him that he asked me to do something in Lincoln at the State Capitol building two years ago, in February. I asked his forgiveness for not following up on that. It was a very emotional time for me, and after I referred him to Uncle Walter, Leighton advised me to do nothing to endanger our immediate family.*

Sarah placed her mother's crocheted cross bookmark in the journal and set it on top of others. Soon, there'd only be placemats and a centerpiece, and she'd once more have room to eat without table clutter. She slid a glance over the documents, but ignored the compulsion to charge back in to the collected information on the unsolved case.

Instead, she wove her way down the hall to check e-mail. Nothing drew her immediate attention. One client said he'd been called out of town on family business and wouldn't need the presentation for a month. He invited Sarah to send anything she drafted for his input.

Mom had done library research, but Sarah had an advantage. Internet access.

*Well, Jesus, if You can spare the time, how about helping me do a little sleuthing? I'm sure curious.*

Sarah searched. A person could find most anything with a few clicks, such as the recommendation for consulting an attorney to fill out the Freedom of Information Act form. She skimmed instructions and mentally added up the cost. Those in charge didn't make the process an easy one.

She followed a link to Nebraska and leaned back in her chair. The State Patrol wasn't federal. Records only become open to the public after a trial. In her family's case, it was personal rather than public. Though she found investigative work rather boring, she kept on with relentless purpose. After a while, Sarah concluded the exercise a wasted effort.

It was past time to change activities. She switched mental gears and pulled up her work project. Time sped while engrossed in her creative zone. Sarah fiddled with pictures, adjusted the colors, and finally called it a day concerning work.

The baby jabbed an exclamation point.

She laughed. "I agree, little one. This activity felt great compared to dwelling on the material your grandma left behind. Let's you and me go shopping."

# Seventeen

There were times Ford's job shouted for a break to connect with family. He swung his state vehicle into his sister's driveway. The subdivision in northwest Lincoln grew between his visits. Tyler and Tanya ran to the edge of the deep stoop, jumping and whooping, waiting for him to shut off the engine.

Once his car door was shut, he crouched in the driveway with open arms. The kids ran and jumped in. Standing, he hooked an elbow around each waist and swung them around twice. He joined their laughter and plopped them on their feet. "I need to tell your mom to quit feeding you so much. Pretty soon you'll be too heavy for me."

"You'll always be strong, Uncle Ford." Tyler giggled around his words. His blue eyes appeared larger since Suze had his hair lopped off. He looked more like a boy than a preschooler.

Ford ran a hand over the top of Tyler's head. "Before you know it, you'll beat me at arm wrestling."

"Give your uncle a break, kiddos." Suze held the door open then swatted Ford with a kitchen hand towel. "Nice to have you drop by."

"I'll never rastle," Tanya announced, twirling on her bare feet, and then losing her balance. "I'm gonna be a dancer."

"I wouldn't want a pretty little girl like you to wrestle. I'll always love you both no matter what you become." Ford addressed Suze. "Is this the weekend Marty's in training?"

"Nope. He was the weekend warrior last week. Why?"

"Something smells good."

"Marty's baking chocolate chip cookies. Do you need him?"

"Naw. Came to see you. I'm going to get more tied up because I'm involved in two cases. I wanted to make sure you weren't going to be alone."

"Ford, I'm all grown up. You need to find someone else to hover over like a male mother hen."

"I can't shake the job of worrying about you." He wrapped an arm around his sister, pulled her in for a side hug. "I got so far with one old case and saw how genuinely cold it is. The other leads me to believe there's a link, thanks to a woman who contacted me."

"Oh, a woman in the picture, huh?" Muscular Marty spoke over his shoulder then bent to peer through the oven door. "A pretty young one?"

"If I'm honest, yes on both counts. The woman has pulled me in as much as the case. She saw the picture in my office of Tanya and Tyler, thought I was married."

"Does this *she* have a name?" Marty tossed a hot cookie between his palms, threw it to Ford.

He caught the fragrant glob and blew to cool it off. Tossed it in his mouth, where he chased melted chocolate and butter around on

156

his tongue. "Sarah. Sarah Bishop. You know Travis Clifton, who wrote that wild graphic book?"

Suze and Marty nodded.

"Sarah was engaged to Travis."

"Bicycle accident, right?" Suze handed her children a cookie on a napkin. "Take them to the table, please. Don't ask for another before dinner."

Ford grabbed a cookie and joined the kids at the table. "Yes. On the trail where I run. Sarah has scads of documents to cull, thanks to her mother's files regarding her grandfather's murder. It's pretty cold, but you know me and my instincts. The hair's lifted on the back of my neck a couple times."

Marty swung around a chair and straddled it. "Admit it, bro, the woman's doing that to you."

"Watch for little ears." Suze swung her head from one child to the other.

"No worries." Ford winked. "I have seen conflicting evidence and way too many questions. There were a horde of suspects as well. Something in the shadows tells me the two cases are connected. I need to hole up and get deeper into this thing."

"Hole up with Sarah, you mean."

"Marty. The children." Suze said it on a laugh, swatted her husband, then kissed the top of his head. "Can you join us, Ford? I'll add a turkey burger for the grill."

"Can't say no to that."

The twins finished eating first and picked at each other while the adults tried to converse.

Tyler folded his arms, his pure blue eyes watery. "Uncle Ford, Tanya wants to lick my eyeball."

"What?"

"I did not. I told him I wondered what his eye would taste like. They're so pretty."

"The same as yours, I imagine, but that's enough." Suze slid back her chair. "Time for baths. Behave or there will be no book reading before bed."

Tyler lowered his head. Tanya pouted. Their eyes met, and they left the table giggling.

That comment about licking an eyeball would be embedded in Ford's memory forever. He'd have to tell Sarah.

Two hours later, Ford tucked Tanya and Tyler into bed. He flew down the stairs to the front door. "Never forget children are a gift of the Lord, you two."

Suze reached up on her toes and pecked his cheek. "That they are. Go do your thing. It's way past time you had a life of your own."

"Don't fool yourself, wife. Our Ford has a bitten-by-a-love-bug gleam in his eye." Marty punched Ford's shoulder. "Pleased for you. I take it she knows Christ?"

"I'm not convinced on that one. I know her mom had a deep faith." Ford turned his back, hiding his own goofy grin. Had to admit, Sarah filled his thoughts every bit as much as the cases. It was a toss-up which one called to him the most.

*Lord, if You're not residing in Sarah's heart yet, I pray you'll stake Your claim there.*

## £

After her walk, Sarah passed over day-to-day journal entries and started reading at the notation: *Closing in on 15 years…Today I went to the library and read about the Freedom of Information Act.*

*Then I shook in my high heels as I rode the elevator to the fifth floor of the federal building to the FBI. I stepped off the elevator and glanced to my left— through glass doors I saw a huge federal insignia. To the right was a magnetolager (whatever it's called or spelled) archway. Two men with ID on their lapels stood on the other side. The oldest, over retirement age, stepped around to talk to me. He said they have a form but they don't know if the State Patrol uses an FOIA form.*

*His suggestion? I should contact the Attorney General's office.*

*Strange emotions slammed into me. I felt like a child in the principal's office. My stomach churned, my cheeks felt hot. It was auspicious. I was intimidated.*

*My conclusion: The average Joe/Jane citizen has limited rights. Unless he/she has the specific question, there will be no answers.*

How much easier computer access would have been for Mom instead of driving to the FBI office in downtown Lincoln for the FOIA.

*Back at home, I wasn't finished for the day. One more time, I wrote a letter to Investigator Richard Randall, Nebraska State Patrol. A few days earlier, I remembered why I had left those messages for him two years ago. Too many questions.*

*I have yet to see a copy of the autopsy report. The County Attorney in Gaylord probably told him that I saw him in September two years ago for that purpose. As much as anything, I want a clear picture in my own mind as to what happened to Dad. I asked if he had any documents at all that I could see for that purpose.*

*I brought up the Freedom of Information Act, which enables me to have copies of documents that would not interfere with the actual investigation. I said I appreciated his attention. I thanked him for continued efforts on behalf of my family.*

*I asked him the same questions I wrote to Uncle Walter, sincerely believing that I didn't get specific answers because somewhere along the line, in talking with an investigator, I had mentioned I'd like to write about Dad's death. Someday.*

*A week later I've had no answer from Uncle Walter or Randall. So, I wrote to Alexander Gipson. I told him this past February Connor and Mason stopped in Clayton for a Coke. Connor saw an old buddy, who introduced them to someone else in the tavern. This man, Sam Bennett, took Mason aside and told him that he knew Mom's family very well. He also claimed to know an "eye witness" to Dad's murder, who can finger the guy. None other than the sheriff in Gaylord, the one who as a deputy was known for carrying a bat.*

*(It could fit. I vaguely recall hearing that this man had been a suspect.)*

*I told Gipson we planned a trip to Gaylord and could meet.*

*Then I wrote that I'd followed the Stallcup case as much as possible through the media coverage here. I told him Neely was the same age as my youngest daughter Sarah, and asked if he'd been involved in searching for what happened to her.*

*I guess that's why I have always been interested in her disappearance.*

# Eighteen

The jarring sound of the downstairs buzzer shattered Sarah's quiet.

The baby kicked, adding to the building queasiness over what had consumed her. She marked the journal page and crossed the room so fast the abdominal muscles strained across her lower belly. With her hands bookending the baby's weight, she scurried to answer the intercom. "Yes?"

"Hi Sarah, sorry for the surprise visit."

"Is that you, Jeremiah? Love it. Come on up!" She rushed to the landing and caught the top of her brother's head rounding the stairs between the first and second floors.

He took the stairs in half a dozen steps, and his hug lifted her off her feet.

She grunted, giggled, and relaxed in his hold "You won't be able to do that pretty soon."

"Can't wait." He kissed the top of her head and helped steady her. Then he loosened and dropped his arms. He backed up and answered before she asked. "I rode with my roomie, who came back for an extended weekend. He still has my duffle in his truck in case I can't sleep on your couch a couple nights."

"You know you can." She shot her brother an answering smile.

He leapt back down the stairs, and reappeared in an instant.

His coloring was dark, where hers leaned to the lighter side. His dark brown eyes matched Dad's, while hers were more like Mom's with hints of gold and green. They were most similar in the shapes of their faces and mouths.

She held the door open. "Why are you here? Help yourself to whatever's in the fridge if you're thirsty now."

"Just water, thanks." He grabbed a glass and pushed the fridge spout. "What's all over your table? Have you outgrown the studio?"

"Mom's stuff. I'm mostly soaking up what happened to Grandpa. But the reading has turned out to be work."

"You tough enough to deal with that old situation, especially in your delicate condition?"

She exploded with an unladylike snort. "You dare to suggest I'm not tough enough to deal with unfinished business? Besides, what delicate condition? Pregnant women have been giving birth since Eve."

He ruffled her hair and slid out a chair, flipping it to straddle backward. "No reason to get riled. You usually don't let my teasing get to you."

"I'm a bit worn. Mom's illness. Trav's death. Mom dying. Now Grandpa's homicide. The combination has me snippy and teary and tired."

Jeremiah rolled his eyes and opened the notebook of official documents. He gave a low whistle. The first clear folder sleeve held a copy of the death certificate. He read aloud, "*Fracture of skull and hemorrhaging. Blunt traumatic injuries. Homicide. Blows to head by person unknown."*

Sarah inhaled a shallow breath and prayed for patience as she let it out, before meeting Jeremiah's gaze.

He raised one brow, searching deep as he studied her face. For what, tell-tale signs of strain?

Travis. Ford. Jeremiah. What was with these guys? It must be some kind of male protective gene.

Moisture glinted in his eyes, but he straightened his shoulders. "And to think she went through those pregnancy hormones because of me, at the time Grandpa was killed. It kind of makes my skin itchy, to see you the way Mom must have looked carrying me."

Sarah hugged him and laid her head on his shoulder. "Mom wrote that Dad saw Grandpa before his body was transported to Lincoln. Indentation began with a strike in the temple, which extended across the forehead, with blows behind the ear, and across the back of his head."

Jeremy whistled. "Hard to think about, let alone say aloud." He cupped her shoulder. "I gotta hand it to you, little sis. You keep up with work, you're carrying a child, and you stomach all this cruelty. I'm proud of you."

"Thanks. It's decades-old brutality on paper. But it matters because it deals with family." She sniffed. "Didn't you ever think about going fishing with Grandpa Stanley? Or what it would have been like for him to teach you to drive a tractor? It would have been sweet to visit the farm as kids. I want answers for the questions my baby may ask in a few short years."

She picked up the journal. "Just read this."

Jeremiah rubbed his eyes. "I sure didn't expect all this when I decided to come surprise you."

"Sorry. I sort of made a promise to Mom that I'd dig into the mystery."

Jeremiah screwed up his face, a familiar boyhood expression. His face cleared and he nodded.

Sarah continued. "Mom never came across as a victim. To me, that exhibits courage. The least I can do is finish the task she wanted done. The only angle she never pursued was hiring a private investigator. I followed her example by going to the State Patrol. Now I have Ford."

"What or who is Ford?"

Her cheeks warmed. Sarah grabbed a manila folder to fan her face. "Ford Melcher is the current investigator with cases grown cold. He's working on a case that happened close to where Grandpa lived. Ford is looking at Mom's records for a link between the events."

"Really." Jeremiah tilted his chair to study her. "This Ford. Someone I should know about? Check out?"

She rolled her eyes. No way would she admit that Ford was reducing the size of a hole in her heart. Not until she sorted out her own feelings.

"Read the pages out loud, would you? The ones marked with stickies in those two journals, while I find a different pair of shoes for my swollen feet."

Jeremiah gave a salute, a cock-eyed grin, and obliged.

"*March 30. I received response from Gipson…*" Jeremiah raised his voice, "Who's Gipson?"

Sarah balanced against the footboard as she stretched under the bed to retrieve a shoe with her toe. Wrong one. "His first name is Alexander. An investigator who contacted Mom after she had stuff printed in the newspaper. You'll have to read it all to get it straight. It's taken me a while to absorb it."

"Got it." Jeremiah went back to the entry.

"*…and it scared the h___ out of me. No way would I go to Clayton to meet him.*

"*He said, and I quote: 'Burn this, just as I have already burned yours. The information is correct as far as it goes. The name gives you knowledge that could get you three, or your families, killed. I cannot compress 27 years of research into this letter. The best I can do is bare bones.'*

"*I'm not going to repeat all the names he mentioned. According to Gipson, the brother of a Nebraska Supreme Court Justice used to run a ditchweed harvesting operation that took it from a little patch a couple miles southeast of Gaylord to New Mexico and used to cut the strong stuff from Mexico. Needless to say, the smugglers were well protected.*

"*When the kingpin and his successors died, they killed about 40 jobs, leaving a depressed local economy. To compensate, local leaders expanded the ditchweed operation into the first cartel's distribution point.*

"*Gipson said the man I named murdered Dad and a teenager to protect the druggers. They were protected by the county coroner, county attorney, and others.*

"*When things got too hot, control passed to Wallace County. The operation is under pressure and shutting down. There are strong indications of plans to move it back to Gaylord.*

"*Gipson claims the man I referred to is probably from the good guys' side, trying to use me to draw out the bad guy at the expense of danger to my family. I take it Gipson means Joyce, Connor, and Mason's families as well as mine.*

"*Of all things, Gipson strongly recommends (to use his term) I go to Motor Vehicles records in Lincoln and ask for a name run on Sam Bennett and run variations like Bennet, Benton, Benning, etc. He said I would have to pay for the searches. He doesn't want me to look for a record, but a reaction that can be evaluated. (A reaction by whom?) Then Gipson wrote, 'If somebody questions you sharply, CID, Air Force, or Army Intelligence, FBI, NSA, CIA, etc. is using you as bait. In either case, back off.'*

"*Holy baloney. This is scary stuff. Gipson warned that if I've talked to anyone other than him, I need to protect my children, because 'those clowns mass kidnap children.'*"

"Sarah, did you catch all that? What kind of man was this, to say such things to our mother? Did she talk to anyone in the law about all Gipson said?"

"I'm in the closet, but I heard every word. It didn't sound that scary when I read it, or maybe I skimmed over it. Ford will help sort it out. Read on, please."

"*Gipson believes Neely Stallcup was a kidnapping victim, along with a string of thwarted attempts in other places, where they met prepared parents. One pair of 'doper snatchers' was caught in Hardin and released without charges. Gipson said two attempts to grab his grandchildren happened in another state.*

"*He asked me to stop by his home in Canton to listen to the tape he sent Uncle Walter and look over some of his information. Then he gave me directions and said he'd let security know who to look for as per what cars we might be driving. Cloak and dagger stuff.*

*"Quoting the end of his letter: The reason is that it would take a truck to haul the stuff you need to know now that you've been sucked in that far. Somebody somewhere is going to get their knuckles rapped for putting you and your children in danger."*

Sarah came back into the room, her stretched-out flip-flops slapping. "I'm praying Ford will catch anything, viewed from his fresh perspective."

"I need to meet this Ford guy." Jeremiah swung the chair around and sat like people are supposed to. "I gotta find out what happens next. As for Gipson, I agree with Mom. Holy baloney. I don't want to use all my time with you reading what you've already seen. Later, catch me up."

"Will do. I can take a turn reading now. Let me get a drink first." Sarah gulped, sat, kicked off her shoes, and began.

*"I answered Gipson's letter on August 27, but didn't want to go into why I never went to see him...I read a clipping about a televangelist from Clayton, who was killed in Iowa. The reporter claimed it was a planned hit and under investigation. I told Gipson I didn't know the man from Clayton, but the account grabbed my attention because he was my age, and died of head injuries. My family's attitude toward any incident hashed over in a bar is that it was the alcohol talking.*

*"August 31, received a letter from Gipson, who figured I knew about the arrest in the Clayton man's murder. He said I may be right — booze talking. Yet, he takes a dim view of coincidence because he's found so many missing children from coincidental leads...Then he went on a rant of sorts.*

"*October 1, another letter from Gipson…the Federal Grand Jury indicted three men from Gaylord. All are outer layers that protected Dad's murderer and others. Dad's case is in the next layer. The Clayton man's murder appears to have come from an unrelated cult. Then he said to watch for Stallcup updates around November, because it's the first case in Dad's layer.*

"*Am I supposed to know what these layers are?*"

Sarah closed that journal and picked up the next, opened it to the bright pink sticky note.

"*Beginning of year sixteen since Dad's death. It's a new year and it opened with two letters the same day from Gipson. (I missed whatever he referred to supposedly happening last November with Neely Stallcup.)*

"*One of the letters was totally beyond me about gov't oppression, terrorism, and some counterfeit money that came from Nebraska. He told me to be watching for the names Easter or Kruz. According to him, 'It's hot, and there's an outside chance it's linked to your dad.'*

"*April 29, another letter from Gipson, a crazy one that reminded me of Peggy Knipplemeier. Gipson wrote that Dad and two other murdered men learned about some of the cattle mutilations done by an Arizona corporation who prospected, looking for uranium. The mutilations were used to find the big uranium deposit in NW Nebraska that is about to be mined. The early exploration method was based on the newly discovered fact that traces of uranium settle out in bovine eyes, tongues, etc. and can be used to locate deposits. Andrew Keaton's bunch were up to their eyeballs in that mess. The deaths heated things up so much that they haven't killed anyone, according to Gipson, for several years.*

"*What the heck kind of garbage is this? Now it's cattle mutilations instead of drugs? Sounds like a novel, or a scary movie.*"

Jeremiah interrupted. "That's enough, Sarah. I came to visit you."

"Got it. Gipson mentioned several names. I do need to give everything of Mom's to Ford. He's been busy."

"Ford, again, hmmm?" Jeremiah skittered that familiar teasing gleam her way, the one he'd always used whenever a guy was implied in Sarah's life. He finished his drink, then rinsed his glass at the sink.

She shot him a mock glare.

"Okay, no more teasing." He stacked Mom's material in a higher pile, clearing more space on the table. "Agreed?"

"If you say so, big brother."

Their stomachs rumbled a duet. They laughed together.

"And that's our dinner gong. Time to eat, Sis. We cooking or is someone else?"

A cloud descended. "Do you think Mom eats and laughs in heaven?"

He nodded. "Do you remember when we sifted through the photo albums to make selections for the slide show portion of her service?"

Sarah picked up the memory. "We laughed at the candid shots, looked at the guilt in one another's face, then Leah, you, and I all sobered at the same instant. Leah told us it was good for us to laugh. Mom wouldn't want us to be sad. Especially thinking about how happy she is on the other side, seeing Jesus face to face."

"That's my answer. Sarah. We need to believe Mom is having a good time where she is. And past time for you to spend your energy getting ready for your baby."

"Correct, big brother. Think new life, rather than loss of life."

# Nineteen

*For God so loved the world that he gave his one and only Son, that whoever believes in him shall not perish but have eternal life.* —John 3:16

Sunday night Sarah reflected on the past weekend. Ford invited them to his place for Italian food. Jeremiah and Ford hit it off as if they'd known each other for years.

She later endured a lot of brotherly teasing about her new boyfriend.

Jeremiah wanted to go to church Sunday. Sarah suggested they attend Plains Bible Fellowship, where both were welcomed by those she had met at the pot-faith dinner.

Following a movie Sunday afternoon, she and Jeremiah walked through a parking garage in downtown Lincoln. "Did you ever hear Mom or her siblings consider that Grandpa had been struck by the bumper of a truck?"

Regardless of the dirt, her big brother dropped to all fours near a pickup truck. He contorted his body through spontaneous reenactments much more humorous than Ford's same moves.

"I need to see this from a different viewpoint. Pretend I'm drunk." Jeremiah turned all floppy and unsteady and twisted into various positions.

"I don't find that comical at all."

He dialogued what might have happened to Grandpa and went through the motions. Any imaged scenario turned her stomach, but Sarah tossed in ideas of a weapon that included tire iron, bat, metal bar or crow bar, tool handle. Jer shook his head, brushed off his clothing, and they continued their walk.

Near her car, they passed a big truck jacked up on oversized tires. Jeremiah ducked to avoid walking into the side mirror.

Their gazes met, processing. Drunks didn't stand erect to their normal height. They often swayed as they walked. She supposed it feasible for the indentation on Grandpa's forehead to have come from the side mirror of a farm truck, or a milk truck.

What explained the blows to the side and back of his head?

They hardly spoke on the way back to her apartment. As the day neared its end, they went outside to wait for Jeremiah's friend for their return to Denver.

"I'd like you to know, Jer, I've found faith in Jesus." She smiled. An inner calm filled her with warmth from inside out. "I've been transformed. I also believe God formed the baby I carry."

"I'm glad, Sis." Jeremiah hugged her as his roomie's car swung into the parking lot. "It means a lot to me that you've finally found Jesus. You can find everything in Him."

The time came Monday for Sarah to beat a work deadline. Later that afternoon, she called Ford.

"Sarah, I was just thinking about you...I mean, your grandfather's case."

Elation bloomed over Ford's slip. "That gives me hope. Thanks for taking my call, and I look forward to seeing you again."

"I'm here for you, Sarah. I'll come whenever you need me."

"How about tomorrow night? You can go over the mishmash file of correspondence."

"Sounds great. I'll pick up Chinese, if you like."

"I like the sound of that. Once finished, her life-changing Jesus news burst to be shared. "I get it all now."

"Get what?" She could tell he'd broken his attention away from his work duties to focus on her. The mere tone of his voice endeared him deeper into her heart.

"The meaning of Exodus fifteen, verse two. *'The Lord is my strength and my song; he has become my salvation.'*"

"You've made my day. Angels in heaven are rejoicing over you, Sarah Bishop."

"See you tomorrow, Ford. Glad I could help your day with my life changing announcement."

The following day, Sarah awoke praising the Lord. She began a habit like her mother's, seeking a verse for the day from a desk calendar. Sarah went from John to the book of Psalms in the Bible and read for thirty minutes. Mom had done the godliest thing while she waited for answers that never came. She sought the Lord.

Expectant for more time with Ford, Sarah again immersed herself in the past. She played with a pen, having a hard time believing the claims Gipson made in his letters. Did any of that conspiracy still exist, especially with computerized information?

Mom referenced the missing girl, Neely Stallcup, as the same age as Sarah. Gipson had used her name as well, saying she'd been kidnapped.

Rattled, Sarah fell into her desk chair, then keyed the girl's name into the search engine. Old articles popped up, along with a clear picture. Goose flesh covered her arms, chills ran down her legs. In the age enhanced photo, which explained why the event bothered Mom enough for her to keep the newspaper clippings, Sarah caught the physical resemblance to herself.

Neely's clothing had been found in a nearby field three months after she disappeared from her babysitter's doorstep, but her body was never recovered. A couple of articles referenced the man serving a life sentence for Neely's kidnapping, but no conclusive evidence had shown up regarding her death.

*Tell Ford.* She registered the time, surprised to see the day had fled. *He'll be here soon.*

The buzzer went off.

She held the door open to the smell of Chinese food. Her stomach murmured and her baby turned. Their lives were so in tune.

"I've got sweet and sour that is not supposed to be hot, cashew chicken, broccoli beef, noodles, rice, and veggies." His offering lightened her heavy thoughts. "Tried to go mild for you."

"My stomach will love you forever." Sarah wished she had a photo of the look on Ford's face, almost as though he'd asked silently if *she'd* love him forever. She pointed to the plates already on the table, and latched the door. "Set the boxes on the counter, please, and thank you." She gave him a full-watt smile. "My baby also thanks you for feeding us."

"Hey, you're feeding me all this information of your mother's."

They spooned into the savory smelling containers and dished the entrées onto their plates.

"Say grace?" Sarah reached for his hand.

He shook his head and pointed a fork at her.

Bowing her head, nervous, but ready for the task, she dove in. "Thank You, Lord, for keeping my baby healthy, for my mother's legacy, for family. And I thank You for Ford, this food, and all You've done for us. Amen."

"See? It comes as natural as conversation."

She answered his grin with one of her own. "Well, it is a relationship."

They smiled at one another and the sparkle in his eye affirmed they had more going on than the business that brought him to her door.

Sarah indulged her first bite, closing her eyes in appreciation over a mouth-watering chunk of chicken with cashew. Heavenly. Then again, next to her sat a handsome, heaven-sent hunk. Hormones again, or a more meaningful reality? Dare she consider how comfortable and at home Ford was, sitting at her messy table?

"How about I just read through these while we eat?" he suggested.

Sarah nodded, enjoying the blissful tang of individual spices. "I'd like your opinion of Gipson's letters, especially where he tells Mom to be on the lookout for the names Easter and Kruz. The guy sounded as though he wanted Mom to help investigate. He suggested some wild goose chases."

Ford sat erect, ignored his food, and scanned the letters. The building buzzer sounded and they both jumped. "That's great timing." Ford took off his glasses and rubbed his lids. "My eyes are crossing."

"And my leg is numb." Sarah got up to answer the intercom.

"Delivery for Sarah Bishop."

"From who? I haven't ordered anything."

Ford eased by.

A moment later she entered the hall and heard an exchange of male voices. The door closed.

Ford returned, holding up a box with a baby stroller graphic.

"You are a dear, dear man. Is that for my baby?"

"Yes. Wheels for baby, delivered by my brother-in-law Marty."

"How did you get your hands on such a nice, expensive stroller?"

"My sister. Suze never told me why she couldn't return it, but this is an elite stroller that almost drives on its own power."

"And why didn't she use it herself?"

"Twins don't sit well in a stroller built for one."

"Right. Well, thank Suze for me." Sarah refrained from peeking. "On second thought, please give me Suze's address so I can thank her myself."

"No problem. I'm sure you'll meet soon. I'll just tuck it in a corner of your room for now. I can assemble it later." Ford returned, and she opened her arms to give him a thank-you hug.

She savored his arms around her, more than the food they were eating. She closed her eyes, and listened to his heartbeat. The rhythm picked up, singing through her veins until it pounded to a crescendo. Why did she fight her attraction? Paying attention to her reaction to this delicious, kind man gave her hope for their future.

The idea of delicious reminded her of the lemon pie in her freezer. Crazy, pregnant lady thoughts. She pulled back.

"Pregnant or no, pursuing answers keeps my mind free from feeling sad. I'm ready for you to take over. I plan to bookmark the next letter and put the whole mess in a box for a bit. That's the only way I'll totally set it aside in order to get some of my own work done. As for now, I have a frozen pie that will thaw quickly on the balcony."

He donned that stern, official persona of a lawman. "So you're about done letting this case work on you? You'll hand it all over?"

"I am. I will. It's a trial of trust, much like what I'll have to do from now on, handing off my troubles to God."

"That's the way it works to achieve a peaceful heart. Both gobbling the pie and setting this case aside. I'll add a better idea. Trust me, the trained professional, to peruse what comes our way and do my job. In fact, let's box it up together, and I'll get it out of your sight for a time."

"I've offered it all to you, and the day for that will come soon, but I'm still learning more about my family." She took the pie out of the freezer.

"If I've learned anything on this job, it's that every family has its crazies, what society once called black sheep, as well as family secrets. Such intrigue is enough to worry lots of people and it gets other people, like me, excited." Ford rubbed his hands together as though ready to dive into a new adventure. "I'll get the door for you."

She set the pie on a patio chair warmed by the sun.

Back inside, she glared at the mess strewn across her table. "How do you keep from taking it home with you at night?"

"Also in the Bible, Ecclesiastes says there's nothing new under the sun. Murder has been around since Cain killed Abel. David ordered murder by proxy. You can't tell me he wasn't into his cups the way he danced naked in the street. There comes a point we have to put everything away that we're not personally responsible for, and have a good night's sleep."

"Interesting you should mention King David. God called him a man after His own heart."

"You're reading your Bible." Ford pushed his glasses up with a finger.

"No one has the right to snuff out another's life. Even King David."

"Judgment is not our job. Forgiveness is, with God's help. He is after all, in the forgiveness profession." Ford strode toward her studio. "Speaking of jobs, what's your next project?"

"Actually, I may be branching out. Leah asked one of her college friends to contact me about being her virtual assistant."

"What's a virtual assistant?"

"A way to use my skills. My potential client is an author. She'll have several e-books released this coming year. So I'd use administrative skills, graphic design of course, create a new web site, bookmarks, and book trailers. Stuff and such."

"I like this side of my Sarah Bishop."

*His* Sarah Bishop? Her pulse kicked up its beat.

"Forget all these gritty details of the past. Get on with your life in the here and now. We have before us the serious task of eating pie." Ford had trouble slipping a letter back into the plastic sleeve.

"Is it caught on the envelope stuck between the letters?"

Ford eased out the envelope. "There's a sticky note here, catching the paper." He handed it to her.

Sarah read.

*"The family has heard a story, but it remains unproven, possibly unreliable. I've been told the man in question was considered an undependable witness, lost in the obsessions of his own mind, after an interview with an investigator. What he revealed could have happened at another time, with different results. He may have related a fantasy. Or told of a conversation, with the plan not carried out—only the perpetrator knows the details. Does someone close, like Connor, know this man? Should we be scared?"*

"You mentioned an unreliable witness when we first met. Do you know who that was?"

# Twenty

*"Never will I leave you; never will I forsake you."* –Hebrews 13:5

Ford froze, taking time to form an answer. "The key is here in your own mom's words."

"What are you talking about?"

"Lena highlighted the key words in the note." Ford's calm voice grated. "Your mom wrote, '*Unproven, Unreliable.*' She referenced a potential assailant who turned out to be an unreliable witness at the time. I'll check into it again, to see if we have more on the original witness mentioned in the file. Speculation doesn't equal fact."

Sarah flipped the pale pink paper over. Nothing but a date on the back. She reached into the plastic sleeve until it gapped open. Nothing else lay within.

"If your mom heard the name of a possible suspect, could she have been too scared to write it down?"

"I have no idea. This notation is a date. Mom's journals are in those crates. Could you please find the one that matches the date?"

He handed her the diary for the appropriate year, and Sarah found the November entries.

"This is curious indeed because she mentions Kruz again. Do you recognize that name?"

Ford stilled.

Sarah drummed her fingers on the book cover. "You need to see every single thing Mom has here. You know what to look for. I have no idea what the investigators involved over the years may have known or not known."

"I'll have more time to check on things soon. The names of the men who played poker with your grandfather the night he was killed might be important, but you need to watch out for yourself."

"And my baby. Got it." She heaved a mental sigh, but deep down, she had to appreciate his solicitude.

Ford deposited the volume back in its crate, then left his chair to stand behind her. The knots loosened as he kneaded her neck and shoulders.

She wanted to release every care and melt into his marvelous touch. Forget the past. Take Ford into the future with her along with her baby. *Dreamer.*

"Give this a rest and get on with your own lives. Yours and the baby's, with the Lord as your guide. I'm reminded of Isaiah forty-three, verses eighteen and nineteen, where God tells us to leave the past and seek a new beginning. Your baby is your new beginning. I'll be glad when you can leave this job for the cold-case guys, meaning me."

Ford's low voice resonated through Sarah's whole being. He rested his hands lightly on her shoulders and kissed the top of her head.

Wow. She somehow managed to lift her hand and pat his, and then retrieved the pie from the patio. "Just in time. Longer, it would have melted. Shall we sit near the window?"

Over the tang of her second taste of lemon cream, she asked, "How did you come to believe in Jesus?"

"I pretty much grew up in church. The youth pastor reminded us—this pie hits the spot, almost as good as homemade—we couldn't rely on our parents' salvation, but had to reach a point of personal choice. I was a sophomore when the guys in our youth group toured the state penitentiary."

The sun brought out all kinds of colors besides blue in his eyes, gold, silver, dark blue rimmed irises. She gloried in the colors painted by God, the Master Creator. "Scared you, huh?"

Ford pinched off a hunk of piecrust. A couple flakes dropped. He let them fall on his plate, and looked her in the eye. "I knew I wanted to stay on the outside of steel bars and the legal side of life. A few months later Mom commented on the attitude change she'd seen in me. I knew the Lord had become real in my life. Can't say a specific day, but I was convinced I had the Holy Spirit."

"It's an amazing gift, isn't it?" She finished eating and leaned back. "Tell me more. Anything."

"The prison visit prompted me to go into criminal law. I've been back to visit, sometimes to question an inmate, but mostly I tag along with a gifted Bible teacher, my friend Chan. He facilitates a study at the prison, and he played soccer with me that day in the park."

"I remember. Blond, short and fast. He reminded me of a cocky rooster."

Ford snorted a spout of milk from his nose, and his shoulders shook with silent laughter. "Bantam rooster. That's good. Chan's a man of God, Sarah. And believe me, God works behind bars."

"So God called you into law enforcement. Why take on these unsolved situations?"

"I had so many questions after Mom and Dad were gunned down. I could blame no specific person, only indiscriminate terrorists, so I made it my mission to seek justice for those families who may still feel violated and helpless in their search for resolution."

They rested their forks against plates at the same time. "I imagine just talking to you cold case guys gave Mom hope. You have an eye for detail and show compassion. Did you always live in Lincoln?"

"Born and raised." He grinned. "What else? You already know I love Runzas, sorry you don't. I read the Bible, stories about Christian martyrs, maybe to understand more the reason and cause that killed missionaries like my parents, and graphic novels. I like classical music except for when I run. Then I need a fast beat. Can't catch the bad guys if too much belly fat accumulates."

Sarah turned serious. "What do I do now, Ford?"

"What do you mean?"

"I don't know where to go to church or how to learn what's in the Bible. I'm a baby when it comes to this Christian stuff. Sorry. That's an awful thing to admit."

"Not at all. You have your mother's testimony of her faith walk. I assume you have her Bible. Continue reading. You can check the references your mom used to get the context. I can give you a devotional guide. Come to Plains Bible with me. If we don't make you feel at home where your mom worshiped, I'll visit other places with you." Ford's animation gave way to concern. "Your eyes are drooping. We can talk about church stuff later. So you're sure I can take your mom's journals?"

She nodded. "As for church, Jeremiah and I went to Plains Bible Sunday. And yes. Take anything. Everything."

"Great news about church." He rested a crate under his arm. He searched her face, displaying a killer grin that lifted her fatigue. Then he patted her abdomen and whispered, "See you both later."

She shut the door and clicked the deadbolt. Suddenly weary, she slumped, and her forehead bumped the cool wood. Baby thumped in protest. She was almost too tired to respond. The phone rang, drawing her from the door to retrieve her cell off the counter. "Hi. Forget something?"

"Honey, you know I believe in Jesus. I forgot to say that even if we don't know why sometimes, God reveals Himself. What matters is Who with a capital W, rather than any whys we can come up with."

"Thanks for that, Ford. I am so thankful for my recent commitment to Jesus. And, thanks again for feeding us."

"My treat. Any time. Can we meet for lunch tomorrow?"

"Give me a couple days. I really am drained, and I have to get some work done in order to pay the rent."

"I understand. Another time. You take care now."

She could get used to him watching over her. She was already used to his touch.

As for the future, much lay ahead to fill her hours. Time spent with Ford, her job, and preparing for baby.

For now, she sought her mother's journey in seeking answers to old questions. Mom claimed four years after her search initiated, she wrote to the original, retired State Patrol Investigator, and asked a lot of questions. Sarah determined her mother never received an answer.

Alexander Gipson sent many rambling letters, the last arrived five years after the first. Mom wrote: *They always come as a surprise. The last one ended, "I don't see any real possibility that this will bring satisfaction for your dad's murder, but one never knows. The Swanson County and other murders made things pretty hot for Andrew Keaton."*

*Yada yada...he named a series of attempted kidnappings, including four of his own grandkids, as well as two contrived auto "accidents" in two days...Dare I try to get something going again?*

At the passing of twenty-four years, Mom contacted a television show. They didn't go for it. The next news to excite Mom dealt with the inception of the State Patrol cold case unit Ford worked in.

*Now, my hope has been renewed! In recent months, the Lincoln paper has been printing articles about Nebraska cold cases. The Sunday issue ran an in-depth feature of Mark Conley of the State Patrol. Connor also read the articles, and I called Mark Conley.*

Mom and Uncle Connor met with that investigator.

She quoted him. "*We had a lot of suspects and followed up on every clue. Unfortunately, most of the people interviewed were either drunk or high on drugs. After so much time, resolution had to come from physical evidence or a confession.*"

*He and a committee will go over the case file to see if it warrants opening up the investigation.*

Nothing new there. Sarah knew better than to keep going, but there were so few stickie notes left in the journals marking the crime.

*Twenty-five years coming up...I'm still wondering who killed my daddy.*

*I drove up to see Connor today, thankful for cleared roads. He keeps moving around, doing odd jobs on farms in Swanson County. Peering into his deep hazel eyes was like looking at our father again. Except Connor smiles more, and is sober.*

*He stops in restaurants and bars in Canton and Gaylord. As it often happens, without preamble, He said, "They still talk about Dad, you know."*

*I told him sure they do. Unsolved murders don't happen in every small town. I asked if anything new besides the usual mention of drugs, or the deputy's involvement had come up.*

*"I met with an old school friend. You might remember—"*

*I interrupted, reminding him I didn't attend the same high school he had. I never lived in Canton.*

*According to Connor's friend, the investigators have been in both towns. "Everybody's" talking about Dad's death again. There's a State Patrol office across the street from the café on Main Street. Supposedly, the talk has been active for six weeks, following a notice of sorts in the Gaylord paper. One of the poker players in Canton even claimed, "Everyone knows Deputy Keaton did it."*

*All conjecture, or are there facts that point to the former Deputy?*

# Twenty-one

As he exited Sarah's building, Ford responded to a work text and pocketed his phone. He hurt for her and her whole family. Yet he was praising the Lord at the same time. Inside his truck, he prayed. "We're equally matched now, Lord. Thank You for coming into her life. I'm thinking I'm in love, here, Lord. And it's clouding my perception of facts because my feelings are getting in the way. Please show me where to turn in this investigation."

He drove past an entrance to the mall that housed the furniture store where he went with Suze five years ago. Hard to believe the twins would soon be going to school.

Time for the Stanley family...had it flown, or dragged by?

Thirty minutes later, Ford perspired on the Pacific Trail on the south side of the city. He thundered through the back entrance to the golf course, jogging in place as he checked for north-south traffic. He crossed the street. Sweat ran in rivulets down his face and neck as he studied the white cross and wreath of lavender and yellow lilies.

He spoke to the heavens. "You'd be pleased with your daughter, Lena. The cross is real to Sarah now. I promise to do everything I can to bring your family closure." He stared down on the memorial. "Travis, I'm sure you were a decent enough guy, but I'm thinking I may steal away your girl. Maybe I'll even thank you for the baby someday."

Ford exhaled and took off at a run.

*I believe we'll know soon.* Familiar prickles stung the back of his neck. *I feel it in my gut.*

However, his gut churned. He didn't want to imagine Sarah's reaction to the fact he'd been aware of who the unproven, unreliable witness was all along.

Sarah was in her element. Taking on the author as a client was a smart business move. She updated her resume with the addition of Virtual Assistant. Creating a book trailer for the romantic suspense author proved to be a blast.

She'd also gone on early morning walks and taken sporadic naps, waking from dreams of both Travis and Mom. In one dream, Mom assured Sarah, "Everything will turn out fine. Not to worry."

Travis appeared in a dream so real she wondered if it ranked in the category of a vision. *Mom, I'm thinking like you.*

"Go on and have a good life," he said. "You are free to love someone as a soul mate. Later, our baby will need a daddy."

Sarah spent lunch reading the daily journal entries. Had the term PTSD existed at the time of her grandfather's death, the whole family might have been diagnosed. No one had escaped gloomy days, mood changes, and times of distress. All circling back to the homicide.

"Conundrum is a good word, Mom. I love to get lost in your world. I often hear the sound of your voice as I read. I hope Ford and I can bring it all to a conclusion before I go into labor."

For a change of scenery, she decided to go to the grocery store. While she pushed the cart and scanned shelves, her thoughts were a humming honeycomb. Peace over understanding where her mother now resided mixed with anticipation of the impending baby's birth, and her ever-present crazy attraction to Ford. Most of all, she took joy being alive in Christ.

How could she feel such a pull toward Ford when her heart still held remnants of sadness and grief? She ran into an immovable object with the grocery cart and snapped out of her musing. "Oh, excuse me." She looked up and gaped. Her heart did a double take. "What are you doing here?"

Ford graced her with an indulgent smile that made her senses go fuzzy. Then he spread his hands, holding a peach in one and a plastic sack in the other. "Shopping. For fruit."

"I'm sorry I bumped into you. I mean, I'm sorry my cart bumped you. I'm glad to see you. I was preoccupied."

His low chuckle washed through her senses as though he'd whispered sweet nothings in her ear.

"I can tell you're sorry. Do you have plans for the rest of the day?"

"Only have to finish my grocery shopping. I need a rest. This concrete floor has made my back and legs ache. Could you come to dinner tomorrow? Say, seven?"

"Sounds good. But only if you let me help you buy a crib. I stopped by the furniture store where Suze and I went shopping for the twins. Found a couple nice ones to choose from."

"You did? You're quite a man of action."

"Wait, I have a question." He moved his cart and leaned in close. "You don't seem excited about purchasing a crib. Are you so caught up in all this past business that you're ignoring preparations for the baby?"

His warm breath trickled from her neck to her knees. Had they been standing so close in a more private setting, she'd probably turn her cheek and meet his lips. Such crazy notions. Had the time come to quit blaming her reactions to Ford on pregnancy hormones?

"Sorry, if I'm way out of line here. And I know I've asked before."

She searched his eyes. Ford's genuine concern filled one of those hollow spots in her heart. She liked the warmth. Her siblings cared, of course they did, but they were far away. How could she have forgotten how it felt to share concerns with a man who cared? She needed hugs, and someone to listen.

"I'm not neglecting the baby's needs, I just feel as if I need to get my mother's quest out of the way. Could be I'm even delaying my grief." She backed up to put space between them, added a lilt to her voice. "I still have time to buy stuff and get the baby's furniture set up. We can talk tomorrow about doing those things."

"Tomorrow, then." He ran a hand through his hair. "I'll take the next journal when you're ready to pass it on."

At home, she ate a huge salad and indulged in a double dark chocolate brownie for dinner. She spent the evening searching the internet for information on some of the names that she'd jotted down. Except for a few mentions in archived documents and old photos, nothing jumped out at her. Perhaps Ford would find something fresh that didn't lead to a dead end.

It wasn't until she was lying in bed preparing to sleep that she realized how natural it was for Ford to offer his help in readying things for her baby. Almost as if he was the baby's father.

£

Sarah had spent all morning contemplating baby supplies. What to buy, what to have in a diaper bag, what to do if her baby had colic, or a fever, or was teething…all the things a mother-to-be asked her own mother, to gain experience in raising a child.

"I miss you, Mom. I wish you were here to talk to…" The empty space in Sarah's heart morphed into a wad of choking emotion. She hadn't cried much after Mom's death because she felt numb. Then she decided not to let her loss dampen her upcoming joy. Now, she couldn't seem to stop the tears.

Without a thought, she dropped to her knees, hands cradling her unborn child. Her forehead sagged to the edge of her leather couch. "I am Yours, Lord. I've never been so aware of Your Presence. This thing Mom faced with Grandpa had to involve faith. I'm convinced You are the only reason she held on to her sanity. I need You in my life. I ask for Your will to be done in me. Please, take care of me and my baby. And thank You for this baby I carry, Lord. I will never believe the baby isn't in Your plan. I believe God sent You into the world to save us all, Dear Jesus. May Your will be done in Ford's life as well. And I place my future in Your hands, thanking You ahead of time for anyone else You will bring into my life, dear Jesus. Amen."

She sensed the presence of Another. Another Entity Who filled her up from the inside out. The Mender of the brokenhearted healed gaping chasms. Mom had referred to a peace that surpassed all understanding. Sarah now got it. The spiritual fulfillment washing over her soul replaced the vacancy.

Rather, completion replaced the emptiness. She'd take her faith walk one tiny step at a time, by putting herself out of the way of God's plan as much as possible.

A silly sense of giddiness grew. She opened her eyes, stood, and went to the balcony to retrieve a jug of raspberry sun tea. A hummingbird thrummed over her shoulder. Enthralled at the swift action of the buzzing wings, she watched the tiny creature hover over a deep purple delphinium on a nearby balcony. "Thank You, Lord. Mom would have loved this touch of Your presence in nature."

She took the tea to the kitchen counter. For the first time, Sarah considered buying a blank journal of her own. Maybe she'd begin to journal, and write to her baby.

"Oh, little one, what a gift you are. I could begin: To my unborn baby from your mommy, Sarah Bishop." Her voice sounded like a shot in the silent kitchen. "You were in my tummy when my mom went to heaven. Sad for you, too, because you'll never know your grandmother Lena, whom I'll name you after if you are a girl. We're all a part of one another."

Her gaze landed on the last journal on the kitchen table. What a valuable link to Mom. Sarah had determined to know her mother on a deeper level, and succeeded. Writing had assuredly kept Mom focused on God, the source of her strength.

Could God be that strong for Sarah? A sudden rumble of thunder rattled the windows and diverted her thoughts. The sky had turned dark. Instead of continuing with her work, she shut off electronics before the crackling lightning did it for her.

She'd always loved storms and wanted to experience this one from the balcony. The ringing phone stalled her intent.

"Just checking on you." Ford's voice made her smile. "It's raining cats and dogs here. There's a threat of wind driven hail. You all tucked in?"

"Fine, thanks, I am safe and secure." Her heart glowed from his warm consideration. She wanted to say, "Wish you were here," so they could experience the storm together.

"You take care, now." A roll of thunder and snap of lightning ended the call.

Sarah caught the beauty of the sky through the balcony window, and scurried for her camera. Captivated by the changing colors of the sky, time meant nothing. The sky lightened as the storm passed. God had to be smiling over His creation of simultaneous golden sunshine and opalescent raindrops. The clouds parted. A dazzling rainbow arced above the horizon.

Hope. She longed to always carry hope in her heart.

# Twenty-two

*He will be the sure foundation for your times, a rich store of salvation and wisdom and knowledge; the fear of the Lord is the key to this treasure.*
—Isaiah 33:6

Sarah awakened slowly, brushing away layers of filmy chiffon from her mind. Once alert, excitement built for the road trip to her family roots. She pulled up the map app on her phone while still in bed, and looked up all names of the small towns Mom had referenced. Sarah didn't want to weigh herself down by taking any papers with her.

The phone rang while she filled a cooler with water bottles. Ford.

"I hit redial last time we spoke and it didn't go through."

"I know. I forgot to charge my phone."

"Are you still planning that trip to Swanson County? Would you reconsider and go a later time so I'm free to go with you?"

"I'm sorry you can't go now. But today's the day for me. I'll be fine."

"You know anything can happen to a woman traveling alone. I'd feel better going along. Unfortunately, I have a couple appointments today." She pictured him with that endearing creased frown, loosening his tie in frustration. "Why put yourself out there to have an accident on purpose? You could come in contact with a murderer and not even know it!"

She regretted her mention of the plan. Was his tactic meant to scare her? He sure came close to crossing the gap between letting her keep her own freedom of thought and being too overbearing. Was his job to blame, or being responsible for Suze so long?

"I'm a big girl. Ford, I want to see the place Mom wrote about. I trust you to do your job. I'm not going to let what happened all those years ago overwhelm me until I bust out in some kind of breakdown or whatever. On the flip side, I won't let this mystery go until I've taken my own action to discover the answers Mom sought."

"I understand the need for completion." He cleared his throat. "It's my profession to investigate so families don't have to, and it enables them to have closure."

*I'm thinking like my mother. She hated the word closure.*

"You know what? That word rubs me the wrong way. Anymore, *closure* strikes me as a cliché. I'll know what I'm seeking when I find it. Any kind of answer will do to give me peace. I'll go as far as I'm able. Plus, I'm looking for a visual here, not tracking down a killer." *I hope not, anyway.*

"Sarah, you make it hard to help you. I definitely don't want anything to happen to you. Or the baby. I can't keep you safe if you're that far away. See you later then." Irritation colored his last statement.

It wasn't Ford's job to keep her safe.

*I promised Mom I'd try.*

£

A gorgeous early summer day greeted Sarah, encouraging her high sense of adventure. She had her route plugged into her phone and water in a cooler. She was more than ready. The few wispy clouds billowed in suspension. Birdsong, varied greens, and calm traffic carried her through south Lincoln.

She passed the sign announcing the distance to the first I-80 ramp and took her foot off the accelerator.

A siren blipped behind her. She checked the shoulder for how far to the right she could go. The blinking bubble light in her rearview mirror stayed on her tail. The cruiser didn't speed up and go around her. She'd never been stopped by the law in her life.

"What do I do?" She braked and came to a stop a few feet from the ramp entrance. Glanced in the mirror again. Her heart pounded.

Sarah fumbled for her purse, and dropped it. She let it go and reached for the glovebox.

The car rolled forward. She forgot to put it in park.

Hearing nothing now but her heartbeat, she retrieved her purse. She waited, holding the registration and license in her hand, staring in her side mirror for an invisible officer.

A tap on her passenger side window made her jump.

Ford's face appeared. He knuckled the glass and circled his finger for her to roll down the window. "Follow me back to the patrol office so I can park. You're not going alone."

She checked traffic and managed to get back on the street to follow him. Several minutes later, she found herself in the passenger seat of her own car.

He loosened his tie and tossed it onto the backseat. Then he leaned in and adjusted the driver's seat to accommodate his long legs. Once inside he put the car in gear, and glanced her way. "Did you check the oil and tires?"

"You sound like a father. I've been driving by myself for a long time."

"No need to be touchy. I live to serve and protect." The corner of his mouth twitched as though he fought a smile.

"All right, I give. Drive on, gallant trooper." Rather than watch out the window, she ran her gaze over his profile as he expertly handled her car. Too bad his shades hid his breathtaking eyes. The corner of his mouth twitched. He knew she stared. She didn't care.

One thick brow raised, he checked his mirrors and merged. "Do you plan to while away the hours checking me out, or is there a specific thought on your mind?"

"You are a mighty handsome man, Ford Melcher. What's your middle name?"

He grinned. "Winston."

"Distinguished." She diverted her attention to the open road, where I-80 miles blew by. Traffic was as heavy as evening rush hour commuters on O Street, bumper to bumper, minus slow speeds and stoplights. The bright sunshine touched the land with hope.

"Mine's Caroline, by the way. As a little girl, I'd stumble over Sarah Caroline Bishop."

"It's a mouthful."

"Speaking of mouthful, it's kind of nice to not be talking around food, or about Mom's words. Where'd you go to high school?"

Ford answered more of her questions and had some of his own. They discovered as many likenesses as opposites about themselves. Somewhere along the line, she admitted, "I'm glad you stopped me. I thought I wanted to be alone, but having you with me is good."

Miles later, he took the off ramp. The never-ending cerulean sky, wild flowers blooming in the ditches, and the call to discovery sang through her as they traveled. *Thank You for life, Lord. Before You opened my eyes, I didn't pay attention to the beautiful blessing of Your creation.*

She spent a couple hours of soaking in the summer landscape. Ford made two stops to stretch their legs. She read signs as he detoured off the main highway to follow the business loop into Hardin.

Ford's voice startled her. "I thought you might like a glimpse of the main street where your mom went to the newspaper office. The patrol's annex is on the other edge of town."

"Thanks. I don't get out much. I've had little exposure to small-town living. Mom described aspects of life in farming communities, and claimed many hadn't changed much over time. I figure, due to the Internet, out-state Nebraska has shrunk."

He silently drove on.

The high Hispanic population of Hardin, no doubt due to meatpacking plants she noted signs for, surprised her. The news office on the main drag was easy to spot. So many years had passed since Mom and Aunt Joyce passed through the front door for their interview.

At the highway junction, as he'd promised, Ford pointed in the direction of the State Patrol office. "It's just a nondescript building a few blocks up."

Seven minutes out of Hardin, Sarah blinked on the outskirts of the tiny village of Clayton. "Wasn't that Alexander Gipson's town we just blew through?"

"Yes. It's no larger than a blip. Gipson wrote his letters from there." Ford slowed for the next village.

"You contacted Gipson at the retirement facility. Did he remember corresponding with Mom about Grandpa's murder when you reached him?"

"I tried. It was a short conversation. The old investigator said his daughter had taken all his files to her home in North Dakota. He's recuperating from surgery and claimed he had visitation restrictions."

Sarah thumped her temple for a memory. "Do you remember, way back, when he mentioned a woman's involvement in one of his letters to Mom?"

"Right. Good catch on your part. I've seen no other mention in any notes of ours, that a woman had a part in his death."

They swished through a couple similar towns before coming to the river bridge that denoted a turnoff that triggered another recollection. "Ford, could you turn at the bridge, please? I want to see the farm with the native pasture Mom mentioned often in her writing. I'm pretty sure we went there once when I was a girl."

He used caution on the narrow roads with ridged gravel. "Never been this way. The height of the hills surprises me. Show me where to turn."

She counted the miles. Sadly, the farm where Mom grew up had given ground to multiple acres of corn. Sarah's heart pitched. "Mom would hate this. She loved the cottonwoods and grasslands. I think she called those dry places where the sand is blowing, blow-outs like the dunes of the Sandhills during the depression years."

"I'm guessing she has green pastures in heaven."

"Thank you for saying that."

Finally arriving in Gaylord, Sarah grew quiet as Ford followed Main Street to the town square, where the Swanson County Courthouse stood proud. He parked the car in a slot.

The excitement jigging in her stomach turned into a constant drumbeat. Few people came and went as she stared at the main entrance.

Out of the car, the baby let her know he or she was glad for some freedom of movement. Sarah arched her back and massaged the sore spots near her tailbone with her thumbs. She grabbed her purse.

Ford locked up her car, and tossed her the keys. "I'm going to check in with the sheriff's office, just because."

They headed for the double doors to the picturesque stone building. Once inside, she located the restroom sign and took care of the pressing need to relieve her bladder. Back in the entryway, she approached the room-length counter. Three clerks worked on the other side. Two women ignored Sarah. The third rose from her desk with a smile of greeting.

Sarah addressed her. "Hi. I have no idea what I'm looking for, or where to start."

"Well, the Clerk's Office is a good beginning. How may I help you?"

Leaning on the counter now, Sarah wondered if Arlene, according to her nametag, had lived here all her life.

Sarah caught herself almost panting. A deep breath proved harder and harder with each passing day. She'd be so relieved once her baby no longer held a position that robbed her of oxygen. "Okay. My mom grew up here in town. Unfortunately, my grandfather was a homicide victim in the county. I've never been here before. Could I please see what you have on file under his name?"

"Oh. We don't have crimes like that happen much around here. What's your grandfather's name?"

"Dieter Stanley."

Arlene didn't write down his name. "I'll see what I can find."

Sarah scanned the directive signs to other offices, and noted county memorabilia on the walls surrounding her. Several photos captured men in sheriff uniforms, including Andrew Keaton.

Was Keaton the reason Ford went off to that office?

The clerk reappeared, still smiling. "Here you go. Not much here besides a newspaper article in with the record of deeds. Anything to do with the actual case regarding your grandfather is at the Nebraska State Patrol. Vital Statistics in Lincoln would have birth and death certificates."

"Yes, I've been in contact with the patrol." *In fact, he's my personal escort today.*

"Sorry I can't be of more help. I can show you the location of your grandparents' farm on the county plat map." Arlene walked away from the counter.

An inner door scraped open on the concrete floor. Sarah looked up, expecting Ford. A man in uniform approached. Severe heartburn hit with a vengeance, accompanied by the certainty she had no clue what she could do to facilitate solving a case that had so far eluded law enforcement.

The big deputy sheriff stomped up to the counter. Sweat trickled down her back. Why? He didn't resemble Andrew Keaton in the least, but he stood tall and formidable.

Sarah glanced at his face. "Full of himself," one of Mom's expressions, entered her mind. Her second look told Sarah the puffed-up deputy looked young enough to "still be wet behind the ears," to coin another of her mother's descriptions, in need of active duty.

Unease niggled and grew, but Sarah couldn't put her finger on the exact cause.

The younger Keaton had supposedly given Grandpa a hard time on occasion. Since the old deputy held a city position now, according to the Internet, the man may well be somewhere in the building at that very minute.

Maybe Ford's caution had been warranted. Did Sarah have any real business sticking her nose in these criminal matters? He'd advised her to leave the job for law enforcement. *But sometimes you have to find out for yourself.*

The deputy nodded after he signed for some paperwork, touched the brim of his hat Sarah's direction, and left. Sarah thanked Arlene, anxious to put behind the town of her mother and grandmother's youth.

With no family ties in Gaylord, no grand architecture to check out other than the building in which she stood, Sarah was finished here. Yet, she couldn't help but consider her family roots. If the case ever came to a jury trial, it would be held somewhere in this building.

She left the courthouse with the certainty she'd never return.

# Twenty-three

*…and great will be your children's peace.* —Isaiah 54:13

Sarah sat on a concrete bench in the shade with the sheriff's office in sight. Her grandparents picked up their marriage license here at the courthouse. Thoughts jumped to a picture of the death certificates her mother had saved. Grandma's stated cirrhosis due to acute alcoholism as cause of death.

Was unbearable grief also to blame? Mom believed secrets accompanied Grandma to her grave. Did she know details about Grandpa's death, never revealed to anyone?

At sight of Ford's tall form exiting the courthouse annex, a welcome sigh of relief burst forth. *Silly woman. I can't imagine I'd be a threat to anyone after all this time.* Feasting her attention on him did wonders for taking her mind off any possible danger.

His smile set her stomach aflutter. He reached for her hand and pulled her to her feet. "Hungry?"

"You know it." He held her hand until they reached the car. Her heart kept up its fast beat and finally slowed as he backed onto the street.

Rounding a curve on a hilltop where the highway turned, she spied a java and smoothie sign. "I can get something here. There's a drive-through next door if you prefer a burger."

He dropped her off. As she entered she kept her car in sight through the windows. The fragrance of fresh fruit and the whir of a blender caused her tummy to gurgle. The girl behind the counter flashed a mega-watt smile, showing a lot of teeth. "Are you new here or on your way to somewhere else?"

"First time through. But my mom's roots are here." She didn't give any more information, except what she wanted in her smoothie. She paid with cash, and while she waited, grinned at sight of Ford's broad shoulders across the lot. He pulled her car away from the order window.

The young girl set the smoothie on the counter. "Here you go. My gran always says children are gifts of God. According to my mother it's in the Bible."

"Your grandmother is a wise woman." Sarah glanced at other patrons as she moved toward the door. Everyone in the place appeared far too young to have known Mom and her family.

Ford parked and came inside with the smell of burger and fries emitting from his bag. She led him to a booth. The frozen yogurt and fruit settled the sourness in Sarah's stomach. She hoped it benefitted the baby.

Her baby.

Sarah was three weeks old when Grandma Stanley died, four years after her husband. Though heartbreak may have contributed to Grandma's alcoholism, cancer also showed up during autopsy, the same kind of cancer that destroyed Mom's body.

*Enough doom and gloom for the moment.* "How's your burger?"

He answered around a big bite. "Must be a half pound of cow in this thing. I'd say it's the best I've ever had. Help yourself to a fry."

"Maybe it tastes so good due to the company."

She loved the sparkle in his denim blue eyes. They finished eating in silence, and were soon on their way.

She took the wheel. Once on the road again, Ford received a text and busied himself with his phone. A blacktopped county road soon led to Canton.

Thirty minutes later, Sarah slowed for the reduced speed at the south end of town, and a dark heaviness settled low in her stomach. How had Mom and her family faced entering the place where a killer might still be walking free?

An uneasy feeling shivered over her. Murder happened here, at this dot on the Nebraska map. What caused the sense of evil?

Oppression threatened to bear down as though it lived. Sarah's skin crawled as her car crept along due to the low speed limit.

Ford tapped her hand on the wheel, and pointed to a small building. She almost missed the VFW, an ancient tiny structure on the west side of the highway in Canton. It might hold a dozen people, a few more if they stood. That building was the last place Grandpa was seen alive. Across the highway and up a block, she read *Lily's Place* from the brightly painted façade higher than other rooflines. Once Rusty's Tavern, Sarah surmised.

She had no desire to enter either establishment after viewing enough television shows for a clear picture of what to expect behind such doors. The gravel road west out of town was easy to find, thanks to the proximity of the now closed Canton Creamery as a landmark.

According to the odometer, and with the small town in her rearview, she approached the place where Grandpa's body had been found in the ditch. A foreign foreboding flooded her soul.

Ford remained quiet. His mind no doubt took in everything, including the spot where a body once laid. She turned in the driveway where her mother had never lived, and years before a deputy carried the tragic news to Grandma of her husband's death.

Sarah sat with the engine idling, and stared at the kitchen window. Her ancestor had kept vigil, based on Mom's writing.

Ford opened the door. So lost in thought, Sarah jumped.

An eerie feeling snaked up her spine. Maybe Mom had written about her own creepy revulsion, but Sarah hadn't soaked in all the journals yet. She focused on Ford and followed his steps to the edge of the road.

Disengaging the brake, gravel crunched beneath the tires as she rolled into the drive and stared at the house. Was it the same kitchen door where Mom had greeted neighbors with their gifts of food and expressions of sorrow?

A gaggle of boys tossed a football behind the house that needed a serious facelift. In the far corner of the yard a charred burn barrel tilted atop a mound of clumped ashes. Sarah imagined an earlier time, envisioned her great uncles burning trash in that corner. What would the current boys' mother say if Sarah knocked on her door and said, "Hello, my grandfather once lived in this house. Until someone hit him in the head and killed him."

*Yeah, right.*

Whoever occupied the house now had to be too young to remember; but surely had heard all the gossip and rumors over the years. Notoriety went hand-in-hand with living in a small town where a murder once occurred.

Sarah stared at the side door, her mind racing with potential scenes of long ago. She couldn't imagine any woman in her family raising a skillet to strike her husband in that kitchen. Mason had been the only other person in the house.

Troubled teenagers had the capability to kill their parents, but Sarah seriously doubted Uncle Mason harbored such malice inside himself. She'd read his letter to Mom. Grandma sounded too gentle and kind.

Family had not done this.

The sound of sliding gravel drew her back to the boys who lived here now. She rolled down the window.

"Whatcha need, lady? Are you lost?" A freckle-dotted boy with plastered sandy hair balanced a fluorescent green bicycle too big for him. He nodded at Ford. "Did you lose something?"

"No. I'm about to turn around. Just got lost in thought for a moment. Thank you for asking." She imagined her uncles going down the road to do their farm chores had looked much the same as these boys.

She reversed and parked on the side of the road next to Ford. She unbuckled, got out, and took the passenger seat. She shook too much to drive on. Emotion clutched a strangling hand at the base of her throat. She searched the ditch surrounding Ford's feet, placed an imaginary body lying there in view of a milk truck driver, cowboy boots facing the onlooker.

Then she experienced Mom's anger. Sarah's hands fisted. She blinked moisture from her vision and imagined the scrim of rainfall taking its toll on existing evidence. Physical clues washed away that life-altering day, along with her uncles' dreams of farming with their father.

She fixed her gaze out the windshield at the cornfield. A light breeze waved the giant clacking green leaves on the stalks, emitting humidity from the field where men once walked abreast searching for signs of anything that had to do with the slaying of her grandfather. Her heart ached again over what her mother's family had gone through.

Sarah caught movement over her shoulder, and the fanciful thoughts fled. The boys didn't venture too close. They remained at the end of their drive gawking through the rear window, no doubt curious about the crazy lady, not brave enough to approach the big man.

Ford turned at that moment, the look on his face hard. He'd probably had puzzle pieces circling through his head concerning law enforcement or names he'd read, and far too many questions gone unanswered through the passage of time.

£

Ford lifted a hand to Sarah. His phone pinged a text from his partner, who was nearby. Without a doubt, they'd soon wrap up the Neely Stallcup case. The anticipation prickled the hairs on his neck.

He caught Sarah's gaze and kept eye contact as he headed to the car. She'd been lost in thought, yet smiled at him now.

"I take it you want me to drive?"

She opened the passenger door. "I did, but I've changed my mind. I need to do this. I can't be so close and not see where my grandparents are buried."

"Good for you." They clicked their seat belts in tandem. He chuckled. "I like your spirit, Sarah Bishop. Tyler and Tanya still tell me they like to do things for themselves. Know where we're going?"

"I checked it out before I left Lincoln. GPS is great, huh? I retrace the route through Canton. Turn left at the highway, and go north through town. The cemetery is on the hill, west side." She started the engine, checked both ways, and pulled onto the road.

His phone dinged with another text. He bit the inside of his mouth, tingles roved up and down his spine over what he read.

Sarah followed her tech guide, and soon slowed the car to a crawl through pillared iron gates.

He looked up. "Pretty setting. Nothing like a calm cemetery in the middle of farm country to make me feel the city is far away."

Sarah giggled. "It sure is. We're a hundred and fifty road miles from home."

They opened their doors simultaneously. A whispering breeze blew, wafting a hank of Sarah's hair across her cheek.

She tucked it behind her ear, and graced him with a smile. "Such an error to say cemeteries are a place of eternal rest. Only remains lay beneath the grass. Their souls have long departed."

They closed the doors with soft snicks instead of slams, appropriate for the place, and not disruptive to the beauty of a lark's song.

"Mom loved a meadowlark's trill, but I don't see a bird with yellow breast and black V beneath its neck."

His phone rang. The progress his partner made picked up Ford's adrenalin, but he shrugged for Sarah's benefit. He couldn't take her along if he had to follow up on this lead.

"I need to get this." He answered his partner, "We're close. Let me know."

He studied Sarah over the hood of her car. Sarah's shoulders straightened and she stood taller. *Tough Woman.* He followed as she meandered between the rows of markers, searching names on the gravestones until they completed a U-shaped jaunt through this small cemetery.

"Here they are." The Stanley markers stood near the entrance, on the opposite side behind her parked car.

He would have seen them, had he turned around to answer his phone.

"This is real. My grandparents, my roots, lay here at my feet." She visibly shivered and rubbed her arms.

Ford drew close enough to touch her. "You okay?"

"Remember that letter Mom received about killers who sometimes returned to the graves of their victims? It's creepy, the idea of stepping where a killer may have trod."

His own insides gave a turn. "It was a long time ago, Sarah."

A crow cawed its raucous warning.

Another text alert interrupted. "Some days are like this."

"I wish you could tell me what's happening. Whoever claimed cemeteries are restful needs to see my feet quivering in my sandals." Sarah raised her chin and slanted him a slight smile. A tear glistened on one eyelash.

He longed to shield her from all future hurt. He answered with a quick text. Then reached out his arms.

She covered her mouth with both hands, buried her face against his chest. But she didn't cry.

"You're strong, sweet Sarah. Don't be afraid. I'm here."

# Twenty-four

*"Be still, and know that I am God."* —Psalm 46:10

*Fear not, I am with you.*

The still small Voice following Ford's assurance soothed Sarah in an instant. Darkness of soul disappeared as fast as the despair that had stormed in without warning. What a relief.

"Thank You." She stepped out of Ford's embrace. "Thank the Lord, and you."

She trilled her fingers over Grandma's name etched in granite, and reached toward her grandfather's marker. The stone felt warm from the sun. Sarah found it somehow comforting.

All sense of harm to her spirit scattered like dandelion seeds blown in the breeze.

Ford stayed beside her as she moved behind the stone markers. "I found what I came for. I've discovered a sense of the place. I can't fault Mom for never bringing me here to visit. Her family roots were fixed in her memory, but overshadowed by trauma."

"I'm glad if you're glad, and I'm proud of you." Ford scrubbed his nape as though it itched. "About the calls and texts. Something's come up I need to take care of. You know I can't take you, because it involves a witness."

"Where are you going?"

"Not far. A hayfield close by. There's my guy now." He pointed to the dusty black SUV pulling in the entrance. "Do you want to wait for me here, or in town?"

"I can stay here. No way do I want to see anything in that town. What's your guy's name?"

"My partner's name is Ken." Ford kissed her cheek. "This is a quiet place, but if we were outside any bigger town, even Hardin, I wouldn't leave you. If you get nervous, or anyone shows up, go to your car and lock the doors. Call me. There's no reason to think anyone followed us. I'll be back as fast as I can."

The man tied her up in knots. He gave her the impression he'd do anything for her, far above being protective on a lawful level. Maybe he made things personal due to her pregnancy. Working a case, yet he felt the need to come with her. Could his hovering turn into smothering?

"Lord, now that I know You, please show me what Ford is supposed to mean to me and my baby. I like him. A lot."

Travis had been the best friend a gal could've asked for. He'd always accepted her, never tried to change her, and never judged when she acted silly or made poor choices. At times, he had more honest motivations than she had for herself.

The constant knowledge she'd never felt the stirrings of romantic love assured her their marriage wouldn't have lasted. Baby or no baby. Besides, he'd scoffed at Christian beliefs. Then again, she hadn't believed when he was alive, either. She was a different person now.

Trav never made her heart sing the way Ford did. She couldn't picture getting old with Travis. But Ford? Now, that man caused a flutter of excitement within.

Just thinking about him did something crazy to her pulse rate. He was barely out of sight, and she yearned to hear his voice again. Losing herself in those dreamy blue eyes made the cares of the world disappear.

Dreaming got her nowhere, out here in a country cemetery. "Let's take a walk, little one. I'll read names out loud so we both can hear them. I know who you are if you're a girl, but a boy's name has yet to catch my attention."

Ford's middle name, Winston, had a nice ring to it.

$$\mathcal{L}$$

Ford kept his gaze on Sarah through the side mirror as he conversed with Ken.

"If a glimpse tells me anything, I can see how Sarah caught your attention."

"Drive, Ken. Let's meet this man of yours. I have high hopes he'll help break our case wide open."

Investigator Kenneth Larson grinned the whole time he guided the SUV from the cemetery. Moments later, he gingerly traversed the rough entrance to a hayfield. He parked facing the road.

A bright bronze, older model pickup with a loud muffler pulled up beside them. The driver waved and they followed the truck behind a row of stacked round hay bales. Hidden from the road, the drivers shut off their motors.

The witness proved himself a spry man with thick white hair, a deeply sun-ravaged face, and snappy brown eyes. He belied his age by skimming the running board rather than step on it as he slipped to the ground.

"Name's Chuck Stopher, Bonnie Easter's my sister. I might be of help to you. Let's chat a spell."

"Care if I take notes?" Ford didn't wait for an answer, but pulled out his phone.

"I been around some time now. Lived near here and in the ranching communities of the next county my whole life. I worked for my brother-in-law, Bonnie's husband. The Sandhills have been my backyard. She had a couple boys that were good fer nothin' scalliwags. Their daddy was a mean, whiskey-lovin' old coot, but he knew his cattle. I'm gonna tell you a story that you'll find hard to believe. Then again, people been sinners since the Garden of Eden, so here goes."

Ford squinted. Sometimes, he missed the trooper hat. He wouldn't show any kind of weakness by shading his eyes. Sunglasses would have to do.

"We worked thousands of acres of pasture land for grazing cattle. Those acres went deep into the hills. Unfortunately, people can hide in those hills. A man who was murdered years ago was at our place the day before he was kilt. Dieter Stanley. The women liked him back in his prime. I just lost Bonnie to lung cancer. What my daughter found cleaning up the place took my appetite for a week." Stopher spat on the ground.

"Take your time, sir. Didn't you say your daughter found this questionable evidence in your nephew's old room?" Ford exchanged a glance with Ken.

"In the boys' room upstairs. Bonnie's hip stopped her from going up the stairs years ago. My girl cleaned out the closet and found a cubbyhole behind some loose boards. Seems that boy and a couple others liked to hook up with young girls. They took those girls and used 'em up until they got knocked up or they keeled over dead. One of them girls was Neely Stallcup."

Ford wanted to punch his fist in the air, but he held it all inside. He drew on everything he had to keep his expression stoic.

"Turns out Neely wrote between the lines of a book and told all about how a friend of my nephews nabbed her right off a sidewalk in Hardin. Only nine years old. They kept her naked and mostly starved, for those boys' sick pleasure. No idea why my nephew kept that book, maybe it gave him some kind of thrill. I do know from piecin' things together over the years, the man who grabbed those girls was named Kirby Kruz." Stopher spat again.

Ford's gut seized. "Are you sure about the name?"

"Written right here in my truck in black and white."

Ken and Ford both stood to attention.

"Little Neely listed the people who came to buy cattle while she was held captive. Dieter Stanley's one of 'em. I'm guessing here, but I'll bet my favorite Angus bull, Stanley caught sight of Neely or another of the girls. Kruz is in prison now, for drugs. And that's how my nephews paid him for nabbing the girls. In drugs."

Divine strength alone kept Ford's jubilation under control. His heart pounded. The hairs on his back were so full of electricity they could stand and shake hands. It all came together. Kruz was mixed up in the Neely Stallcup mess. Kruz and Dieter Stanley had a blow-up over keeping Connor away from drugs. Kruz was a piece of work.

Ken stepped closer to Stopher's truck. "You said you have that book? May we see it, please?"

"I got that dastardly piece of words locked in my glove box. I pray, off my hands, off my mind." Stopher placed his hands above his knees and pushed himself off the running board. He lunged a sideways skip to the passenger side of the pickup. "Never want to see the thing again."

Ken received the book wrapped in a brown paper bag.

Ford couldn't wait to get his hands and eyes on it. The verse from John 8:32 wove into his mind. *"Then you will know the truth, and the truth will set you free."*

He wanted Sarah to be free of the past. His heart beat a staccato rhythm at the prospect of putting on gloves to study the book in the SUV on the way back to Lincoln. He'd never do that to Sarah. Ken would take the evidence back.

She waited for him now. The idea of gazing into her golden brown eyes wiped out present eagerness to discover young Neely Stallcup's revelation.

£

While she waited, Sarah had enjoyed butterflies dancing amidst wildflowers, and finally glimpsed the pretty meadowlark. She now gulped a bottle of water while leaning against the roof of her car. Ford better hurry. She wanted to get home.

As though he'd heard her think his name, the SUV drove up. Ken kept the engine idling while Sarah took in Ford's face. He expressed excitement, rather than tension. He climbed out, tapped the roof, and Ken was off.

She tossed the bottle in the backseat to recycle later. Feasting her eyes on him, her hot, cold case investigator, created music as pretty as the lark's song. "I hope this trip's been profitable for you."

"Invaluable." He hugged her. "I can't talk about details until we get it closed up."

"I understand. Want to drive?" He accepted her keys, and she took the passenger seat.

His face lit up, enhancing a sunburst of appealing lines that fanned near his eyes. "This is hard to describe to another person, but when a clue is uncovered, or a break is about to happen in solving a case, I get this electric feeling underneath the skin on my neck and back." He checked both directions, and pulled onto the gravel. He chuckled. "Habit. Never know if a tractor comes along. As per the case. What we've found out today points straight to the missing girl, and I'm hoping, your grandfather."

"Neely Stallcup and Grandpa? Sounds like quite a coincidence."

"No such thing as coincidence. When it comes to timing, God holds the whole situation in His hands."

Her senses went on full alert. Sarah grasped a deeper measure of faith. "In other words, you're saying Mom never had an answer just so we could make this trip to Canton today."

"I believe it. There is no happenstance with God. If you haven't read it yet, read the book of Ruth, and note chapter two, verse three."

"I'll do it. After today, I get how God holds the big picture in His hands."

Ford pulled into the gas station in Canton. The girl at the counter was as young and friendly as the one at the smoothie shop in Gaylord, except this one had too much black goop around her eyes. On the road again, Ford circumvented Gaylord via the bypass.

Praise songs from Mom's CDs blared through the speakers. "Do you think people in heaven can see what's going on here with us?"

"Good question. I don't have an answer for that. We're spiritual beings, here and in heaven. Maybe there's a way God lets heavenly souls know what happens with family on earth."

Sarah panned the area in front of her car. Grasses gone to seed waved and rippled from the breeze in the ditches, reflected gold and silver and bronze by the sun. "Do you mind answering more? Can we talk about Grandpa's case on the way home?"

"Good a time as any."

A cluster of T-shaped electric poles stood like a sentry of crosses. She'd never have seen Jesus in that image a short while before. Her mind hummed much like those wires.

Wouldn't it be something if what Ford and Ken uncovered here bore weight regarding her grandpa's homicide? "Have you heard from that specialist, the forensic pathologist you mentioned?"

He nodded. "He got back to me earlier today. And speaking of earlier, I'm sorry about my phone blowing up. As a result, though, we've got tangible evidence."

"No prob. You're a working man."

"Nothing new from the pathologist. Your grandfather had no scrapes or bruises on his hands or arms. We're still not sure about the weapon because nothing ever showed up. The mark across his forehead was deep. No way to determine which blow came first. Wherever it struck, the blow stunned him to the ground."

"I no longer consider Grandpa a stranger. I've come to know him through what Mom wrote about him."

At the last rest stop west of Lincoln, Sarah walked a bit. They drove through sporadic sprinkles and a short-lived rain shower. Eventually, a golden haze colored the earth, a familiar glow that often followed twilight rain during summer.

Petunias perfumed the air where Ford stopped for his car. She stretched. Weariness struck as she rounded the hood to take the driver's seat.

Ford reached for her hand. "You rest tonight. I've got to get on the other case, pull it together."

Did that mean Grandpa's case would then take priority?

At home, Sarah dropped her bag on the kitchen counter, rushed through her mail, and nuked dinner. Like a thunderbolt, the day of travel took its toll. Her body was done in, but her mind kept ticking. Once she reclined on the couch, her thoughts returned to the details of Grandpa's death with renewed vigor.

Curious investigators fit clues to evidence day after day, filling in the blanks. But the human aspect couldn't be easy unless those people exercised cold-hearted detachment. She knew first-hand Ford's heart was warm. Those in law enforcement faced emotional, even erratic relatives, dealt with misinformation, inconclusive bits and pieces, and handled all the fragile fingers of correct ways to enforce the law.

It made her brain hurt, just trying to puzzle it all out. She'd taken action by following her heart and made the trip to the courthouse, even if Ford went with her. Her mother's cancer had made her feel helpless. At least Sarah had a sense of accomplishment, as well as a sense of home, since she'd seen where her grandparents had lived and died. The day had given her empowerment.

This trip also exposed the type of mind Ford must have, he and other investigators in different areas of jurisdiction, as they carried their skills to work out their duties. She respected him on a deeper level. Sarah still had questions. Would they even matter now, in light of this new information?

Wait. That break came for Neely Stallcup's case. Ford hoped for a clue to Grandpa's murder.

Though tired, she pushed herself up from the comfortable chair and into the studio where e-mail waited.

Her inbox bleeped to let her know all the messages had flowed in. She opened one with an unknown address. The subject line read "courthouse visit."

*Let the past alone, little girl. It's as dead as your grandfather.*

She cradled her baby as though struck.

Sarah read the ominous message again. Her blood ran cold.

# Twenty-five

*Now faith is being sure of what we hope for and certain of what we do not see.*
—Hebrews 11:1

**M**id-morning Sarah yawned through her exam as she waited for her nurse practitioner/midwife to give her the latest update regarding the little one's development.

She was already looking forward to a good night's sleep, but it was far from the end of the day. She'd slept in after lying awake until the wee hours, attempting to put faces and names to who could have sent that e-mail. Who indeed? Did Andrew Keaton have such a far-reaching arm?

Dare she overlook that frightening message, or turn it over to Ford?

She tuned in with half a brain to the professional in the baby business, but alerted when the midwife said, "It's time for you to find someone to attend natural childbirth classes with you. It's usually the baby's father, but a friend or relative works just as well."

Travis would have been the logical choice.

As soon as she returned home, she called Ford, and jumped right to the subject. "Glad you answered. Baby checked out great this morning. I'm so excited. What if it's a boy? I still don't have a boy's name picked out. Thanks for going with me yesterday, Ford."

His warm chuckle washed over her, and she wished to see his face.

"Hello to you too. I'm glad the trip was worthwhile. You sound good, but tired."

"I'm fine." He wasn't hovering, he cared. "It did me a world of good to physically be in the places I've been reading about, to put the geography in perspective. I'd never seen the graves of my grandparents. It's a road I needed to travel. Have you looked over that new evidence?"

"In the process. Profitable facts for both cases." His chair squeaked.

"Imagine you're itching to get back to it. Would you mind if I stop by your office later? I have a question for you, unrelated to my grandpa."

"Tomorrow's better than today. As far as the case goes, I'll tell you a couple of the names in the kidnapping case tie the two cases together. Your mom also mentioned these men."

"Wonderful news. I'm happy for you and I'm happy for my family. See you tomorrow afternoon, then."

Sarah worked in the studio. She didn't even look at the kitchen table while she ate lunch standing against the counter. Then she braved consuming her mother's close-to-final written words. She flipped back to sporadic journal entries, written over the course of Mom's last few months on earth.

*Thirty-three years, and here we go again. Mason was back in Canton for a high school reunion. He told Connor (why not me?) about another rumor circulating. Kirby Kruz struck the blow that killed dad. Connor denies knowing anything about the possibility—there was talk years earlier of his friend—he did say there's new talk about the deputy doing away with the weapon.*

*I've heard it all before, especially the reference to these two men.*

*Rumor or speculation? Does anyone know the truth besides God?*

*I hadn't heard about the deputy angle regarding the weapon. Mason told me the teenagers used to torment Keaton, never really breaking the law with their mischief, but eluding him when he gave chase.*

*The weapon is all conjecture, be it tire iron, broken ax handle, narrow edge of a board.*

*Am I all confused from the cancer and drugs, or has time muddled the events?*

*Leighton claimed the murder weapon was an ax handle with a hole drilled in the end. I think he dreamt that. That old-fashioned way to organize tools with a cord for hanging was his habit.*

*My mind has turned fuzzy, recollection and memory faulty. Could this be an advantage? My physical healing will take place as soon as I see Jesus. I have faith. God knows the killer, and it will all work out in the end, because justice is in His hands.*

*This could be an advantage, knowing my time on earth is short. My celebration of life is planned as far as the music goes. The message is one of hope, encapsulated in one Word, one Person. Jesus.*

The names Kruz and Keaton jumped off the page. Again. Mom's words swirled through a mist of my tears. She ended life on a positive note.

Everything was coming together. Even Ford said so.

Gipson and his ramblings had held truth after all.

*£*

Early the following morning, Sarah looked up Jeremiah 17:7. The words accompanied her to Ford's office. *But blessed is the man who trusts in the Lord, whose confidence is in Him.*

She also had confidence in Ford as he stood to greet her. His desk separated them, piled with her mother's records and a manila folder. Did the folder hide his current case, or Grandpa Stanley's file? The folder rested within proximity to Ford's fingertips, as though he'd closed it upon her approach.

There was nothing cold about her investigator. He appeared better looking every time she saw him. The blue of his eyes, complemented by the tiny turquoise plaid of his shirt, stood out. The expression in his face invited her in for a chat. It was really hard to focus. Much more jumped around in her stomach than a baby's gymnastics. She looked on this accelerating attraction with a sense of awe.

A flicker widened Ford's pupils. "You look pretty in yellow."

Did he feel the same gravitational pull? She no longer cared if her emotions for him grew apparent. *Focus, Sarah.*

"Thanks. Baby seems to grow overnight these days. And now it's time to grab a partner for birthing classes."

He gave a deep laugh. "I took those classes with Suze, big brother in the substitute father role. Some of the guys joked with me about the heh-hee panting and blowing. Those were terrific hours of labor my sis went through."

"I can't imagine having two babies tumbling inside me at the same time."

"There were a few tense moments before the babies came, even talk about emergency caesarian. I'm still proud of the way she handled the process."

Sarah's gaze lingered on Ford. His strong defined jaw, the inviting shape of his lips. He spoke with love and pride when it came to his family. Best to lift her gaze. He'd cut his hair and she wanted to run her finger over the bottom edge where the sun hadn't tinted the skin above his ears.

Wearing a wide grin, he pointed to the picture of adorable kids and their dog. "That's Tanya and Tyler. Their dog Flash."

She studied the family photo she'd only glanced at the first time she came to his office. She still needed answers concerning her grandfather, though, so she looked him in the eye. "We talked about the autopsy photo on the way back from Canton. Does the patrol have anything else to pursue from his file?"

Ford wouldn't meet her eye. At the moment, he drummed his fingers. Out of character for sure.

Had she hit a nerve?

Then again, had the case become personal to him because of an interest in her?

231

Ford was a dichotomy. He appeared to be the friendliest guy in the world one minute, and the toughest Navy SEAL-type the next.

Even though a stabbing pain in her calf caused her mind to hiccup, she kept going. "I'm really confused about so much. Why Great-uncle Walter, since he was a cop, never came clean with Mom about the crime. He had to have figured it out."

Ford remained silent. Was he being evasive? He leaned back and clicked his pen.

A sudden clenching pain clawed at her leg. She grimaced, held onto the armrests, and tried not to yelp.

He dropped the pen and rose. "What's wrong, Sarah?"

"Cramp," she managed between clenched teeth.

Ford's face showed nothing but concern. He came to her side in two seconds. "Where?"

"Calf." She indicated her left leg.

He jumped up, swiveled her chair around as though she weighed the same as his niece or nephew, and faced her from the other guest chair. Before she formed a protest, he lifted her leg. Then he slid off her sandal, and flexed her toes.

His warm hand massaged her calf in an upward motion. She concentrated on the touch of his fingers rather than previous pain. He worked deep magic on that calf muscle from ankle to the hem of her capris.

"Easy does it, the muscle is relaxing."

The baby pressed against her diaphragm, and she sat taller.

"That's it, slow and steady. This is great breathing practice, by the way. Preparing for labor, I mean."

"Are you good at everything you do?" She slanted him a grimace.

The solicitous boy-next-door exterior went ramrod straight. "Not so great at everything. If I had all the answers, more cold-blooded killers would be doing time for their crimes."

"You can't be responsible for what doesn't come out in the open."

"Like the weapon regarding your grandfather's slaying. No matter what you've read or heard, it's never been identified. Never shown up." He pinched her big toe, replaced her sandal. "I'll be back in a sec."

Ford returned with a bottle of water, handed it to her, and rounded the big desk to resume his chair.

She nodded her thanks and downed half the bottle. Their gazes collided and remained fixed while she twisted on the lid.

"Calf cramps often come with dehydration. I learned that when Suze was pregnant. In your situation, the heat and humidity of summer add to it."

"Thanks for helping. It's a mystery how you make my troubles seem to lighten."

"That's why God put me here, to help shoulder your burden."

"I don't see pregnancy as a burden," she spouted. "Since you went through the birthing classes with your sister, would you have time to go with me?"

She'd held the idea inside too long.

He flashed that killer smile. "You're offering me a gift. I'd be honored."

"The next two Thursday nights, 7:00."

"You can count on me."

Sarah's focus switched from the warm, circulating tingles remaining in her leg to her reason for being in Ford's office. "I think I can relax now. What about the four men who played poker with Grandpa at Rusty's Place? You should have seen that list Mom put together. Did the patrol follow-up on those men?"

"Sarah, I don't have to remind you that the investigators checked every angle, conducted numerous interviews. Why do you think so many polygraphs were given?"

"They had to follow every lead?"

"My responsibility is doing the best job I can with the information available. So yes, even the card players. Two of the men are really old, around ninety. One is behind bars."

That answer somewhat settled her nerves. She scanned the notes in her hand. "Okay. I'm going to forget the long list of questions. I suppose it was too early for DNA, had there been anything under his fingernails."

"You've been watching too much television. The officers at the scene were used to giving speeding tickets and breaking up drinking parties. You shouldn't get so worked up. In real life, answers don't come as quickly as a couple slides under a televised microscope."

"I have a question of my own, and we'll leave it at that. Where is the evidence box with Grandpa's clothes and boots? Surely, with today's technology, forensic investigators can go back and conduct DNA testing."

Ford bounced and slid forward so fast, his knee banged against the desk. The look he gave her was way out of investigator character. Instead of one line between his brows that told her he was in deep thought, twin vertical lines marred his features.

"What?" She mouthed with open mouth and hands spread wide.

"You've covered some unanswered questions. My job involves proven facts. And the giant fact is…" he glanced off to the side, avoided her eyes, "…there is no evidence box."

# Twenty-six

*"I have told you these things, so that in me you may have peace. In this world you will have trouble. But take heart! I have overcome the world."*
—John 16:33

Sarah stared at Ford across his desk. "You can't be serious. No evidence box?"

He brought his gaze back to hers, and uncrossed his legs.

She'd had a picture burned in her mind for what seemed like forever, of a lidded box marked with Dieter Stanley's name and details of his death. She wanted to see the word CLOSED in heavy black permanent marker.

"A paper case 'file…'" Ford used air quotes. "…in this manila folder is all I've ever had to work with."

He removed his glasses and rubbed the impressions from the pads on both sides of his nose.

She wanted to kiss the tender spots on his nose.

"We have a few pages of typed notes and those black and white, grainy autopsy pictures that the forensic pathologist blew up."

Her heart reached out to him. "What an undertaking for you, facing a project that has no foundation of evidence. Until now. I hope you received a clue that day at the cemetery. I don't blame you personally, Ford."

His face cleared. "Your grandfather's has been one of the most frustrating, nagging, perplexing situations I've ever dealt with. I'm thankful to have read Lena's info. I'm praying Neely outlined the information we need when she scribbled in that storybook."

"Have you seen the name Kirby Kruz, Uncle Connor's old friend, as well as the references to former Deputy Andrew Keaton?"

His gaze darted over her shoulder then back to her face. "I am familiar with the names."

His simple words eased her tension. She strove for a lighter tone. "A few minutes ago you said, as a rule, homicides aren't so perplexing. Did you mean that?"

"Homicide is pretty basic." He slanted a slight shrug and replaced his glasses. "We follow the evidence and fit the pieces together."

"And in my grandfather's case, there is no physical evidence to build on."

Ford glanced at his laptop screen, she surmised to check the time, and then closed the file folder in front of him. "So far. As I said, I'm banking on what just came to light."

"I've used enough of your time. What basis did Alexander Gipson's ridiculous requests of Mom and my great uncle have to do with anything?"

Ford answered with closed lips and a shake of the head. "I still don't know what to make of this Gipson. If your grandfather had information to pass on to law enforcement, why didn't he go to your uncle in the beginning?"

"How could a detective in San Francisco have any input on what happened in a small Nebraska town, even if he is part of the family?"

"Makes sense to start with the people you know."

"Thank you for being patient. I was curious as to what had been kept from Mom." She smiled for the first time since entering his office, stood, and touched his hand. "See you for that birthing class?"

"I'm not going to wait that long." He rounded the desk to escort her to the door.

Did he want to give her a hug as much as she needed one? "I hope the new evidence is a case breaker."

£

Ford's thoughts went into high gear as he studied her path to the elevator. Stanley hadn't trusted Deputy Keaton or his boss the sheriff. It made sense that Stanley went to his cop brother at some point, and may have followed Walter Stanley's advice to drive to Omaha for the taping of his testimony. Sarah's family hadn't known of any tapes except through Gipson's reference.

Memories of Sarah intruded and broke concentration on work. At the touch of the soft skin of her leg, his cognition had turned sideways.

Talk about a professional getting way too close. She'd turned into so much more than a victim's family member to him.

Ford knew in his soul he could never love Sarah solely as a best friend, as she'd referred to her relationship with Travis.

He'd love Sarah Bishop with passion.

Back to work. He had a case to solve.

He strode down the hall to a conference room. That familiar electrifying prickle that tweaked the skin on his nape accompanied him.

Big Ken, a hundred pounds of solid extra weight, looked up and grinned. He waved a magnifying glass that looked tiny in his beefy hand covered in a plastic glove. "Check out what young Neely wrote in this book."

"We know it was Neely Stallcup's writing?" Ford closed the door behind him. "You were able to get a handwriting sample from her parents?"

Chan piped up. "Easy. Both her mom and dad saved grade school cards she'd drawn and signed. The writing's a match."

Ford pulled on his own gloves. "Are you photographing the pages first, or examining the original book?"

"Both." Ken pointed to a spread of printed pages on the counter-height table. "They're arranged from the beginning of the book. We handled the edges of the paper in case the lab can lift any valuable prints."

"Stopher mentioned a ranch where Stanley bought cattle. Look for Kirby Kruz's name first. Anything about Stanley, and dates close to his death. If Stopher's correct, Kruz kidnapped young girls and the Easter boys kept them on the ranch as sex slaves."

"Hard to absorb, makes sense in a sick way." Chan bent to use his own magnifying glass. "Been going on since Bible times."

Ford reviewed the first few copied pages, took note of the highlights. "Stanley feasibly bought cattle the last day of his life. Neely wrote it was a Friday because the bad men came that night for the weekend."

Ken addressed Ford. "Gipson referred to that ranch visit when he wrote to Stanley's daughter?"

"Right." A ton of threads knocked at Ford, weaving tunnels underneath his twitching skin. The names wove together like a chain of intertwined words, much like the minuscule printing of young Neely. He couldn't help but picture Sarah's face as he read the words of the missing young girl.

"Looks like Dieter Stanley's killing happened as a wake-up call to those despicable men." Chan shuffled notes in in his own file folder. "The dates match. They moved the girls shortly after Stanley was taken out."

*Finally, an answer, Lord?* If this latest information held relevant evidence, the book Stopher handed over was the very ticket Ford needed to prove his gut instinct. The Stanley murder had always pointed to Connor's friend, Kirby Kruz.

They had a name written as evidence in the kidnapping of Neely Stallcup.

That warm intuitive rush heated his blood to boiling and stood those pesky hairs on end. "Keep the coffee pot filled. My goal is to seal both these old cases."

The three men worked throughout the day, pouring over tiny squiggles between lines of text and the margins of a storybook.

Ford finished perusing the laborious notations of a scared, lost, and tortured girl-turned-teenager who scribbled horrible details. Man's inhumanity to man defied compulsion. He slipped the book into a plastic evidence bag. "Ready for the lab. Who wants to do the honors?"

Ken reached out his hand and left to take it down the hall.

Ford stripped off his vinyl gloves. Neely Stallcup wasn't the only young woman kept nude and chained in a rustic cabin that must have been the remnants of a sod house on the side of a secluded hill. She described and named Deputy Andrew Keaton, the Easter brothers, Kirby Kruz, other men who abused the girls, and businessmen who had bought cattle on the ranch. Including Dieter Stanley.

For the first time, Ford understood why rape victims washed their bodies repeatedly, yet never felt clean. Only a cleansing of the Spirit enabled a person to feel clean again after being touched by the dregs of evil.

"Chan, pull up everything you can find on the disappearance of the other young girls. Anyone who vanished five years before and five after Neely Stallcup."

Convoluted schemes filled him with such unease that a headache pecked at his temple.

Ken returned. Ford had a job for him. "Notify authorities in Black Hawk County to investigate Chuck Stopher's tale regarding his nephews. I pray they have the funds to call in a cadaver dog."

Kirby Kruz, the creep, now served time on drug charges. After all these years, wouldn't it be a miracle for him to come clean on all counts?

Ford came in contact with people such as Chuck Stopher, who revealed strange tales, weirder than movie scripts sometimes. Ford looked over Chan's shoulder. "I'd like to go in with you the next time you do Bible study at the prison."

The men sorted their findings and chatted about what miracles the Lord had wrought in lives of the incarcerated, many who thought they were past redemption.

"I'm calling it a day. See ya, Ken, Rooster." Ford grinned at his use of the nickname inspired by Sarah, all in good fun.

It had been a most profitable day that began, and would end, with Sarah.

Soon after, Ford closed his office, and with the crate of Lena Bishop's documents in tow, headed for Sarah's apartment.

Would she forgive him for not mentioning he'd suspected Kruz from the beginning?

# *Twenty-seven*

*And the peace of God, which transcends all understanding, will guard your hearts and your minds in Christ Jesus.* —Philippians 4:7

Sarah welcomed Ford with iced coffee in her hand. "I forgot to tell you about an upsetting e-mail message I received the night we got home from Canton. My only conclusion is that a deputy I saw at the clerk's counter in Gaylord asked about me and my business after I'd gone. It makes sense is he must have passed on my use of Grandpa's name."

"Slow down, lady. What are you talking about?" He placed the crate on the floor, took the coffee from her hand, and set it on the table.

She led him to her studio. His hand felt extra warm from the outdoors against hers, which was cool from holding the icy drink. She released him, touched the mouse, and opened her inbox.

The words glared at her. *"Let the past alone, little girl. It's as dead as your grandfather."*

Ford didn't say a word, but his whole body tensed. He pulled Sarah to his side, and hit the contact list in his phone. "Melcher,

243

here. Can you trace a message that I'm guessing came from a courthouse out state?...Sent to Sarah Bishop. Here's her e-mail address...And your guys will take it over from here?...Thanks."

"Bless you, Ford. So I can delete this now?"

"Wait until I give you the okay." He pocketed his phone and wrapped both arms around her.

"That ugly message scared me so much, I put it out of my mind." She snuggled in. She wanted to lose herself in the feel of his fingers on her back and the heat from his body against her baby bump.

He loosened his hold. "Amazing how God orchestrates the people we come in contact with, good and bad. I think we've found our answers, Sarah. In fact, I'm sure this old business will clear up soon. For both cases. Could you go for a nutrient-shot smoothie?"

"That was a quick change of subjects. Sure." She walked him to the door, then filled a glass with water in the kitchen.

She sighed, stood at the table, and fanned the empty pages of her mom's last journal. How long would it have taken to fill the blank pages at the end?

*Hard to believe it's December already. It feels like Christmas has come earlier and earlier in recent years. Sarah decorated a small tree and put up a wreath for me. Christmas. Baby Jesus. Followed by Easter and the cross.*

*I can't get Dad out of my head. We may never know the whole story—what happened during the wee hours so long ago. Each of us has to choose what to do about that lack of answers.*

*Resolution remains elusive. I wonder what is going on in Uncle Walter's life. I would have been thrilled to see him before I die.*

*Closure is the word the world uses these days. It may never happen. If there are no answers, others in the family must decide whether to let it go, or let it eat them alive. The one who chooses not to let go will become an empty shell.*

*I'm not empty. I'm closing out my time in this world filled with eagerness for an eternal existence with my Lord and Savior. I hope, with both my parents. Dad went to church, he knew right from wrong, but I don't' know if he knew Jesus personally. It wasn't stressed in his denomination.*

*Someone once said when we meet God, He'll disclose our whole life and fill in the blanks for us. Then I'll understand why He didn't reveal what happened to my earthly father.*

*Oh, Lord, I pray You protect all my children while I'm gone. I love them so much. I believe time won't matter in heaven. I'll see my present and future grandchildren there someday. As for now, I'm looking forward to reuniting with my Mommy and Daddy.*

Sarah skipped over the doctor appointment dates, and the treatments. She'd gone through them with Mom.

*I've written through the details of my father's death too many times over the years to count. It's a fact my dad was a drunk, an imperfect person. Any sin of his was no greater than any sin of mine.*

*Now that I'm facing the end of my days, I'm viewing cancer as one of God's gifts. I've had hours and days to dwell on the facts of what has touched my life.*

*Guilt. I must have been a bad mother more than a few times when the kids were small. How could I have been fully engaged when Jeremiah was 13, and Sarah 9? Those ensuing months when I was consumed with the letters, the emotions, and the injustice? I was not only consumed, but obsessed by my mission to find Dad's killer; I had to have been as preoccupied with my search then as I have been in recent months.*

*I'd like to think I lived in the moment, but I fear I was more than a little depressed at times.*

*I, I, I. Forgive me, Lord, for my selfishness. And speaking of forgiving. I forgive whoever killed Dad. How could I not? As soon as I knew what loving Jesus is about, and the way He forgave me, how could I not forgive an unknown assailant?*

*No answers then.*

*No answers now.*

*It's okay to take the unknown to my grave.*

*It won't matter once I see Jesus.*

*Psalm 73:25-26 reads, "Whom have I in heaven but you? And earth has nothing I desire besides you. My flesh and my heart may fail, but God is the strength of my heart and my portion forever."*

*I've been blessed because I trust in the Lord, and put my confidence in Him. I've asked the question way too often. Was that an indication I lacked trust? Faith is living without answers.*

*Amen and so be it.*

Sarah had consumed and treasured the words her mother set down before death came calling. She traced a finger over the last words Mom penned that final lucid day, in a hand that wavered over the lines from pain and drugs.

*"I have overcome the pain of this present world. Come, Lord Jesus, take me home. And please watch over Sarah and her baby, Jeremiah, Leah, and her family."*

Did memory change over time? Was it possible bad things became clearer as secrets were resurrected? Mom had struggled to the end, made a brave attempt to unscramble notations, dealt with past grief, and held on to hope.

Mom had the faith, and the peace, to live without answers.

Sarah trusted earthly answers would soon be in her hand, thanks to Ford and his team. She closed the journal and reached for Mom's Bible, where she fed on the holy words. Time passed quickly. "Thank You for Your Word, Lord, and for giving patience as You talk about in Psalm thirty-seven."

She stretched, crossed to the window, and at sight of Ford's approach, waited to open both doors for him.

He entered and set the drinks on the table, then went to the sink.

She followed him. "I've been reading Mom's last words. Her faith inspires me. What do men like Kirby Kruz believe in?"

Ford looked at her over his shoulder. "Unless they're chosen by God from the beginning of time, see their sin, and repent, they believe in the devil's lies."

She slurped the rich berry filled fruit drink. "Do you think it bothered Grandma that one of Connor's friends might have been responsible for Grandpa's death? A bitter pill to swallow, the fact a man Grandma had welcomed into her home, whom she'd looked in the eye, no doubt killed her husband. Mom may have met the guy as well."

"All I can say is that we now have evidence from Neely Stallcup herself. And it points to Kirby Kruz." Ford dried his hands and reached for his smoothie.

"With so many references, he had to have been under suspicion before now." She pondered Kruz's alleged involvement, connected with Ford's gaze for a long moment. Excitement washed through her. "You're pulling it all together, aren't you?"

He raised a thick brow, grinned around his straw, and gave a slow nod.

Mom's attention to detail had enabled Sarah to dig into the whole case with an emotional lens for her mother's loss. Ford, as a trained outsider, used an intellectual microscope. Weaving the two together, Sarah had kept her promise to Mom.

Ford set down his empty cup and covered Sarah's hand. "So strong, same as your mom. We're doing this, Sarah. You're keeping a promise and I'm doing what I was trained to do. God has allowed it all to happen."

"Have you pieced together that Mom and I lived parallel lives? She dealt with, and I'm dealing with, pregnancy at the time a parent died. God blessed Mom with focus on a newborn each time she faced a parent's death. I've set aside much of my grief for Travis and Mom by digging into what she left behind." She broke eye contact and slurped.

"All this sounds good to me. I was concerned preoccupation with your grandfather's untimely death had come close to turning into an obsession. You're fixed on concentrating on your baby now?"

Sarah looked forward to the journey with her own family unit. "This sweet little bit can't come fast enough."

"Best news I've heard in a long time. I'm still hungry."

"Open the fridge."

He reached for a deviled egg, bit it in half. "We still on to shop for that baby crib later?"

She beamed and thumbed to the Psalms. "Food for thought, according to Mom. Psalm thirty-seven instructs believers to delight in the Lord, to be still and wait for Him."

He leaned in close with the remaining egg in front of Sarah's mouth. "And here's sustenance for the physical body. Open wide."

She opened, chewed, swallowed. "See how obedient I am?"

"Sometimes the Bible is more filling than nutrition. A few verses further it says, '*A little while, and the wicked will be no more.*'"

Astounded, the words from months earlier hit Sarah in the heart. Mom had recorded the same verses. Sometimes she spent whole days reading the Psalms. She called it comfort food for the soul. The Lord laughed at the wicked, and the day would come for Him to uphold the righteous.

Sarah laughed, and it felt good. "You know, I think I could lose hours immersed in the Bible. Scripture revealed that in order to go on with my life and experience God's gift of life for me and my baby, I have to accept His ways as higher than my ways."

"God leads us to passages all through life as we grow in Him. He communicates wisdom and insight just at the exact time we need it."

"It's so simple, and I used to make it hard. God has His reasons for unexplained things on earth." She set aside her straw, took off the lid to access the remaining bursts of flavor.

Ford slurped another deviled egg into his mouth without biting.

She giggled at his bulging cheeks, dribbling frozen berry and yogurt down her chin.

Still chewing around the glob in his mouth, he reached out and ever so lightly, thumbed the drop away from Sarah's face. Keeping their gazes locked, he swallowed the egg and licked the fruity nectar from his thumb.

The intimate touch ignited a trail of awareness to her toes. Too bad he hadn't kissed away the dribble on her face. Her turn to gulp at the sudden clog in her throat, she couldn't ignore the pull of this magnetic man.

She wanted Ford to be part of her future. She could manage with Grandpa's case remaining unsolved, though Ford believed it was coming to a close. She was more than ready to be finished with the old business concerning her family's past, fully in acceptance of the unknown. She didn't want to think about having no more reason to be in contact with Ford.

Others claimed spiritual epiphanies. Sarah admitted whenever someone in her past talked about a spiritual experience, she'd been skeptical. Spirituality meant different things to different people, sparked by creation, an animal, the devil, some sign. For her, the revelation came from the Holy Spirit.

*Just as Mom found peace, so have I.* She jumped up from the table.

"What is it? The baby?"

"No, I feel so free all of a sudden I want to dance! No more dismal thoughts and gruesome speculation for me. I'm convicted to be done with this. I've obtained the ability and strength to put history behind me. Would you help me?" She gathered up the last two journals, checked to make sure chronology remained, and placed them in a box for storage with the other notebooks and binders, making sure the earliest volumes were on top, and taped shut the box. She marked the lid with her mother's name boldly scrawled across the top.

"Who would have thought packing away Mom's items would lift such a weight? This occasion calls for bouncy praise songs. One of these days I need to get Mom's CDs on my computer." She turned on a boom box between the couch and table. If she was alone, she'd jiggle her hips, swirl, and raise her hands in celebration.

She twirled and bumped into Ford's broad chest. He smacked her at the hairline, turned her with one arm, and saved the smoothie cups from toppling, all in lightning-fast moves.

They separated, her heart thumping. Both wore silly grins.

Ford scooped up the box and placed it near the front door. "I'm still checking on a couple things, but soon we'll do this at the office, box things up for storage."

She huffed and puffed from exertion and happiness, grabbed his hands and gave them a squeeze. "Thanks for being here with me, Ford. I'll haul them to the basement as soon as possible."

She glanced at the table and pictured a cranberry-hued glass pitcher as a centerpiece, a Bible, and a blank-paged journal of her own. In no particular order, she'd write to her little one, record the final measurements of her abdominal growth, which would only matter to a girl baby someday. Sarah planned to seek favorite scripture references, and anything else to let the sweet baby know about its mother's world during the days preceding her, or his, birth.

"Hold still a minute." His tone calmed her. "Steady now."

She relaxed in his arms as he released her hands and encircled her waist. She blinked away her wandering mind to concentrate on how good, how fitting. Ford's arms were meant to be around her. He knocked aside every scattered thought except expectation as he leaned down.

He lowered his head and she stretched up to meet his seeking lips. The steady beat of his heart against her hand gave her courage. The rightness of their embrace cascaded through her in waves, chasing away anything but sensation.

She finally pulled back.

Ford colored her world.

He gave her another squeeze, released her, and they went out the door to shop for the baby crib.

So relieved after clearing the table of her mother's piles of paper, Sarah drifted off in the car.

She woke to a shiver of foreboding that popped open her eyes, where she feasted on Ford's short hair that called for her touch. She centered her gaze on the curve of his lips.

He turned her way. "You're awake."

Oh, the unselfish care she read in his deep blue eyes. Would she have to say good-bye to him, now that she'd relinquished the hunt for Grandpa's killer?

# Twenty-eight

*"For there is nothing hidden that will not be disclosed, and nothing concealed that will not be known or brought out into the open."* —Luke 8:17

Ford's fingers trembled as bad as a rookie's. The envelope holding copied pages from the storybook shook in his grasp. He was so close to sealing the books on these cases he pictured himself taping up the boxes and scrawling *closed.*

The penitentiary parking lot seemed longer than usual to traverse. He quelled the urge to pick up his pace.

Inside the sally port, he said a relieved prayer as the door closed behind him. *Oh, Lord. If we could all just rest in Your timing. I needed motivation. I needed specifics. You supplied them, starting with Lena's records, our trip, and Chuck Stopher's revelation. Thank You.*

On the secure side of turnkey, he followed the escort guard, eager to face the inmate in the interview room for the first time.

Ford entered the room without looking at the prisoner, opened the envelope, and spread the pages with Neely Stallcup's printing across the tabletop. He punctuated the silent display by slapping his card in front of the prisoner.

"Am I supposed to know what all this is about?" Kruz thumped the table.

Ford had ignored Kruz until he spoke. Now the investigator noted the prisoner's appearance. Balding, straw-colored hair, emotionless eyes, thin to the point of emaciation. Ford waited for eye contact. "A little girl named Neely Stallcup wrote in a storybook. These are copies of those pages. Pay attention to what's highlighted in front of you."

Kruz lowered his eyes. "This supposed to mean something to me?"

"Oh, yeah. She pegged you for nabbing her. I'm closing the case, thanks to the Easter brothers. You write down your role in her life, and where we can find Neely Stallcup's remains."

Ford waited while Kruz looked at the copied evidence, then set a pen on top of a yellow legal pad marked *Confession of Kirby Kruz*. "Finish with that. We'll talk about Dieter Stanley when I come back. According to Neely Stallcup, you knew the man."

Ford reentered the interview room with a cup of water for Kruz, and prepared for a completed puzzle.

Kruz picked up the water. "Yeah, I knew Dieter Stanley. His son Connor and I ran together when we were young and wild. That whole period of my life passed in a blur. I was all messed up. Tested every drug I was asked to unload. It all came back to me when I saw Stanley's picture on a card here in the joint."

"Tell me what you remember." Ford forced his expression to remain impassive, but all senses stood at attention. He didn't want to overlook a nuance of tone or mannerism. This was for Sarah, in honor of Lena's memory, and closure for the whole family.

"Stanley didn't want me around his son. I remember how crooked most of the county bigwigs were. Somebody was covering up or holding secrets over others' heads, bad stuff going down everywhere I turned. Some cops were in on it and other cops ignored what was happening. Hard to keep up." Kruz gulped water.

Ford waited him out.

"The girl told it straight. Stanley saw me at the ranch. He saw two of the girls. I had to shut him up."

"You could have saved a lot of people a lifetime of sorrow if you'd answered straight at time of the polygraph."

"'Course I answered in the negative. Then. I said I never killed Stanley."

He'd been messed up, to use his term, so the test had been inconclusive.

"I got lost in my own head for a time back then. Stanley wasn't the only one who got killed." Kruz met Ford's gaze, shifted to stare at the wall over his shoulder. "To save my own sorry butt, I took out three others. And got paid well. My boss at the time was covered by the coroner, the county attorney in Gaylord, a deputy, others in the law. And a couple dudes that liked young girls. Probably all dead now."

"Go back. Tell me what happened that summer of 1980."

"I was at Connor's, late July, maybe. Stanley came home. We had what you call an altercation. He threw me off the place and told me to never show up there again. Then he said, 'I saw those girls on the ranch. You come near my son again, your secret's out.' My right arm was broke, or he'd a never got by with shoving me out the door."

"How did you break your arm?"

"Fell off a water tower the week before and still couldn't drive. I was on prescription drugs for the pain. I remember running into Stanley the next Friday night, but God only knows who was driving my Mustang. We'd been drinking at a kegger east of Canton." Kruz took another drink.

"We ran out of smokes so we drove back to town and went to the bar. I don't know why, but after we left Rusty's Place, we drove past the creamery. Dieter Stanley was walkin' through the parking lot, nobody else around. Maybe he was there to see Connor at the motel next to the factory. We pulled in beside him. We'd had some weed, and I was drunk myself. I don't remember who was with me. The ghost driver. Had to have somebody along cuz I couldn't drive with a broken arm."

Never in his life had Ford wanted to hurry along an interrogation. Yet, he refused to miss a word.

"We were out of the car. I grabbed a two-by-four, spun on the ball of my foot, and swung. Got Stanley in the head with my left arm so hard the wood bounced and flew. I picked it up. The club felt heavy. I slung it on the floor behind the car seat, and yelled. Don't know what I said."

"Any idea what time it was?"

"Time's kind of fuzzy here."

"Did you see him again?"

"About halfway between Canton and the Stanley house west of town. I said, 'Stop! There he is.' Could be that's a dream. Next thing I know, I was standing in the road by my car, reaching in back for the two-by-four, I think. Like in a slow-motion dream. I've had flashes of this arm swing back and heave something with a handle, maybe it was wood? Far into the field."

Even if they missed two meals, Ford planned to be patient and stay as long as needed. "Back up. You saw a disembodied arm. Before or after you got to Dieter Stanley? Was it your arm? Or did the arm belong to the friend you claim to have forgotten?"

Kruz shrugged. "I've heard phantom voices. Maybe that night wasn't forgot after all. These voices go back and forth in my head. 'There he is, the bas_____. Stop the car!' 'He's drunk. Let him alone.' 'Not on your life. I don't care if he is staggering drunk. Stanley chased me off his place one too many times.' Guess that's me."

"Okay. If that was you, I imagine the fire of revenge raced through you."

"Don't put words in my mouth. I did see red. Dieter was such a poor excuse of a man, couldn't even let me be a friend to one of his idolized sons. Got his courage from a bottle and wanted to fight anybody drunk enough to swing."

Kruz rubbed his eyes, screwed up his forehead, created ridges. "Tires slid on gravel. The car fishtailed, I was already opening the door. I yelled, 'Hey, Stanley, got a drink on ya?' Before he could turn to face me, I swung. The first blow landed with a crack against the back of his skull. I hit him again."

Ford unclenched his teeth, lowered his jaw to relieve the tension. "So, you hit him three times. First, on the forehead, in the creamery parking lot."

"I swung, don't know how many times, hit air at last because he was already down, and stumbled back against the fender. I tried to get in the car. Saw Stanley on his hands and knees, reaching up from the ditch for help."

It took everything Ford had not to react. He unclenched his fist hidden under the table.

"I knew he was done. Half in and half out of the ditch, I kicked him off the road. His body slumped to the grass. Somehow, I got back in the car. The car was in gear before my leg was inside. Pulling the door shut, I didn't know if I should pop the top on another beer or go for the joint burning in the clip. I eventually did both."

Silence. Ford opened his mouth for another question, but Kruz continued.

"We drove as far as Stanley's driveway. Turned around, and headed back to the kegger. Must be where I spent the night. Don't know whose house the party was at."

"What happened in the morning?"

"The next I remember, it was about eight in the morning. Somebody handed me the phone. Connor called up. Have no idea how he knew where I was. Anyway, he said, 'They found my dad in the ditch. He's dead. You and your drug buddies better not have had anything to do with it.' Man, I wished he'd been there. I woulda belted him, cast or no cast."

Kruz finished the water.

"Back then, I had to deal with threats from two Stanleys. Connor and Dieter. I wanted to give it to Connor, too, if I'd seen him. Tryin' to be better than the rest of us, when he partied just as much. Threatening me that way."

"What did you do next?"

"Probably slept it off. The whole town was talkin' afterward. Nobody been killed in Canton, Nebraska, before. Well, a hundred years, back at the turn of the twentieth century, some cattle rustler was hanged. Anyway, next thing I knew, about the whole town was called in for those lie detector tests.

'Course, I always said I didn't know nothing about it. Actually forgot it for a time. Then I saw the picture when we was playing cards in the commons, and it all came back in a flash."

"You can remember details of the altercation. Why can't you remember who was with you, as in a woman, or where you spent Saturday?"

"Don't have an answer. Why didn't it come back to me earlier? I don't know."

"What made you volunteer the information now, Kirby Kruz?"

"Like I said. Saw Stanley's picture on the card. Plus, a guy named Chan has been talking to us about the Bible. I guess, God made me do it."

# Twenty-nine

*"My grace is sufficient for you, for my power is made perfect in weakness." ...so that Christ's power may rest on me...For when I am weak, then I am strong.*
—II Corinthians 12:9-10

Two weeks had passed since Sarah saw Ford for the birthing classes. She'd spent the time nesting. All she needed to do now was wait to go into labor. Ford buried himself in work that took him to western Nebraska. She wanted him back in Lincoln.

On her way to the bathroom, she carried pleasant impressions of baby prep and memories of short phone connections with Ford. She drew a lukewarm, deep bath, and eased her way into the tub. The water soon surrounded her and she caressed her mounded belly.

"You represent all the good things ahead, little baby. You are my family, and Jesus is family. I'd like to think of Ford as family, too, if it's meant to be."

Baby moved, bulging Sarah's belly. He, or she, must have approved. As Sarah relaxed, she watched her belly. The baby rolled like a dolphin through ocean waters. Sarah laughed at the antics. Would her distended bellybutton remain an outie?

The baby settled in a rounded bump against her hand, and she failed to imagine distinct features other than those on the sonogram photo. The tech had offered a 3-D image, but Sarah declined. She closed her eyes with a deep sigh, and basked in the memory of the smell, the strength, the reality of Ford filling every corner of her soul.

The jangle of the phone crashed into her fluid reverie.

£

Ford waited for her to answer. *Will she ever forgive me?*

"Sarah, hope you're well today. I have what we've been waiting for, regarding both cases. But first, how are you and the baby?"

"As big as my kitchen table." She sounded short of breath. "Thanks again for setting up the crib. I have everything ready now. We just need baby to come. Sorry for rambling. Did I hear right? It's over?"

"Don't faint on me. We're ready to be done with your grandfather's case."

"I must be dreaming. You wouldn't say so if it wasn't for real. Is it a sure thing?"

"God does indeed work in ways we'll never understand. I followed up on Chuck Stopher's gift of evidence. A book. I'm more than humbled that against my wishes, you insisted on that drive. God's timing is nothing to scoff at."

"I think I was following His will."

"The State Patrol already had an undercover guy behind bars. Thanks to those playing cards in one of the facilities, we've received some groundbreaking news. And, I want to deliver it in person." He tapped the plain manila envelope he carried against his leg.

"Oh, my goodness. That's startling enough to give me labor pains."

They shared a laugh of relief, Ford's on the bitter side. He'd surmised the killer's identity. No one could prove Kirby Kruz's guilt so he'd kept his suspicions from Sarah. He prayed she'd understand.

"It's beyond explanation sometimes, but once in a while surprises come our way. In the case of your grandfather, I'd say it's only because of divine intervention. Sounds like we have a legitimate resolution to the case. Actually, more than one."

"That's incredible. Can I come see you?"

"It just so happens I'm not far from your apartment. Would you mind if I stop up?"

"Uh, I'm not quite ready. Give me twenty?"

Nineteen minutes later, he pushed the intercom to buzz Sarah's apartment, more nervous than he'd ever been delivering such welcome news to a family member. The building door opened. He bounded up the stairs.

She greeted him at her apartment door with a sparkle that spread across her beautiful face. He paused, soaked her in. Tiny tendrils of blonde hair curled around her face. He painted the picture to memory. The business reason for contact with her was about to end. Being in her presence did odd things to his insides. He couldn't afford the time he'd spent dwelling on the prospect of a lifetime of her kisses.

He wished for super power x-ray vision to penetrate her innermost thoughts. What he wouldn't give to know if she was interested in pursuing a relationship. Could she desire spending time with him the way his soul cried out to be with her always?

His intent culminated with her in his future.

*She'll feel betrayed.*

Cold dread washed over him at the thought of never seeing her again. He reached for her hand, and warmth from the touch of her fingers rose clear up to his earlobes. The baby must have kicked, because she gasped.

"You okay?" At her nod, he followed her inside.

"So the book notations from Neely Stallcup are valid enough to bring this whole thing to a close?" Sarah's voice ended on a squeak, and she slumped against the door jam.

"It is. I wanted to see you, tell you in person." He grasped her wrist, and only let go when her trembling subsided. He was more than ready to bare his heart to her, but it was getting hard to keep it inside. "I'm here more as a friend than a cop."

*What a dumb way to put it.* She'd already had Travis play that role. What he wanted was to kiss her until she trembled. *Set it aside.*

"I wish Mom could hear the answer after all this time. I almost forgot my manners. Coffee or tea?"

He scanned the length of the counter. "No need to brew a pot of coffee. Do you have tea already made?"

Sarah nodded, and filled two glasses with a jar of lemongrass tea from the fridge.

Intense emotions zinged through him. He longed to give her happiness more than anything in the world. "I'm going to tell you a story, based on an actual handwritten confession—yes, you have a right to drop your jaw. You should feel pleased you followed the urge to go to Swanson County. Thanks to our visit, we have more than one major missing piece that'll pull resolution to two cases."

She lifted her glass. Her hand trembled enough to force her to set it back down.

"Anything we consider worthwhile now points to Mr. Kirby Kruz, whose name has come up before."

She gripped her hands together. "Mom wrote about him, hearsay, and rumors. You and I have talked about the old friend of Uncle Connor's. And now you say he's connected to Grandpa?"

"You got it. The patrol investigators considered him a possible suspect at the time of your grandfather's death. He's also the so-called unreliable witness referred to a time or two. Your grandfather had more than one run-in with him. He was a well-known drug dealer, a person of interest in other crimes. Before you ask, I wasn't free to name him." *The only person others saw outside the bar that night. Yet no one agreed to testify as to having seen him.*

Sarah squealed. "How did this happen? What brought it out in the open after such a long period of silence?"

"I mentioned my buddy Chan, who is a Bible study teacher with a heart for those behind bars. Last week I went to his inmate study, and after the meeting, I found a note in the back cover of my Bible.

One of the men had slipped it in. He requested to see me regarding what he heard from a particular inmate pertaining to your grandfather's case. One thing led to another, in fact, we've gained knowledge about several cases. Anyway, after touching base with our undercover guy as well, I met with Kirby Kruz."

Sarah closed her eyes. He wanted to think she prayed.

So would he. *Thank You, thank You, Lord. You orchestrate how and when things happen. Please enable Sarah to put this whole situation in Your hands and leave it there. And show me how to keep her in my life once this nasty business is finished once for all.*

Ford circled the sweating glass, wiped the table free of moisture.

"Did this all happen because of what you and Ken found out near Canton?"

"Yes. Well, the playing cards in prison started it. Thanks to Neely Stallcup writing names in that book, we got what we needed."

"That one item isn't enough evidence to be used in court. It's okay for you to tell me?"

"I don't think there's going to be enough evidence for any kind of trial. It's enough to close things and follow up on other cases."

"Wow. It's over and done with?"

"Since your mom was denied so many answers, I brought the news to you. For the sake of your whole family."

*Lord, please give her strength.*

Sarah blinked twice, drew herself up. Her smile made the memory of Lena proud. Could she be looking down on her daughter from somewhere far above?

$\mathcal{L}$

Sarah couldn't still the quaking in her gut. She squeezed her eyes shut. Then thanked God for Ford, her salvation, and then commanded her thundering heart to slow down. She blinked tears away to clear her vision.

One of Ford's earlier comments screamed for clarification. "You're telling me you suspected Kruz this whole time, without ever telling me?"

It hurt, that he'd kept such vital information from her. She'd assumed they were closer.

The buzzing in her ears escalated. Cold case evidence or not, he should have trusted her.

Nerveless fingers couldn't raise the glass to her mouth. She lifted her gaze to Ford's face as he finished revealing the confession. Her vision blurred from unshed tears, she couldn't see a thing clearly. Words stilled in her mind and her speech was trapped in her throat.

She fought the impulse to throw up. After envisioning the vivid horror inflicted upon Grandpa, she now had to deal with Ford's betrayal.

What next?

All sorts of reeling thoughts hit from what seemed like different parts of her mind. She sniffed. It no longer mattered whether the killer was left-handed, or if Grandpa's body had defense wounds, or if the blows came from behind. The DNA on his clothes or boots was invalid, either burned up when her grandparents' home was emptied, or rotted in a landfill. So what if no one saw Grandpa walking on the road, or who played poker with him at the VFW?

It was over. None of the unanswered details mattered.

Ford stood and grabbed a box of tissues off the counter. His movements cleared away the fog. "The alleged killer has confessed. Conjecture pointed to Kirby Kruz but we had nothing conclusive without evidence. I was bound not to talk about him with you. No matter what happens now, he'll pay someday according to God's judgment. Sarah, I'm so pleased your family has a clearer picture of what happened."

*At last.* She covered her mouth with both hands, unsure of what sounds she might utter if she tried to speak. Rampant thoughts renewed their chase. She pulled her attention back to Ford.

"This confession sounds authentic. We investigators are hoping to discover whether Kruz had company or if he acted alone. Those "buddies" might have been figments of his skewed mind. People are able to drive automatic cars with one hand. If his car had a standard transmission, he needed a driver."

"Do you think you'll ever find out who the other man involved was?"

"It's possible."

"In my Internet research I'm sure I read that some murderers are able to kill and not remember it until an event or a certain way with words dissolves the glue that had sealed their memories. Disassociation is often a key in how they deal with life events."

"We're getting off topic with that one, honey. I haven't read where Kruz has been diagnosed with any mental condition, but those with such issues often fantasize about committing, and even admit to committing, crimes they didn't do."

Crazy thoughts can come out of nowhere. Had Mom ever, as a writer, tried to fictionalize a villain by getting into the killer's head and putting that to paper? Ugh. Too much fixation on the psychotic mind.

*Look to the good.*

"This is amazing. Ford, this is beyond huge. I don't know how I can thank you for coming here and telling me. And I hope you won't get in trouble by revealing it." He opened his mouth, but she went on. "You helped me box up Mom's memories. I don't want to be stuck in time. I want to live now, and move through all the unknowns, no matter what. To think we finally know what happened is almost unbelievable."

Her heart hammered in her ears. Goose flesh raised the hairs on her arms as Sarah imagined the killer, one Kirby Kruz, in that car on a dark country road. She was there in the black of night, and "watched" his car stop near the end of her grandparents' driveway. She had a mind picture after being there in person. Talk about shivers! Rage suffused the order of events in her mind. She attempted to make sense of why and how the man could have killed Grandpa in such a vile way.

Impossible. No rhyme nor reason, it boiled down to sin.

"Remember, Sarah. A confession doesn't mean there's enough physical or circumstantial evidence to convict. As much as you feel relieved, Kruz may never be prosecuted, despite the details that have come to light."

"Why not?"

Ford placed a hand on her nape, brushed behind her ear with his thumb. She welcomed his touch, but not the distraction from her topic. "We're talking about a small-town county attorney's office on a tight budget. They'd want much more tangible evidence than this, plus lots of witnesses. They'd also want to go after who else was involved. Remember, many years have passed. Who'd want to prosecute with nonexistent evidence and the loss of original records? Not to mention the deaths of original law enforcement."

"I still don't get that lack of evidence, as in investigative files. Did those old guys take home their notes and the family tossed them later?"

"Records got lost in many places during the transfer from paper to computer. Look at the bright side here. Your family has a confession from Kruz."

"You said he was a suspect before the confession. Why couldn't you trust me enough to let me know?" She pulled away, sniffed, and blinked. Her dismay must have shown on her face, judging by his guilty expression.

"Things point to Kruz's involvement. The picture isn't complete without knowing who else was involved. At least now you know who the murderer was and your family can rest assured we will continue to look for his accomplices." His voice expressed entreaty. He yanked a tissue from the box and handed it to her. "I wish I could be more encouraging."

"You're an officer of the law, Ford. And I thought you were more than a friend. I still think you could have said something earlier about having a strong person of interest." She tried to pull herself together. With the Lord's help she'd get through this betrayal, which for some crazy reason meant more at the moment than knowing the name of a killer. "Thanks, but you can keep that tissue. It's past time for me to put all the tears in the past."

"You can do it. You've proven yourself strong. You now have the Lord to rely on."

"I need the Lord in my life. With Him, I can make a life for my baby." *With or without Ford.*

She grabbed the table edge to stand. A gush of liquid erupted and flooded the wooden chair.

Her mouth gaped in a soundless *O* of wonder as she stared at Ford.

He reached for her hand and his cell phone at the same time.

# Thirty

*For you created my inmost being; you knit me together in my mother's womb.*
—Psalm 139:13

Sarah had spent time with no one besides Travis and Mom the eighteen months before Mom died. "Thanks for racing to the hospital, Ford. I'm grateful."

They occupied the labor-delivery room where she drifted in and out of pain. Her thoughts between contractions replayed like movie trailers. Add in the kidnapped girls, and it turned into stuff of fictional plots.

Ford squeezed her hand. "You doing okay?"

"I kind of blipped out for a bit. My mind keeps skittering all over the place, thinking about the crimes you've uncovered. For my own mental health, as Mom did, I need to remember the Bible says judgment is up to God. I have faith so I trust. I need to be done with the old crime, and accept what's been revealed as the ultimate answer, whether Kruz is ever charged or not."

"Smart move to let it rest. I know it's hard. Murder is a tragic event that affects the wellbeing of everyone involved. But I'm proud of you for reaching this point. Besides, in case you hadn't noticed, you have another event going on here," Ford pointed out with a huge grin.

Another contraction felt like a knife.

The hope of soon holding her baby gave Sarah relief from her anguished quest.

Would Ford still be in her life now that she was free of what happened to Dieter Stanley the night he died? She couldn't imagine life without Ford by her side. Did she face a broken heart?

"I almost forgot," she said between contractions, "please give Jeremiah and Leah a call. If they were here, Jer would be in some waiting room down the hall, pacing and guzzling coffee. Leah would be where you are, by my side. Thanks."

"I wouldn't miss it for the world."

She clung to his poor hand, bracing for another rolling pain, striving to keep mental notes. She wanted to be coherent in her retelling. Her senses clouded with the gut-wrenching pressure, the increasing urge to push.

"Baby keeps putting its hand up above the top of its head," someone said.

"That's because baby is face up, wrong position," said the trusty nurse practitioner.

Soon, Sarah couldn't be positive who said what, her eyes were mostly closed with the onslaught of contractions that now felt never ending. She wanted to push.

"She's dilated to eight. And I see five fingers on that peeping hand. Baby's pulse is one-sixty."

Sarah had read that a faster pulse indicated a girl.

"Let's dim the lights. Give her some oxygen."

"Ford. Help me remember everything. No time to rest between contractions." Her voice sounded muffled, or maybe she spoke the words in her head. "I want to push. Oo-oo-oh."

Ford encouraged her. "Hang in there. You're doing great. This is a huge moment in our lives. Remember your breathing lessons."

*He said* our *lives.*

"I'll try to help you remember details. You're doing fantastic, Sarah. Hang in there."

Forget trying to identify individual odors. Hospitals smelled alike. She concentrated on the sounds, anything to think about other than pain. So many clicks. So many machines. Somewhere a toilet flushed. Muted music drifted in from the hallway. Muffled voices. The rhythmic beep-beep, beep-beep of the baby monitor.

"Who-o-o." She groaned and blew at the same time. It helped to make noise as one sharp contraction after another ripped through her. "Wuh—ohh."

Later, she'd laugh about the helpless expression on Ford's face. "I'm sorry I can't help."

"You are helping. You're here, but you're not being cut in two. Ouch… a nasty one."

"Can't imagine," he mumbled.

A nurse scanned the read-outs. "I'm going to get the doctor."

Sarah yelled, "I'm ready."

Several disembodied voices gave orders. Sarah heard muted comments all around.

"She pushes, and the hand comes out."

"Just breathe."

"Hand presentation."

"It'll be a friendly baby, it's wavin' at us."

"She's comin' to deliver."

"Try not to push, baby."

Who would tell her that? And call her baby? She obeyed. To a point. "Oh. Okay."

"You're doin' a super job. Super job." She recognized Dr. White's voice.

"Head comin' out?" Sarah unclenched her teeth.

Ford answered, "Its whole hand came out."

Someone snapped latex gloves.

Doctor White instructed, "Push hard, Sarah. Hard. Hard. Hard. Push. Push. Push!"

Her cheeks filled up. She bore down. A huge expulsion of air roared through her mouth. She was about to spill her guts.

Bumps. Bang. Metal. Grating wheels. Plastic. Paper. Ripping.

She heard a wide exchange of medical terminology. How many people were in the room with her? And would she be embarrassed later, having had Ford with her throughout?

"Think your baby washed his hand before he started hangin' it outta there?"

"Are you numb down there?"

"No." Did she want to remember all this?

"You gonna feel a little funny now. Keep your head back. How's that?"

Her head swam. Time stopped for a short moment. She wanted to sleep.

"Ready? Push. Hard. Push. Push. Hard. Hard. Push hard, Sarah. Push. Push."

Ford joined in. "Push, honey, push. Baby's almost here."

She'd forgotten the pants and counting and attempts to concentrate on breathing. She let loose with another gargantuan exhalation. The pain was well worth it.

The clanking of metal sounded extra loud and tinny. What kinds of tools were they using? "Help me. I want my baby out."

"Push down hard, Sarah."

The pain and pressure were so acute, she cried out, "Mommy!"

"Would you look at that? The cord's wrapped around her head. It's a miracle baby's not distressed."

"It's a girl."

What a relief. Sarah entertained the idea of raising her fist in the air, but she only had enough energy to lie there.

"That's the wavenest baby I've ever seen."

The baby girl cried. She sounded phlegmy, as if she needed her throat cleared.

Sarah wanted to weep with relief. How she'd wished for Mom to share this day. Sarah had gone through this experience with Jesus.

And the Lord had provided Ford.

*Even if he has let me down.*

"She's beautiful, Ms. Bishop. Meet your baby girl."

Sarah caressed her baby's velvet skin for the very first time.

"What's her name?"

"Not positive." What would Travis want? She needed to honor him somehow as the father.

"How are you feeling there?"

"I'm fine. Ready to start my new family."

"She's tiny." How did a new mother express awe? Her darling girl's weight fit perfectly in Sarah's arms. A rush of love washed over her and turned her weepy with joy. Hormones. "She's perfect."

"Got your camera?" came from someone unidentified.

"In the outside pocket of my bag, Ford," Sarah answered. "Thanks."

He and Dr. White talked politics while the doc sutured her up. Aware of Ford's fixed gaze on her face, Sarah couldn't turn her attention off her baby's beautiful, rosy features. She tried to ignore the thumps, clicks, and snips coming from her nether region.

"Sorry, ma'am, but we need to have her for a bit. Get her weighed and other essentials."

Her arms emptied and Sarah could no longer see the sweet miracle. Two or three conversations carried on. She felt numb, yet exhilarated and tired, all at once. She floated in and out. Exhausted.

"Look at those eyes!"

"Which hand was stickin' out? Left or right?"

Eventually, she opened her eyes on Ford, more alert. "Am I complete again?"

"You look all together to me, better than ever." What a guy, to compliment her when her hair was plastered to her head like she'd just run a marathon. "I stepped out for coffee."

"I'm glad. All of a sudden, I'm starving. Hope to eat good tonight."

"That can be arranged." A nurse handed Sarah the swaddled wonder. "Here's your baby. She's perfect."

Sarah's new daughter again filled her arms. She pictured herself leaping up to cry and laugh and dance and twirl. Not quite yet.

"Hi sweetheart, are you looking at Mommy?" Baby stared back at Sarah, unblinking. What did a newborn see when she stared so intently? "Did everything wrong, didn't you honey? Looking for milk, huh?"

A nurse turned to Ford. "If you've got family out there, I've gotta clean up before they come in."

"I better call my sister." Ford laughed. "Suze's not going to believe I went through a birthing again."

"Thanks for everything, Ford. I'm so blessed by your company." Sarah hoped he couldn't see her blush.

"Baby is gorgeous just like her mama."

"Would you mind grabbing my phone so I can text Leah and Jeremiah? Maybe check to see if you can find me a cup of that coffee somewhere?"

"You want coffee instead of rest?"

"I'll sleep well tonight."

He kissed the baby's forehead, and grinned at Sarah. "Be back in a flash."

If only Mom was here to meet her youngest daughter's daughter.

*Thank You, Jesus, for this miraculous armful. Please guide my days ahead, especially where Ford is concerned.*

£

Later that evening, Ford approached Sarah's hospital door. He'd had no way of knowing what flowers she liked, so he settled for a grand pastel arrangement. "Knock, knock, anyone here?"

She reclined on the bed with her baby in the crook of her arm, so radiant his heart threatened to pound out of his chest. He hoped happiness filled her and she'd be too busy to shed tears any time soon.

"Hey, there. A sweet little someone wants to say hello." Joy poured from her wonderful face, bubbled more likely. "Are those bountiful blossoms for me?"

He peeked around the giant bouquet. "They are, but they can't hold a candle to how pretty you look. My whole day is shinier, now that I've seen you. I think you've made my eyes happy."

*Oh boy, did that sound hokey. But I'm thinking you are my heart's partner.*

"What do I answer first? The flowers are lovely. Thank you. Set them down, please. But me, appealing?" Her eyes glittered. Then a curtain dropped. "How can I be appealing until I have flat abs and hollow hipbones again?"

She'd always be beautiful to him, no matter what. He settled the cobalt vase on the shelf across from her bed, where the tip of the spray reached for the ceiling, and stepped her way. "Oops. Let me sanitize my hands. Out of practice."

"Good thinking. I would have asked you to do just that. I'm so glad you went through this with me."

He was back in sixty seconds. Instead of reaching for the baby in her bed, his gaze locked on hers. Without breaking eye contact, he leaned in, wanting nothing greater than to kiss her. "I don't care about flat abs and hollow hipbones. God sees into the heart. And you should know by now, I look beneath the surface."

He moved closer. One corner of his mouth hit hers. The other caressed her cheek.

She slid her face away. "You should have known I prefer having no secrets between us."

Ford reared back. "Please understand professional rigmarole prevented me from saying anything I suspected about Kruz. On a personal level, my heart wanted nothing more than to reveal my suspicions. We needed proof, or that confession, to fit together the pieces."

She yawned and closed her eyes, a soft smile of tranquility gracing her face.

He waited, and cuddled the infant while they both slept. Much later, he rose to leave.

"Ford."

He stopped, but didn't turn from laying down the baby.

"You're a good man. It's okay. I understand about Kruz. No hard feelings."

Forgiven, he left his heart in that hospital room.

# Thirty-one

*For God will bring every deed into judgment, including every hidden thing, whether it is good or evil.* —Ecclesiastes 12:14

Ford had signed off on his final reporting of Neely Stallcup's kidnapping. As for Dieter Stanley, he'd revisit the details when and if the case went to trial, which he doubted. He'd be prepared if called to testify. For now, he needed a good hard run. His phone interrupted him while tying his running shoes.

"It's a brand new day." Sarah's voice brought out the sun. "Any chance you could give a couple girls a ride home?"

"See you in seven minutes." He changed clothes again. All the while, his heart raced as though he'd just finished running five miles. Her ability to forgive made him want to split open his happiness and spread it around.

He reached the hospital in ten. He hadn't considered the time to park. He ran through the lot and took the stairs instead of the elevator.

At her hospital door he came to a screeching halt. He gasped at the beautiful sight of Sarah. Enthralled, what a beautiful word. He was enthralled by this new mother who surpassed any kind of beauty other than motherly love. She sat near the window in the oversized chair, absorbed by her baby girl.

"Well what a couple of beauties." Ford could care less that his voice sounded raspy.

Sarah glowed with the blush of new motherhood. "Our paperwork isn't quite finished yet."

He leaned in close. "How about picking up where we left off last night?"

She turned her face to help him hit the target for a perfect kiss.

A rushing tide hammered through him. Fireworks exploded behind his now closed eyelids. Nothing existed outside this room.

He pulled back, yet wanted nothing more than to kiss her forever.

She opened her eyes. Time held no meaning as they searched the depths of one another's eyes. The three of them, together. They were on the same page of life, ready to begin a chapter together.

"Have you decided on a name?" he croaked.

"None came to me except Lena."

"I'm guessing your mother would be pleased."

"Lying here, I've thought about Travis. I'll remember him as my best friend from my youth. To honor Travis, his mom's name was Anne. So, may I introduce you to Lena Anne Bishop."

"Well, sweet Lena Anne." He held out his arms. "Let's get a good look at you."

Sarah sat up straighter and placed the tiny gift in the crook of his arm.

She entrusted him with her baby. He readjusted her fit and held Baby Lena close to his heart.

Sarah retracted the footstool on the recliner and swung to her feet, albeit stiffly. She caught her fingers in the excess fabric of the ivory top she'd worn to the hospital. "I'm so ready to say good-bye to these fat clothes. You handle my sweet bundle as though she were made of fine glass."

He couldn't help but grin from ear to ear.

She touched his arm. "I saw you in the park that first day and it hit me how nice it would have been to know you as the boy next door. And look at you now, here with us. You're a natural with my baby."

Ford cupped Baby Lena in his hands and gave her a small bounce. Head and butt fit just right. He settled in the recliner next to the window, rested Lena's bottom on his thigh and removed her cap. Downy blond hair. He loosened the blanket.

"I'm in awe of you, little miracle. And while I'm taking you in, I want to know if your mommy would consider having me around for a while longer."

Her mother made no comment.

*Am I the only one feeling so squishy here in the presence of a miracle?*

"You're already another beautiful Bishop female." He continued to talk to Baby Lena while re-swaddling her. "I caught a glimpse of your mommy in the park. Then we met at a party and I could hardly believe she'd eat with me. She intrigued me. The whole beguiling package. You put a glow on her face, and she's blessed to have you now, little baby girl."

He glanced up to gauge Sarah's reaction. Sure enough, her cheeks were rosy. They shared a knowing look.

Tucking Baby Lena with a gentle bounce, Ford continued. "Yup. I'm a busy kind of guy who familiarized myself with your grandfather's, oops, great-grandfather's case, so your mommy and I had reason to keep talking. I would have made up a topic to discuss, just to stay in her company. And her sexy voice on the phone tickled my curiosity."

"Excuse me. Watch your language, please. How about talking to the lady instead of the baby?"

To the tune of an ancient lullaby, Ford crooned, "Your future, and your baby girl's life, are entwined with mine. Rest in the Lord..."

Sarah giggled. "Ford, what am I going to do with you?"

"A whole bunch, I hope."

"Okay, nothing has really been said, but judging by the bouquet, the kiss, your exuberance, you might be interested in spending time with us?" Her full-wattage smile could light a basement without windows.

"I want to be all yours. I have nothing new to interfere with me telling you I have been at your calling since our first meeting."

She licked her lips, clearly nervous. "I give. You must be the real deal if you found a victim's huge pregnant family member attractive."

What a mouthful. He waited her out, unable to stop the happiness that hummed within, or the giant grin that had to be plastered across his mug.

Sarah sucked in a big breath, blew it out with gusto. "I said I'd thought about Travis, while in here. He was my friend half my life. He comforted me one night after I broke down over dealing with Mom dying. Wrongfully, we got carried away. But God ordained this baby's life, so I can't ever say again our coming together was a mistake, though I know it was a sin. We each woke up knowing without a doubt that we loved each other but were not *in* love with one another. He did the noble thing and offered to marry me, so at the time of his death we were engaged, which I had to come to terms with because I loathe mediocrity.

In my heart, I was upset as much with settling for Travis as with the embarrassment of finding myself pregnant. I've asked the Lord to forgive my actions. I've also worked through guilt over not grieving for Travis like some people thought I should have. Losing Mom was enough grief to handle."

Clearing any censure from his countenance, he said, "You have come so far. I don't think I've ever told you how much your single-mindedness drew me to you."

"Let's agree to not talk about Travis until Lena is ready. My heart is light, I'm so full of love for my daughter. You've been open and up front with me. I learned you sacrificed your job and your time to raise Suze when you were both young. God's plan for you is to be protective."

"That's good to know. I thought you held it against me that I smothered her."

They shared a laugh, gazing into one other's eyes. My, but she did awkward things to his insides.

*If you give me the chance, I'll love you passionately.*

She looked away as though hearing his thoughts. With poignant intensity, she told me, "I'll tell Lena about Travis and his life. He's her father, after all. I will make sure she knows he wasn't the love of my life."

"You've got plenty of time to prepare for that discussion." He drew the baby close and kissed her snuggly cheek, intently tracking his gaze over her face. Baby Lena's fingers wrapped partially around his pinky.

He raised that perfect digit to his mouth. "How could anyone not be a goner for this beautiful baby girl?"

He met Sarah's golden brown eyes, enthralled anew by the striations of color in her irises that only God could create.

"What do you think of me courting your mommy, Lena girl? As soon as you can go out in public, little sweetie…" He dropped Lena's finger to lift Sarah's chin. "I invite you both on a date. That is, if you both agree."

"You could have asked me first. Lena and I say we like that idea."

# Thirty-two

*"I have set my rainbow in the clouds, and it will be the sign of the covenant between me and the earth…Whenever the rainbow appears in the clouds, I will see it and remember the everlasting covenant between God and all living creatures."* –Genesis 9:13 and 16

"In the morning…" Sarah sang while clanging pans around, and pulled the chosen 13x9 out of the cupboard. A baritone vocalist had given the song a spiritual rendition at Mom's service. The Lord used the lyrics to impact Sarah later. "…give me Jesus."

Sarah grinned at her six-week-old baby. Lena opened her mouth, exposing her gums. "Oh, my. Did you just smile at me? I think you did."

"All my life, my mother baked cakes and brownies in this pan, a wedding gift to her mother, she said. You, my child, will be the fourth generation to bake love in this pan."

Sarah turned on the oven, her heart overflowing with love for Jesus, Baby Lena, and Ford.

The rich chocolate batter of Black Magic Cake always reminded her of Mom. Sarah greased, and then swished the whole grain flour, covering the bottom and sides of the pan. Lena held her gaze on Sarah, and she wondered at the baby's thoughts.

"Grandma's recipe, little girl. Someday soon you'll be old enough to talk and I figure you'll agree that this batter smells good. One of these days, you'll ask to lick the spatula. I'll have to say sorry, not with raw eggs." She spread the batter in the pan, the rich coffee color close to the same as Ford's hair, and swirled the spatula from side to side.

She continued to sing "Give Me Jesus," mixing up the lyrics and the chorus, while talking to Baby Lena. "Ford is going to love this cake, baby girl. You will, too, when you're a bit older. Coffee makes the frosting taste so good."

While the wonderful aroma of baking chocolate filled the apartment, she mused. So much had happened to change her life. She lost her best friend, whom God chose to father her baby. She lost her mother, who now resided in heaven. She met Ford, the love of her life. Jesus called her to salvation. They found answers to the family mystery.

There were rocky moments she'd questioned her ability to trust Ford. She eventually gave him the benefit of the doubt. He'd been doing his job. She'd never be alone again, thanks to the Lord in her life. She had so much to look forward to.

The family seemed to be satisfied with Kirby Kruz's confession, whether it would ever stand up in court or not. Mom's quest, which evolved into Sarah's search, had come to an end. Mom died without having a definitive answer. Had she known about his coming forward, she'd feel as reassured as Sarah from a couple verses in Romans, chapter twelve.

God commands His people to not take revenge, but leave room for His wrath. "I will repay," says the Lord.

Sarah believed Mom had been too hard on herself. There had to be a psychological term for how she claimed she didn't remember a lot of her life around the times Sarah and Jeremiah were babies. Amnesia caused from a traumatic event, or whatever. Were they to talk, Sarah would remind Mom that such guilt comes from the enemy, not from God. She and Jeremiah and Leah were just fine. Maybe suppressed grief enabled Mom to function on automatic pilot. Whatever took place, the Lord carried them through.

Sarah wouldn't have that problem as a new mother. She believed accepting the love of Jesus, and her love for Ford, had wiped out grief. Since Sarah wasn't living underneath a cloud of trauma, she determined to remember her moments with Baby Lena.

Jeremiah, Leah, and Ford agreed it was way past time to go on with their lives as victors in a battle that had spanned generations. The shadow of murder had been replaced by a canopy of the Lord's peace.

There were still unknowns. No one knew if an officer of the law hid Grandpa's clothing. Or, if indeed, Grandma burned them in the barrel behind the house. At the thought of Keaton's name, she remembered she'd never asked Ford about that threatening e-mail message.

It no longer mattered.

Unless Kirby Kruz suddenly regained a pure memory, it would remain unknown if he acted alone or there were others involved.

Local authorities had found the skeletal remains of Neely Stallcup along with other missing girls. Law agencies were dealing with the cases in outstate Nebraska.

Sarah now had the responsibility of teaching her daughter about Jesus. She'd share the times of protection under the umbrella of His wings. She'd share how God became reality, overriding evil.

£

Later that evening, Sarah sat on the balcony with Ford and Lena partaking in the close of the day. An earlier shower brought welcome relief from the blast of the sun. Sometimes in Nebraska, rain left the air heavy with humidity. Other times fresh and invigorating, like this day, with air fragrant as a bouquet.

Ford slid his iron patio chair away from the table and stepped to the rail. Sarah watched, at times unable to train her eyes off the man. What was he thinking about?

As so often happened, he answered her thought. "There's a verse about time I mull over sometimes working through the old files. According to Psalm ninety, verse four, *"For a thousand years in your sight are like a day that has just gone by, or like a watch in the night."*

"How about in coming days and nights, you share a lot of God's Word with me?"

"I'd say I like the sound of that assignment."

Ford seemed mesmerized by the sky opposite the setting sun. He leaned way over, stretching his runner's torso. He reached back with his hand and invited, "Come see."

She glided to his side, too short to detect what caught his attention in the southeastern sky.

"Grab Lena so we can look out another window." Ford toted the tray with remnants of their meal.

They did their little crowded dance in the small balcony space. Sarah unbuckled the baby from her carrier.

Inside, free of the dishes, Ford slung his free arm over Sarah's shoulders and guided them to her studio. Through the window, the wonder of a rainbow drew gasps of delight.

"Dear God, You are in the details of our lives. Thank You, Lord, for granting us the experience of this sight," she prayed and hugged her baby. "Lena, girl, your grandma loved the unique meaning of a rainbow. She would have been so tickled by you. I'll read you a story she wrote about the way God put a rainbow in the sky to comfort her and the family after your great-grandfather went to meet Jesus."

They stood there until the pastel hues faded into deep blue. Sarah knew with every fiber of her being that she, Ford, and Lena were meant to be on this spot at this designated point in time. God's time, as He proceeded to write the book of her life.

Lena squirmed in Sarah's arms.

"I'm sure she's had enough. Thanks for spotting the rainbow."

"Wait." Ford stepped from her side to face her. "It would please me to have your undivided attention."

Her heart melted. Her handsome cold case investigator, Ford Melcher, dropped to one bent knee.

He reached into his pocket and offered Sarah a blue velvet box.

"My dearest Sarah Bishop, I love you with all that I am..." he waved a hand and reached out to tweak Lena under the chin, "...and sweet Baby Lena...would the two of you do me the honor of becoming my family?"

"Yes!" Sarah pumped Lena's hand up and down, and they twirled. Lena flashed her gummy smile, and kicked her legs against Sarah's arms. "I've been waiting since you said something about lifetime love in the hospital. I have finally discovered true love. God first. A mother's love for her baby. And now, a lifetime love with you."

Ford eased to his feet and wrapped his arms around them.

"I like the sound of Sarah Melcher, it rolls off the tongue."

"It has a sweet flavor, My Sarah. Sweeter yet, we've both been sealed into God's promises by the blood of Jesus."

"Praise the Lord," she echoed. "Mom said the same thing, God sealed us into His covenant."

*£££*

Dear Reader,

The cold case alluded to on these pages is based on my father's unsolved homicide. Lena's portion of the story is recorded in my own journals.

The account of my father's murder has been written twenty different ways. After all, I only know the event from my perspective at the time it happened. The rest is conjecture and left up to my imagination.

Over the years I got worked up enough to attempt to get things moving in the investigation. The quest for answers caused me to struggle with many uncertainties. Going through my files always stirs up myriad emotions as my mind travels back. Some memories have grown dim with time, others may carry the impact of immediacy forever.

I've imagined all kinds of conclusions to close this albatross that hovers over my family. I can still get riled over what I think was handled wrong initially. I've pictured a scene of death and a scene of justice for each alleged speculation.

My whole family has faced and dealt with the absence of resolution, or not.

As Lena expressed in this story, I believe faith involves living without answers. God holds those answers, as well as control of the justice that belongs to Him alone. I know that. Yet, also knowing a killer went free has never left the back of my mind.

I have entrusted God with the long chapter of my life story that has an ending known only to Him. Even though there will always be questions regarding my father's homicide, the ultimate answer remains in the Lord's hands.

Thank you for reading my story with a happy ending, as all true romances wrap up. If my words tapped a memory or emotion, a positive review posted on Amazon would touch my heart. Authors appreciate reader support and reviews that encourage others to purchase stories with a God-honoring message.

I praise Him for victory through grace.

~LoRee